DEATH AT THE DOUBLE

JO ALLEN

Copyright © 2025 by Jo Allen

All rights reserved.

No part of this book may be reproduced in any form or by any electronic or mechanical means, including information storage and retrieval systems, without written permission from the author, except for the use of brief quotations in a book review.

❀ Formatted with Vellum

To Gill
May you always drink it while it's fizzing xx

AUTHOR'S NOTE

The characters in this book are, of course, figments of my imagination and bear no resemblance to anyone alive or dead. The same can't be said for the locations, many of which are real.

Others, however, are not. I've taken several liberties with geography, mainly because I have a superstitious dread of setting a murder in a real building without the express permission of the homeowner, but also because I didn't want to accidentally refer to a real character in a real place or property.

So, for example, you won't find Jude's home village of Wasby on the map; and while you may try to place the fictional Eden's End in the context of the (real) places around it, I have done my very best to make sure that you won't succeed!

Although I've taken these liberties with the details, I've tried to remain true to the overwhelming beauty of the Cumbrian landscape. I hope the many fans of the Lake District will understand and can find it in their hearts to forgive me for these deliberate mistakes.

ONE

It was a foul day, one of the foulest imaginable, but had Connie ever expected anything else? She'd always loathed winters in her home county, blighted as they were by the thick fog that settled like a roll of cotton wool over the wide, coiling River Eden, striking deep into the bones of anyone foolish enough to step outside their front door. In midwinter (and January, and November) the daylight barely lasted long enough to allow the lights to be turned off and rarely grew bright enough to cast a shadow. By early adulthood she'd grown weary of getting up in the dark, going out in the dark, coming home in the dark, chasing rare rays of sunshine in her lunch hour and never seeming to catch them. She'd always been susceptible to depression and this joyless absence of light only emphasised it. By contrast Australia, where she had wanted to believe she'd settled and was happy, was blessed with an irresistible brightness that had proved balm to her mind. Yes, the light could be harsh and the heat cruel, so much so that she had perversely found herself seeking the deepest shade she could find and sheltering there for hours, but it was better than the grinding cold and grey that clung like a leech to a Cumbrian winter.

It was early December. The bones of a recent snowfall lay high on the slopes of the Pennines, lingering in the ridges of the fields and shadows of the hedges lower down as the taxi crept decorously along the winding road, fixed in its place in a queue of traffic. In front of her the driver made irritable conversation with someone in an office somewhere, complaining about how late he was, how it wasn't his fault. Listlessly, Connie thought she probably agreed with him. Everyone knew how slowly traffic moves on country roads and whoever was in the office must know it too, but was yet impatient and probably only looking to vent their own bad temper.

She turned her head. On the other side of the road a tractor and flail battered the tall summer's growth off the top of the hedge, spraying splinters across the road to trouble cyclist and horses. This seemed to have been the cause of the holdup because once they were past it the line of traffic picked up speed and bowled merrily towards Langwathby, past verges by now below the snow line, slick with red mud. Beyond the woods they turned right, decelerating as they passed along a tarmac drive that had crumbled badly in the cold until it frayed at the edges, just as she felt she was fraying after her long flight back from Sydney, and pulled up outside the care home where her father had finally agreed to spend the rest of his days.

'There you go,' said the driver, slamming on the brakes in a way that betrayed both his irritation (was he, too, tired of this endless winter?) and his impatience to be away to pick up his next passenger. 'Eden's End.'

Damn. Now she had to get out and get on with it. Just at the wrong moment the exhaustion of the past few months, and in particular the past couple of days, had caught up with her. She wanted to fall asleep where she sat and if she couldn't do that she would almost settle for sitting down on the sodden grass in front of the building and falling asleep there. If no-one noticed it would end in death, but didn't everything? People said dying from the cold (never a risk in Australia) was easy and peaceful, and it seemed infinitely preferable to the alternative.

But *I wants don't get*. She'd heard that too often, from both her parents. Maybe this was why she'd spent so long chasing after what she did want and been so determined to get it, and it galled her immensely to realise that they were both right after all, and it had all been for nothing. Her father would know that, and he wouldn't let her forget it.

'Thank you,' she said to the driver, and reached for her purse. 'Card?'

'Cash only, I'm afraid.'

'Really?' God damn it. The place was even more backward than she remembered. Thank goodness she'd taken out some cash against emergencies when she'd arrived at Manchester. It took her a moment to find it among the vast number of necessary things that crammed her handbag, and she must have passed over it at least once before her fingers closed on it in a side pocket. 'Keep the change.' It was a mean tip, just fifty pence, but she had no coins so it would have to do. 'Can you pick me up here in an hour or so?'

'You can book a pick-up with the office.' The driver, clearly insulted by her meanness, was scowling at her as she took too long to get out of the vehicle. 'I'd do it now if I were you. We get busy round this time.'

Surely people used to be more friendly? Contemplating the prospect of being stranded with her father for hours if a taxi proved unavailable, Connie yawned, watching as the car shot into a rapid three-point turn and headed back towards Penrith. And that was it. She was committed.

She turned towards the building. When her father had gone into Eden's End nursing home some years before, it had had the reputation of being luxurious and had been highly sought after but even then, as she'd clipped her quick way around it on a brief inspection, she'd sensed the beginnings of a downturn. Now she wished she'd listened to her gut. At the time she'd been in a tearing hurry and her father had been an increasing burden on her, so all that had mattered was that it was good enough. It seemed pale and tired and she regretted the actions of her old self. The gravel apron outside the front of the building was rutted and uneven, pooled with melted snow and sleet. The paint on the front door was peeling and the bare woodwork of the external window sills was bleached by that infernal wind. The extensive grounds, which had been well maintained , even in winter, now seemed sad and unkempt with moss accumulating in the gravel of the paths, the flowerbeds clogged and black with leaves that no-one had cleared away.

It had been thirty degrees in Sydney and here, as the sun plummeted in the west even more dramatically than she remembered it doing, the temperature barely clung on above freezing. She shivered. The sooner she got this over with, the sooner she could get back to the roaring fire in the lounge of her hotel, settle down with a large glass of wine, and think about what she'd do next, what would be the next step on her journey now that the last, like all those that had preceded it, had gone so badly wrong.

She struck the bell harder than was necessary, rewarded by its harsh buzz from deep within the building. After what felt like an age she rang it again, with the same result. As she raised her hand (with rising impatience) to try for a third time, the door eased open.

'So sorry,' said the harassed young woman who answered it, her hands encased in sticky Marigolds and the rest of her wrapped in a white plastic apron. 'We're a bit short-staffed right now. Everyone seems to have the 'flu. They always do at this time of the year.'

Connie allowed her brows to contract in disapproval. She hadn't put her father in this place and signed up to spend most of her inheritance (if not all of it: the Sheldons had long-life genes) to have him neglected, but it was hardly her place to comment, especially as she hadn't been the model daughter he'd always wanted. There were so many regrets. She wondered if he felt like that, too. 'My name is Connie Sheldon. I'm here to visit my father, Edwin Sheldon. Could you tell me where his room is?'

The girl's brows contracted in her turn, but in perplexity rather than irritation. 'Sorry, I haven't been here that long. I'll have to check.'

She bustled into the tiny office. A black and white cat jumped up on the table in the reception area and stretched its pink nose up for a fuss. Connie, who liked cats, put her hand down to it and let it investigate the smells of travel — stale sweat and spice and lemon-scented towelettes — which must have accumulated on her clothes and her skin in the half-circuit of the world she'd completed since she last had a shower.

'I'm awfully sorry,' said the girl, coming back out of the office. 'We don't seem to have an Edwin Sheldon.'

'Of course you do.' At least inside the place it was warm, though it smelt as stale and tired as she did. Connie loosened the scarf she'd bought for an extortionate amount of money in a designer shop at Manchester Airport when she'd stepped off the plane and remembered the feel of winter. 'Do you have the name right? Sheldon. Edwin Sheldon. He moved in here five years ago.'

'We definitely don't have anyone of that name.' The girl glanced at her watch. 'Are you sure you've come to the right place?'

How dare the girl dismiss her like that? 'Yes, of course I'm sure. I settled him in here myself. I think I need to speak to the manager.'

'You'll be lucky,' said the girl, with more than a touch of impudence. 'We don't have a manager right now.'

'Don't have…?' Just when Connie thought she couldn't feel any more weary, another wave of tiredness swept over her. It was like being buried, hour by hour. 'How can you not have a manager?'

'I mean we do, but she's off sick, too. I don't know when she'll be back.'

'Just find whoever's supposed to be in charge right now so I can speak to them, okay? I mean, someone has to be in charge, don't they?'

The woman's mutinous face implied she was about to say there wasn't anyone available, but instead she shrugged her shoulders and turned to where a woman in a nurse's uniform had appeared in the doorway.

'Everything okay, Liz?' the woman asked.

'This lady's looking for her dad but he isn't here.'

'Is that right? Leave it with me, pet, and get on with what needs doing.' The nurse shooed her out of the way and turned back to Connie as the girl disappeared. 'Let's see if we can sort this out, eh?'

'Sort it out?' Connie heard the tension in her own voice. 'It's not as if you've got hundreds of residents, is it? There can't be more than thirty.' They traded on that. They called it *exclusivity* and *personal service* and charged a ridiculous premium for it.

'There are twenty-five residents,' said the nurse briskly. 'I'm Ellie Jack and I'm the head nurse. I've been here for years so if your dad's here I'll know him, right?'

Connie vaguely recognised Ellie Jack from her initial visit. She had been pointed out from a distance to illustrate the top level of medical care that Edwin could expect, but she'd been busy with a patient and they hadn't been introduced. 'Yes. He's Edwin Sheldon.'

'What?' Ellie straightened up. Her expression was wary. 'I'm sorry, who did you—?'

'My father. Edwin Sheldon.'

'I didn't know Edwin had another daughter.' Ellie was looking a bit flustered, now. She shook her head and her dyed blonde bob swung furiously. 'Oh dear.'

'What are you talking about? He only has one daughter. That's me. My name is Connie Sheldon.' She'd forgotten; her married name would be on their records. Perhaps that explained it. 'Connie Armstrong as was. I've come from Australia to see my father, so would you please take me to him?'

The world stopped for a moment, still and silent but for the purring of the cat at Connie's side. Ellie Jack's eyes widened and her expression transitioned from wariness to shock.

'Okay,' she said with care. 'Okay. Look, Ms Sheldon, maybe you'd better come through to the office. I think there may have been a misunderstanding.'

TWO

Jude Satterthwaite slammed the front door behind him, blocking out a bad day and a wintry night and wrapping himself instead in a domestic silence which, after almost eight hours of meetings, confrontation and general ill-temper, was exactly what he needed. He stood in the hallway and savoured the moment — no phone, no voices, nothing but the wind rattling in the front door and the fussy ticking of the clock — but the moment of respite didn't last. He'd barely hung up his coat and scarf and run upstairs to change out of his suit before his sense of dissatisfaction with life reasserted itself. By the time he'd switched on the oven and set the yellow-stickered ready meal he'd picked up on the way home in to heat up, he was once more in a full-on bad mood. Putting the trials of work behind him only revealed domestic issues to try his patience. An evening of pre-Christmas chores lay in wait and he'd been procrastinating (unusually for him) for the most flimsy of reasons. He had no idea what, if anything, he should get for Ashleigh O'Halloran, the colleague with whom he'd been engaged in a relationship for the past few years. The flame between them was burning out, as he'd always known it would, but they remained close friends. Which was why it had become so complicated.

He would have to get her something. When the lust and the illusion of love had evaporated they'd left a rock-solid friendship behind. A gift was in order, but exactly what was appropriate? The problem was the more complicated because, although she hadn't told him, he strongly suspected she was moving ever closer to a reunion with her ex-husband and knew that such a move would be a disaster. She knew it, too, and had admitted as much on more than one occasion, but she couldn't help herself. Now Jude not only had to decide what was appropriate for a man to give his ex-lover but also to consider if it might cause offence to the ex-husband he'd really rather she had nothing to do with.

If he'd been the type to interfere he'd have made sure a huge bunch of red roses arrived at her door, preferably when Scott Kirby was there to get the message, but Ashleigh's love life was nothing to do with him, and he knew it. While he was as keen to know everything outside his work as he was within it (he was a detective) he was wise enough to think carefully before he intervened. Yes, Ashleigh's relationship with Scott was a dilemma, but it was none of his business. He went to the fridge, helped himself to a can of Coke, and wrenched it open, knowing that when the evening ended he would have done all his shopping early and online, except for that one, complicated, gift.

The doorbell rang, breaking that welcome silence. Not expecting anything, and with the online shopping yet undone and no deliveries in the pipeline, he took a long drink while he ran over the possibilities of who it might be and whether he was obliged to answer. Unable to think of anyone other than Ashleigh (and it was too much to hope that she'd have seen the light or even opted to come to him for advice and be in the mood to listen to it) and consequently intrigued, he went to the door. On the step, hunched under the streetlamp in chilly misery in a drizzle that had thickened in the past fifteen minutes and now looked as if it might be turning to sleet, stood a woman in a long coat, hooded and with her face swathed in a bright, multicoloured scarf.

'Jude?' she said, pulled away her scarf and flipped the hood back to reveal damp hair plastered to her forehead. 'It's Connie. Connie Sheldon, as was. Connie Armstrong, now. Anything goes, call me whatever. But you remember me, right?'

'Of course.' He'd recognised her the minute she'd revealed her face. He had a memory for details and Connie, with her angular yet somehow attractive face and eyes his mother had once described as *black as the Earl of Hell's waistcoat*, wasn't someone who passed a man by. 'Come on in out of the cold.' Because he had questions. So many questions.

She needed no second invitation, but stepped over the threshold, shaking herself vigorously and spraying the narrow hallway and Jude himself with icy droplets. 'I don't want to interrupt. I know you're busy. You always are. But God, Jude, I need to talk to someone and I couldn't think who else to ask.'

'I thought you were in Australia,' he said.

'I was, until about thirty-six hours ago, but how I got there and why I'm back is a story nearly as long as the flight,' she said with a theatrical sigh.

Part of the reason he'd become a detective was that he couldn't resist a teasing story and this promised to be just such a one. 'Take off your coat and come and get warm. I was about to put the log burner on.'

'I shouldn't put you out.' But she was already slipping out of her coat and handing it to him, quick to find her way into the living room and sink into the sofa before he'd even hung her coat on the hook beside the door.

She hadn't changed. There had always been a superficial confidence about her and he knew it to be misleading. He suppressed a smile at the thought of old times as he followed her through to the living room. He'd laid the fire and not intended to light it but it cost him nothing but the wood and the thirty seconds it took to touch a match to the kindling. It would give the place some warmth, some soul. Maybe, if for no other reason than that, he was glad to see Connie again.

'Cup of coffee?' he asked, closing the front of the wood burner and standing up.

'If it's not too much bother I could handle something a bit harder. I've had a hell of a day and my body thinks it's five o'clock. I think it is, back in Oz.'

'It'll be five o'clock in the morning there, though,' he said, with a smile, and went to the kitchen to open a bottle. He hadn't thought of her for a long time and now he remembered that she'd always amused him. As it happened it was six o'clock, and a perfectly respectable time for a drink.

'You always were a pedant,' she called cheerfully, 'but whatever.'

In the kitchen he turned off the oven, opened a bottle and poured a generous glass of red wine for Connie and a more miserly one for himself. Back in the living room he found she'd made herself comfortable and was inspecting the pack of tarot cards that he kept, as a curiosity, on the side table.

'Surely these aren't yours,' she said, fanning them out and then yawning. 'You're far too literal for this kind of nonsense. People change, I know, but not you. Not this much.'

'You're partly right,' he said, handing her the glass. 'They are mine. They were a present for me from an ex-girlfriend. As a joke.'

'Is Becca into the tarot then?' she said, replacing the pack on the table and applying herself to the wine. 'I never had her down as the type.' She reached out again, fished out a random card and brandished it at him. 'Which one of these is you? The Magician? The Emperor? The Judge?'

'None of them. And not that ex.' He sat down, a smile twitching at his lips, thinking of another picturesque expression his mother had used about Connie. *More front than Blackpool, that one.*

'The detective, then?' She raised her glass at him and winked. 'My original point stands. Joke or not, that's not a valid policing tactic. Don't look like that. I know all about your doings. I'm still in regular touch with Adam and you know he loves a gossip even more than you do.'

He shook his head, his amusement snuffed out. 'Then you'll know I won't want to talk about it.'

'Touchy,' said Connie, reaching out and patting his hand as if he needed to be soothed. 'But all right. We won't if you don't want to.'

Anyone else, veering into the territory of a long-term friendship damaged beyond repair like that which existed between Jude and Adam Fleetwood, might have annoyed him but he couldn't bring himself to resent Connie. Besides, she'd easily be steered away from talking about him by the simple expedient of letting her talk about herself. 'Tell me about your bad day.'

It worked. She took another large swig of wine and

leaned forward. 'God. Yes. I'm so jet-lagged. You wouldn't believe it.'

'Go on,' he said, as he sensed she wanted him to do.

The dark eyes widened. Under her antipodean tan her face was as pale and drawn in the light of his living room as it had been under the yellow streetlight. 'Right. God. Well, anyway. I've been Down Under for a while now, seven years give or take a few months, and you know how it is. I kept meaning to come back but things kept me there. The family. All that sort of stuff. I'll tell you about it some time if you can be bothered to listen. But to get to the point. Did you know my dad was in a care home?'

'I didn't.'

'He's been there for about five years. He's eighty-nine, ninety next week. Or do I mean eighty-six, coming eighty-seven?'

'You don't know?' He couldn't help it. She'd always made him want to smile.

'That's the mystery.' She nodded at him. 'Of course, the first thing I did when I came back was go and see him. I checked in at the George, dumped my bags, didn't even stop for a shower. I called a taxi and went straight over to Eden's End, to get there before tea time to be sure they'd let me in. Do you know the place? The big old house up Edenhall way?'

'Yes.' He knew the nursing home too well and had been there too often, but he shrugged that aside.

'Right. So I turned up there this afternoon to see him, it must have been just before five, and he wasn't there.'

He allowed her pause, which was intended for effect, to extend until she had to carry on. Everything was drama with Connie.

'Apparently he's dead,' she said, and frowned.

'Apparently?'

'Yes.'

'And they didn't tell you?'

'They did not. And thereby hangs a tale.'

'Is it suspicious?'

'I should bloody well say so.'

Her laugh was thinner, this time, and had a quaver to it that threatened a dam-burst of emotion. Jude, who wasn't normally judgemental of other people's drinking, found himself wishing he hadn't poured quite such a large glass of Merlot. Twenty-four hours without sleep wasn't going to help her stay sober. 'Then don't you think it's a matter for the police?'

'Yes!' He was right; the wine had gone straight to her head. She pointed a finger at him and laughed. 'Do you think I'm here to report it to you officially? Right now I feel so knackered I ought to be on the way to the glue factory, but I'm not quite out of my mind. Of course I phoned the police straight away and spoke to a very nice woman and she left a message for a detective who texted straight away to say she'll come out tomorrow and see me. But because you're a detective and because we go back such a long way, when I realised I needed to talk to someone, of course it was you I thought of.'

Of course. He sat back in his chair and sipped, fastidiously. If she'd reported it then the matter of her father's death was in hand, something he needn't concern himself with when he had so many other things he had intended to do. He'd done his social duty by offering her a glass of wine and it was in her own interests to go back to her hotel and try and get her body clock back in balance rather than sitting drinking wine in his living room all evening, but she'd piqued his interest. *Thereby hangs a tale*.

'Go on,' he said. 'Tell me everything.'

THREE

God, but the wine tasted good. Connie had taken a few glasses on the flight, probably more than was good for her, though she'd justified it on the grounds that she was stressed beyond measure, but it had been poor quality and harsh on the palate, and the only effect if had had on her was to stop her sleeping. Not that she ever slept well on a flight (she was as anxious about travelling as she was about everything else) but the alcohol had jerked her awake every half hour or so leaving her with a dry mouth and a grittiness between her eyelids and the surface of her eye that seemed to grate every time she blinked. The flight seemed light years away now, but the dryness and the grittiness felt as if they'd been there for ever.

Enough of feeling sorry for herself. Here she was, in a warm and comfortable living room with a fire leaping in the grate, a glass of decent wine, and a ready listener. She'd thought for a while before deciding to turn up on Jude's doorstep but it was the right decision. She'd known him a long time and trusted his judgement and as she'd expected, he was ready to listen.

'Well?' he said, settling himself and looking at her with the half-raised eyebrow she remembered so well. In the old days it had preceded an inevitable question, but he was twenty years older now and probably sophisticated enough to realise that the eyebrow did the job alone. He'd always been darkly attractive rather than handsome, and Connie found that single gesture added disproportionately to his appeal. Or maybe that was the wine, playing havoc with her loneliness.

'I don't think you'll have heard anything like this,' she said, ready to spin the story out now that she was over the initial shock and could see the entertainment value.

'I'm intrigued.' He lifted his own glass and took a fastidious sip. He'd never been much of a hell-raiser, even as a teenager, and it seemed nothing had changed, but she got the sense that responsibility hadn't dulled his dry humour.

'So you should be.' She relaxed. 'Shall I start at the beginning?'

'Go on. There's nothing on the telly. And I like a good story.'

And Connie was, she knew, a good story-teller. 'You remember my dad?' She didn't wait for him to nod. Of course he'd remember. 'You know how close we were, when I was younger.'

'I remember you were very close.'

Close? She thought of Edwin's zany sense of humour, his delight at a prank. The twinkle in his eye. The way he'd adored her, his darling daughter, and she had worshipped him in response. 'Yes. But after my mum died he changed. We were still close, but when it was just the two of us he became very difficult, as if he blamed me.' And maybe she'd changed too, or maybe it was just that her mother had been the buffer between two over-similar characters and after her death they had bumped and sparked until there were flames, and there was no-one there to put them out. 'I think that's where it started to go wrong.' If she'd been a better person, more forgiving of his temper, his grief, the demands he had made on her, what had happened might have been avoided. 'You remember how keen I was to go to university. That's the reason, and it's why I was so reluctant to come back here.'

He nodded again, because this was something he already knew. What he didn't know, and what she would struggle to explain, was how she'd made mistakes and failed to learn from them, made them again and failed to learn, until she'd become trapped in an unbreakable cycle of failed relationships, all of her own making.

'It's not unusual,' he remarked. 'I know plenty of people who viewed university, or any other life change for that matter, as a chance to start again, for one reason or another. And, as you say, you'd lost your mother. Your circumstances make it understandable.'

'Yes. You can get trapped in your life. I think I felt like Dad wanted me to replace my mother in a strange kind of way, and of course it was impossible. I'm not her. He should have gone and found himself someone else but instead he focussed on looking after me.' It hadn't helped that he was a much older father, over fifty when she was born and set in his ways. 'Anyway, to cut a long story short, when I did come home I found living here — living with him — very stifling and so I went to London and met someone and got married.'

'Didn't you come back?' he inquired. 'I'm sure my mum said—'

'Yes, I came back when my marriage broke up.' It had

only taken months before both she and her husband had realised the magnitude of the mistake. 'And then I married again.'

'Did you?'

If he was tuned into the local gossip, which he almost certainly was, he should surely have heard this and her initial reaction was disappointment to find that he either hadn't known or didn't think it important enough to remember. 'I married someone from round here.' On reflection, it was perhaps for the better if Jude had really heard nothing, so why should she enlighten him? Neither she nor her second husband, who at the time had been married to her one remaining female friend from her schooldays, had behaved very well to their previous partners. 'Dad didn't approve. I barely spoke to him after that and he barely spoke to me, although I thought of him often and I like to think I did right by him. Matthew — my husband — and I moved to Australia and had twin sons.'

'And your father stayed here.'

'Yes.' Connie was an only child and her father the same. Her mother's family were getting older themselves and more preoccupied with their own children and grandchildren, and in any case Edwin had never been a man to reach out to others. It was easy to see how he'd become isolated. 'I didn't deliberately cut him off. If anything he did that to himself. I called him regularly, to begin with at least, and he'd end the calls after a few minutes with barely an excuse. The time always seemed to be wrong.'

'Literally,' said Jude, in what felt like an attempt at a joke.

'Maybe. It was always either very early or very late when I called here. I never thought that what was a good time for me might not be for him. I'd send him gifts at Christmas and on his birthday and he never acknowledged them, or reciprocated. He never sent anything for the boys, and when we did come back over for a visit when they were babies so that he could meet them, he didn't show much interest in them. Naturally enough, we let things drift. It was such an effort doing anything else.' She swirled the wine in her glass, willing herself to drink it more slowly. It would be so easy to slug it down and ask for more, but when she drank too much she always ended up disliking herself. There were too many unpalatable truths in the bottom of a wine glass.

'I understand that. Relationships are difficult and we have no entitlement to them.'

There might, she thought, be a tale behind that but she wasn't about to ask him. Whatever his story, it would be neither as dramatic nor as immediate as hers. 'We have obligations, though. I don't want you to think I forgot them.' If she wasn't careful she would get teary. 'His health wasn't great. We came back for another visit about five years ago and I was shocked at the state he was in. He was very proud, as you may remember.'

'I didn't know that, but I can imagine.'

Could he, though? In Connie's experience, pride too often crystallised into stubbornness. On a walk in the outback a few months earlier one of her sons (into rocks and dinosaurs) had prattled on about the rocks being the hardest in the world, and she had looked closely at the example he'd presented for her inspection and the glint of some mineral or other had reminded her of the flint-like snap in Edwin Sheldon's eye. 'I saw at once that he couldn't look after himself. We had a huge row about it, and a lot of unpleasant things were said, but at the end of it he finally agreed to go into a home, though he wouldn't give me power of attorney and kept full control of his affairs. Matthew and the twins went back and I stayed on for a while to find him somewhere suitable and settle him in.'

'That was Eden's End?'

'Yes.' Her father, she knew, had left her everything in his will but he'd almost cursed her as he'd crowed over how much the home would cost and how he'd live for ever so she would never get what she was entitled to. 'I wrote to him regularly, and he never wrote back. I called and he rarely answered. And so, I'm afraid, I rather got out of the habit.'

The glass was empty and she set it down, saw Jude eyeing it up and then, reaching a decision, looking at her and nodding towards it. He was so predictable. 'Another?'

'Just a small one.' She felt her lip wobble. It cost so much effort to be strong. She thought she might be getting to the end of her tether. 'I really do need to get some sleep. Anyway, recently I had a terrible personal crisis. My marriage broke down.' Her husband had left and had taken the boys with him and they, pulling the rug from under her feet, had gone willingly, adoring him just as she had her father, to the exclusion of her mother.

'I'm really sorry.' He tilted the bottle and poured a generous amount into the glass.

She'd always found Jude warmly sympathetic and she sensed that still. Professionally he must hide it, but he wasn't being professional now. 'It was tough. Really tough. But it happened.' She'd been as bad at being a mother as she had at being a daughter, but how was she to learn when her father had been so unpredictable and her mother suddenly and irrevocably absent when teenage Connie had needed her most? 'So I decided to come home. Take some time, assess my options. That sort of thing.' For all she cursed its diabolical climate, the Eden Valley would always be home and had offered her what only home could: security. 'Of course the first thing I thought I'd do was go and see him. I arrived at Manchester around lunchtime, got the train across, checked in to my hotel and went straight to see him. And he wasn't there.' She held up a hand to stop his questions. 'And as I said. He's dead. He died almost three years ago.'

'And they never tried to tell you?'

'That's exactly it. I was only in the place once, very briefly, when he first went in. It seems that for the last year of his life Dad was regularly visited by a woman who told them she was his daughter, Connie Sheldon. Me. Except, not me.'

'And nobody there had any clue?' He said it as if he wasn't really surprised. Perhaps Eden's End had a poor reputation and she had somehow missed it.

'No-one had visited him for a long time. He had no friends left alive. The home had a high staff turnover anyway, so they probably wouldn't have known much about the regular visitors. No-one who's there now had ever met me, and it seems he told them this woman was his daughter, Connie. When he died she dealt with all the admin and then she disappeared.' This interloper. This stranger. Words failed her. She drank again.

'What about the paperwork?' he inquired, sitting forward slightly as if he'd sensed an irregularity that could be pointed down. He must be thinking about fraud, which had unquestionably been committed. 'Didn't they cross check what she said against that? Surely you gave them some proof of your ID when the contract was signed.'

'I did, but no. No-one seems to have checked.' She put the glass down and felt in her pocket for a handkerchief, against the inevitable tears. 'Apparently the nurse went along to the funeral to represent the home. This woman, pretending to be me, had the cheek to lead the mourners at my father's funeral. And then she disappeared.'

She had his interest now. He sat even further forward, on the edge of his seat, and the firelight threw shadows across his sharpening expression. 'Wait. This is impossible.'

'It ought to be, but it isn't. I can only imagine Dad was easily confused and she somehow persuaded him that she was me.' She dabbed at her eyes.

'Has anyone tried to contact this woman since then?'

'They didn't have any need to. The head nurse called the number they had for her this evening, when I was there. It's unavailable.'

'Ah. And what about his—?'

'His will? Unless he changed it, he left everything to me. Obviously I've called the solicitor but I didn't get an answer. They'll have gone home. It was nearly six when I rang. But I fear the worst, Jude, because of course I went straight to the house, which as far as I was aware hadn't been sold, and there's someone living in it. I knocked on the door and there's a family I don't know living there. They say they bought it last year.'

She reached out for the glass and drained it, all in one desperate gulp. 'I must be dreaming. It must be the flight. I keep thinking I must have missed something really obvious but I can't see what. My dad's dead and buried and the house is gone. I don't know how, but someone's defrauded me of everything. Not just the money. But of him.' Of any chance of repairing that broken relationship.

Jude stared at her for a moment. 'And you say you called the police.'

'Straight away.'

'And were we helpful?'

She sniffed. 'Yes, very. As I said, someone's coming to talk to me tomorrow.'

'Excellent. Do you happen to know who it is?'

'Yes, a Sergeant O'Halloran.'

He nodded. 'I know her well. She'll see you right.'

'I don't see how anyone can see me right. I don't know what they can do. She's gone, and he's dead.'

'Give us some credit,' he said, and almost laughed. 'We'll find out who this woman is and what's happened, and we'll sort it out so you can get your money back.'

'But my dad—'

'I know.' His expression sobered. 'There's nothing we can do about that, and I'm incredibly sorry. But we'll do what we can. If there's been a crime you deserve justice and we'll do everything to see you get it.'

'Of course there's been a crime!'

'It certainly sounds like it. I'll have a chat with Ashleigh before she comes to see you, and in the meantime I think you should probably go back to your hotel and get some sleep. Where did you say you're staying? The George?'

She nodded, sniffing. He was right. There was nothing that could be done that night and she desperately needed sleep, but it was so warm and comfortable, and such a pleasure to have a sympathetic listener. 'Yes.' Shoving the handkerchief back into her pocket, she struggled to her feet.

'I'll walk you down there,' he said, 'and make sure you haven't forgotten the way.' He smiled, and she knew he meant it as a joke but it felt uncomfortably close to the truth. 'And tomorrow you can tell Ashleigh what you've told me. You'll find she's very easy to talk to.'

'She's your girlfriend,' she said, as he passed her her still-damp coat and she thrust her arms into the sleeves. 'Isn't she?'

'You're not right out of touch with the local gossip, then,' he said, cheerfully, 'but you're a bit behind. These days we're just friends.' He paused. 'You're still in touch with some folk back here, obviously.'

'Only Adam, as I said, but you only ever need to be in touch with him, don't you? He's like GCHQ, always listening.'

He laughed. He and Adam had been friends and there had been a bitter falling-out, of which Connie only had Adam Fleetwood's version and she was far too smart to take that at face value. There might be a time to ask Jude to tell her his side, but just then she was too busy dwelling on her own feelings, her failings and her imperfections to be concerned about anyone else's.

'I behaved really badly today,' she said, as he ushered her out onto the pavement and locked the front door before falling into step beside her as they made their way down the hill towards the town centre. 'To the staff at the home, I mean. But I was so shocked and the woman who spoke to me looked at me as if I was stupid, and I was so tired. I'm not normally that rude.'

'I'm sure she'll understand.'

'I know.' She watched her feet as they slid a little on ice. She'd forgotten how brutal it was to live in cold weather. There were Christmas lights in the windows of the town but their brightness seemed cold and artificial. 'But it isn't like me. God knows these people have enough to do. It wasn't her fault there was nobody there who knew what's going on. I'll go back tomorrow and apologise.'

'We'll find out exactly what happened,' he said, with a degree of confidence she couldn't bring herself to feel now she knew her father had disappeared from her life — from his own life — as suddenly as her mother had done, but without her having any idea that he'd gone. Had he died wondering why she never visited, desperate for her hand on his, or had he, God forbid, slipped off believing someone else was his daughter? And then there was the money. It wasn't about that, not in the great scheme of things, but she'd thought at least she'd be able to stay in the house while she sorted out her life. Now she had to rethink everything.

They cut through Sandgate and up the narrow ginnel at the end of Burrowgate and there they were outside the entrance to the hotel. Christmas music drifted out. Connie struggled with the date. It was a Tuesday, or so she thought. She was tired.

'Thank you so much for being so kind,' she said to Jude and then, for old times' sake, she reached up to pull his face down to hers and kissed him.

FOUR

It was far from the first time Jude had kissed Connie Sheldon. She'd been the first girl he'd dated, way back (as he liked to think of it) when the world had been a younger place and he had been an insufferable and over-optimistic youth who'd approached the unfolding prospect of the rest of his life with a curious naivety. In the intervening two decades he'd thought of her, very occasionally, when he was in his more melancholy moods, most recently when he'd heard from a mutual acquaintance that she'd left the country. Between those times, and certainly since then, he'd been too busy with his own life to think about an old flame whom he was unlikely ever to see again.

When she'd disappeared behind the huge Christmas tree that adorned the busy, welcoming lobby of the hotel he turned away with a wry smile, trying to analyse the ways in which she'd changed and those in which she'd remained the same. It was no surprise to see Adam Fleetwood loitering on the other side of the street without even pretending to do anything other than stare. Adam, who hated him, was too often his shadow these days, always seeking new ways to create some kind of personal or professional trouble for him, but Jude was learning to shrug it off. In any case he didn't get the impression that Adam's interest in him, though obvious, was any more than passing tonight; the glance at a watch told him that, and the quickening of the step that suggested an appointment elsewhere.

For a change, because he'd normally have turned his back and carried on minding his own business, Jude raised a hand in acknowledgement. Adam would misinterpret what he'd just seen, almost certainly deliberately, and would take delight in beginning to spread rumours about Jude's *new relationship*, but by now Jude was so used to him that he no longer cared. Becca Reid, the woman he loved and had thought he'd marry professed not to be interested in anything more than friendship (though he was sure she still cared for him) and Ashleigh O'Halloran, with whom he had been involved in a romance that served as displacement activity for them both, was now solidly accorded the status of a very good friend. Adam could say what he wanted; he would be unable to influence either of those relationships and with neither of these women to consider, Jude had no need to explain himself. Let Adam misinterpret what he'd seen, and spread what rumours he chose. He could do no damage.

The raised hand brought no response. Adam checked his phone and sauntered along to the Market Square, turning up the hill without giving any further indication of being interested. Nevertheless, with the caution he'd acquired early in his career, Jude waited until he was sure his former friend had gone before he got out his phone and called Ashleigh O'Halloran.

'I'm not disturbing you, am I?' he asked, in a way he would once not have bothered to do. This recasting of their relationship now allowed for the fact that she probably had another man in play and if she did it was certainly the ex-husband whom everyone, including Ashleigh herself and probably the ex-husband too, knew was damaging to her emotional health.

'Not at all,' she said, cheerfully. 'You've caught me being very efficient and doing my Christmas wrapping weeks early and I'm already bored with it, so I'm glad of the interruption. Is everything okay?' That, too was a sign of how their relationship had changed. Not that long ago they'd have called one another for no reason at all and never needed to ask why.

'Yes. I can just about see my way to doing you a favour.'

'Is that right?' she said, and laughed. 'Are you going to finish my Christmas shopping for me? That sounds like an offer I can't refuse.'

Across the square Penrith's Christmas lights flickered as the wind got up. He stepped back into the relative shelter of the doorway to the local department store, its windows full of the type of gift you might buy for an elderly relative in a care home — cherry red soft cardigans, slippers, shawls. 'A little bird told me a very interesting case landed on your desk just before you left work today.'

'It's your job to know that kind of thing, I suppose.' Jude was a chief inspector and thus, being two ranks above her, her boss. 'Having said that, I'm impressed you're that much on the ball considering how late it came in. I only got the message about maybe six o'clock. The only follow-up I've done is phoning about a meeting.'

'I have my sources. It happens I was at school with the person who made the original call.'

'Connie something? I don't have my notes to hand.'

'Connie Sheldon, married name Armstrong.' There

would be a previous married name, too, though he didn't know it. 'I've just been talking to her. She's just back from Australia and popped in to say hello and tell me all about her woes. Fraud, by the sound of it, and a particularly cruel one if what she says turns out to be correct.' Though it would require a strange set of circumstances for Connie to be wrong.

'Okay,' said Ashleigh, and he detected a note of caution in her voice. 'All I have is a message to speak to her about a problem at Eden's End. If that place is still as chaotic as it was the first time I went there, I can imagine it wouldn't be that hard to pull off fraud. I'm only surprised it hasn't come up more often.'

'It's not just fraud. There's identity theft. Connie will tell you all about it tomorrow, and be a lot hotter on the detail than I will be, so I'll leave it to her. But I have a bit of time in hand tomorrow morning and I can tell you now that someone's going to have to go down to Eden's End and chat to whatever temporary manager they have in there this week. So I was going to offer to take that on for you.'

She laughed again, and he could imagine her shaking her head. 'Faye's going to love that.' His immediate boss, Faye Scanlon, was an officer who set great store by rank and expected interviews out of the office to be undertaken by her junior detectives. Jude's fondness for keeping his hand in and making contact with the general public was a constant irritation to her.

'I think I'm well-equipped to do the job,' he said, gravely, 'so she can hardly complain.'

'Not on that score, no. But yes, to your original point, if you're offering to take on some of my workload, be my guest.'

'I was good friends with Connie at school,' he said,

'though I haven't seen or heard from her for years, but we do go back a long way. I have a personal interest in this case.'

'Does Becca still drop in to Eden's End?'

'I've no idea.' Becca was a district nurse and was called upon from time to time to visit the nursing home. It was true to say that when he found himself up at the place he did wonder if she might drop by. But he thought of Becca often, in all sorts of places, and as she lived opposite his mother he saw her regularly, for whatever that was worth.

'She might be able to give you some information off the record,' she said, 'that's all. I know you don't need me to tell you how to do your job so don't think it's that. But you can't expect anybody at Eden's End to give you any kind of clear answer. If there's been something wrong at their end, whether it's cock-up or conspiracy, we all know they're going to be covering their own backs and throwing each other under the bus.'

He expected that, and would be ready for it. That was part of the pleasure of interviewing, sifting the truth from the obfuscation. Being in management took away some of the simpler joys of policing, or so he sometimes thought. 'I'll enjoy it.'

'Then we have a deal. I'll speak to Connie tomorrow and you can go and make what you will of the chaos I expect you'll find at Eden's End.'

'I'd leave it until later on. She'll need a long sleep.'

'Noted,' she said, sounding businesslike. 'I'll aim for noon. And in the meantime is there anything you feel you can tell me about Connie Sheldon-slash-Armstrong?'

He thought for a moment as he turned, slipping down the narrow alley into Burrowgate and towards home. As he reached the corner the smell of fish and chips tickled his senses and reminded him of that lasagne, left in the oven while his evening had been overtaken by events. He was suddenly very hungry. 'I'm not sure. She'll tell you her history herself, I've no doubt.'

'Do you know her well?'

'I would once have said I know her very well. We went out for a while in our final year at school. But when you're that age you don't know half of what you think you know, and people change. The impression I have is that her life right now is all over the place.'

'I'll be gentle with her, then,' she said, although there was never any question in his mind that she wouldn't.

'I imagine she'll be experiencing a significant sense of guilt,' he said, still thinking of Connie as she used to be. 'She always followed her heart and not her head.' Something Ashleigh herself was too prone to do. 'I don't get the impression that's changed. She wasn't in contact with her father at all during his latter years, although I don't think I'd say she was neglecting him. She tried, but he was difficult and not receptive. He was very much older than her mother, from what I recall.'

'Poor woman,' said Ashleigh, briskly. 'That sounds like an interesting case. I'll look forward to speaking to her.'

'We can catch up tomorrow,' he said.

'Shall we aim for early afternoon, as soon as I've spoken to Connie?'

They agreed a time and he let her go back to her wrapping, slipping the phone back into his pocket and standing for a moment outside the chippy, trying to decide whether to get himself fish and chips or go back to that half-cooked lasagne. The chips won and he headed to the counter. Walking briskly back with the bag of fish and chips warm in his hands and the tang of vinegar rising from it, he found himself wondering about Connie. Given his job it wasn't surprising that she'd come to him for help, but he was more concerned to spot a vulnerability he hadn't expected. But then again, she was exhausted, she was alone and had just discovered she was both defrauded and bereaved.

He let himself in to his house and went through to the kitchen. That was the other thing about Connie. As a teenager, as a spoiled only child, she'd been needy in a way that Jude had struggled to deal with. He had the feeling he would be seeing a lot more of her in the near future.

FIVE

Eden's End, Jude thought as he pulled up the car at the edge of the sodden and uneven gravel apron in front of the building, was a case study in chaos and bad management. He knew the place of old and it had never recovered its reputation after a scandalous murder case a few years before. He was reasonably confident of what he'd find there — nothing helpful, only a morass of neglected administration, incomplete records and a lack of any accountability. Those circumstances could have made it ripe for a crime such as that which had been committed at Connie's expense — which begged a question. As well as Connie, could there also have been some other lonely and vulnerable old person whose dying and inheritance had been so ruthlessly capitalised upon?

He paused for a moment before he got out of his Mercedes. Extreme chaos didn't preclude a wider conspiracy at staff level. That was one reason why he'd been so keen to conduct this particular interview himself, despite the possibility of incurring his boss's wrath. He knew the place well. Before coming out he'd checked to see if there had been a recent inspection but there had been nothing for four years, when the place had barely scraped an *adequate* rating. They would be due another one, soon, and that report would be worth a read, for sure.

It was only just after nine and the dark shadows of the Pennines stretched a long way west at this time of day, this time of year, so that it was barely light. He got out, made his way across the gravel where an array of cars was parked, and leaned on the bell.

They must have been looking out for him. The door opened immediately, a young woman peering round it with a fearful expression. She stood aside to let him in.

'Good morning,' he said, stepping over the threshold and producing his warrant card, which he handed to her. 'I'm DCI Satterthwaite, here to speak to the manager, Cindy Rushall. That's you, I take it?' She was wearing a smart suit and so was not a carer but she was so young and so uncertain she couldn't possibly be in charge. To appear to think she might be would give a fillip to her self-esteem. Besides, in situations such as this it was often useful to have a member of staff who thought kindly of you.

'Yes,' she said, to his confoundment, 'that's right. I'm sorry if I seem a little unprepared. I only picked up the call to say you were coming around ten minutes ago. Good morning.' She held out her hand for the briefest of touches before turning away and leading the way down a narrow corridor to an office and waved him to a seat at a tiny table below the window. On the other side stood a desk with a computer, phone and a bulging in-tray. He looked twice at that. With so much admin done online, it was a fair bet that this was old paperwork, neglected and needing to be caught up on. He wondered how long it had been on the desk and if it would ever be dealt with. 'Coffee?'

'Thank you. Just black.' He cast a quick look around.

This room, too, had worn badly since he was last in it The paintwork was shabby; there was a dark mark beneath the window to show how the frame was creaking and an accompanying draught to suggest where the water was coming in, and the carpet was uncleaned. The office, he supposed, was the last place the proprietors would spend money in such a public-facing business, if they spent it at all.

'I'm sorry,' she said as she busied herself at the machine, selecting a shiny green pod and sliding it into the slot, 'did you say you're an inspector?'

'Chief Inspector.' He'd got Ashleigh to call ahead and warn them that someone would be coming and to make sure they had any relevant paperwork, but at his request she hadn't told them who. He was, after all, well-known at Eden's End and his arrival was unlikely to be welcome. Cindy Rushall, and anyone else who had an interest, had had half an hour's warning of his arrival, which should have allowed her enough time to find the information the home held on Edwin Sheldon but not enough to put together any complicated kind of deception. He had hoped his seniority would surprise them and it seemed to have done the trick.

'Have you been here long, Ms Rushall?' he asked, as she placed a mug in front of him and turned back to the machine. The coffee pod she selected for herself was, he noticed, a fierce dark blue in colour. He guessed it was the strongest available.

'I'm afraid not, so I may not be much use to you. I'm actually only the temporary cover while they recruit a permanent manager.' There was a slight pause, and he thought she covered it with a sniff of disbelief, as if the process was not ongoing and she feared she might be landed with the job. But the sniff might just have been a symptom of her obvious heavy cold. 'I'm normally based down in London.' Another pause. 'This is my first managerial role,' she said, as if to warn him not to expect too much.

He sipped his coffee and waited for her to take her seat at the table. There was a brown manila folder in front of her, and she put her coffee cup down on top of it in a gesture that was almost defensive.

'Thanks for taking the time to speak to me,' he said, keeping his voice brisk. 'As you know, I'm here to speak to you about one of your former residents. Edwin Sheldon.'

There was a Post-it on top of the file with Edwin's name scrawled on it and she looked down on it as if for inspiration. 'That's right. I believe his daughter…um… called in unexpectedly yesterday.'

'You weren't in yesterday, is that right?'

'Yes. I was off sick.' As if to emphasise the point, Cindy coughed, loudly and deliberately, with one hand over her mouth and the other touching her chest.

'Who was in charge?'

'Nobody, really. I mean, everyone pulls their weight and they know they can call head office in an emergency.' She got out her handkerchief and blew her nose. 'I know what happened. Ellie — she's the nurse — called me last night and so I thought I should come in.'

He nodded. He knew Ellie Jack of old and she was always a useful source of information. She'd been there a long time and would know Edwin. 'I wonder if you can tell me about Mr Sheldon's time here.' He sipped his coffee and watched her.

'Right.' Cindy slipped her mug off the folder and opened it. The contents were pitifully sparse — a printed sheet with a few numbers, a sheet half-filled with what looked like rapidly-scrawled notes. 'Okay. I'm sorry, but there's not very much I can tell you, other than the dates Mr Sheldon joined and then…left us.' She took the printed sheet and passed it across to him.

'You don't keep comprehensive records?' he prompted.

Cindy went scarlet with embarrassment. 'Yes, of course. We're required to do that. But in this case there seems to have been…a system malfunction.'

That was one phrase for it. It was an ugly gap in the records, a matter for the care regulator rather than (at this stage, at least) the police, and serious though it was, it was almost certainly a problem to be handled at a higher level than Cindy's. 'Can the records be retrieved?'

'I've asked head office and they're going to look into it. But I think they might not be. You see, there have been serious issues with record keeping in the past and a lot of the paperwork, signed contracts and powers of attorney and so on, doesn't seem to have been scanned and uploaded onto the system when they should have been. A number of the hard copies have also since been lost. The manager here at the time of Mr Sheldon's…um…stay with us…'

'Karen Grant,' he supplied, with an internal sigh. He understood exactly how this mess had come about.

'You know about it, then? The poor woman who died? I can assure you that was quite an exceptional circumstance. Since then matters have hugely improved in terms of record keeping and—'

She was reading that from the sheet of paper, an obvious line given to her by a panicked senior manager somewhere in head office. 'May I ask, is it only Mr Sheldon's information that's missing?'

'I haven't yet been able to establish…this morning…I only had the chance to look for his details. But yes.' She closed the paper file and took a sip of coffee. 'I expect other paperwork is… incomplete?'

The late lamented Karen Grant, live-in manager throughout Edwin's tenure, had had a disastrous breakdown, so it was hardly surprising she'd left such a mess behind her. Jude could see, too, why no-one had spent too much time and energy on recovering the records of those who were dead and gone. But it would be interesting if it were only Edwin whose record could not be traced. 'I'd like confirmation of that as soon as possible.'

'Of course.' She made a note on the front of the folder.

'What about his medical records? You have those?'

'We don't have them but they'll be lodged with his GP, and we naturally have our own records of his medication and so on, as Ellie was in charge of that.'

'Mrs Jack was here when Edwin arrived, of course.'

'Was she?' said Cindy. 'I don't know. I only know she's been here longer than anyone else. You'll obviously want to speak to her.'

'Yes, very much.'

'I'll arrange that. She doesn't start her round until about ten.' Cindy picked up her phone and sent a rapid text. 'I don't think any of the other staff have been here that long, I'm afraid.'

'And the residents? Are any of them likely to remember him?'

She frowned. 'I think Marjory Hodgson would have been here then. She's our longest-serving resident. But to be honest with you poor Marjory, though a lovely woman of course, can barely remember her own name these days. I'm afraid you'll come across that problem with many other residents, too. But you can ask.' She shrugged.

'Thank you.' He would delegate that to someone else.

'If you could supply details of Mr Sheldon's GP and I can speak to Mrs Jack, I think that'll be all.'

'Yes, of course.' Now that the end of the interview was in sight Cindy was looking a lot more relaxed. 'I shall pass on all the other information we have about Mr Sheldon and also whether the information we hold for others is incomplete. I'm sorry I couldn't help you any further.' They got up, and he followed her out of the room as they headed up towards the main part of the home. 'Good luck with your search, Chief Inspector.' And he almost sensed her unspoken thought: *the mess this place is in, you're going to need it.*

SIX

In the lobby there was a breath of fresh, cold air and the decorations on the large tinsel Christmas tree trembled in the tail end of a draught. Beside the tree, on a table, a pristine sheet of paper headed *Visitors*, lay with a pen on top. Whoever had passed through hadn't signed in, another indication of how things were slipping.

'We're waiting to get a digital sign-in system installed,' said Cindy, before he could ask. 'Until then we make do with paper. It's not ideal, I know. I'm going to ask head office to expedite matters.'

She was more chirpy now the interview had ended. He had found the lack of information frustrating but not, he thought, as much as she had. He'd been too much of a gentleman to ask her age but she'd struck him as very young and had admitted that she'd barely been in the job two weeks and hadn't had time to get on top of other people's record-keeping. There had been an unspoken contempt in her tone and he could hardly blame her for it. Here she was, a young woman shunted into a remote corner of the country (her accent implied she was a southerner) doing a job that no-one else would want to touch, and having to deal with the fallout from a cascade of other people's poor decision-making.

'Thanks, Ms Rushall. You've been really helpful.'

'Do you mind if I leave you to wait for Ellie? As you can imagine, I have plenty of other things I really need to get on with.'

'Not at all.'

'Obviously if you need anything else…' She was away through the door without even finishing the sentence, never mind formalising the conclusion of the interview with a handshake.

Left alone, he took the opportunity to check the place out. The sheet of paper was dated that day; there must be a new sheet each day. Cindy hadn't even bothered to sign him in. He wandered around the lobby and checked the notices on the wall — the health and safety instructions and map of the fire exits, a noticeboard headed *Recent Events* which showed nothing later in the year than Easter, and a section labelled *Upcoming!* which had notices about Christmas carols and a tea party, to which family and friends were cordially invited. He had finished there, and was just looking around to see if there was anything else of interest, when the door that led towards the lounge and dining area opened and Ellie Jack appeared.

'They do say there's no show without Punch,' she said, cheerfully, 'and so here you are. Been talking to Cindy about what happened with old Edwin, have you? You won't have got much out of her. It's not her fault, the poor lass, but she's only been here five minutes and she's right out of her depth.'

'She'll have told you I want a word.' Ellie was good

value, a woman who prided herself on knowing everything that went on on her patch and was prepared to tell it. She had mistakes in her past, for sure, but these days her sense of right and wrong was clear cut.

'You always do. Yes, of course. Let me entice you into the airless cupboard they call my office and give you a scummy cup of instant coffee, and you can ask me what you want to know.'

He declined the coffee and followed her along a corridor, then another, and up a few flights of stairs to a niche at the end of the corridor. She hadn't been joking; it did indeed look as if it had once been a walk-in cupboard with the door now removed, and the table and two chairs barely fitted into the space.

'A nice spot they've given you,' he said, squeezing into the second of the chairs.

'This place was never meant to be a care home. It was a bad idea in the first place and the whole show has been badly run for years.' She shrugged. 'I don't know why I haven't moved on. But I'm the longest-serving member of staff, now, and that gives me an odd kind of seniority, like I'm everyone's mother confessor. I wouldn't get that anywhere else. I suppose it flatters my vanity.'

Jude took a moment to reflect once more on Eden's End. Its history was well-known to him. It was a former country house that had become a very high-end, very expensive care home, the final destination for many of the district's wealthier (and, he had to admit, some of the more entitled) residents until, as so often happened, time had caught up with it. Luxury and individuality consumed money and costs would have rapidly outstripped the fees that residents (and their expectant beneficiaries) were prepared to pay. Staff were harder to come by. The cost of living had risen. He remembered Becca telling him the home was on a downward turn, that it wasn't full, that people preferred to leave their money to their families and the cachet it had had, even relatively recently, had been squandered.

'What's it like here, these days?' he asked, attempting to be casual.

Ellie gave him a searching look. She would know a leading question when she saw one. He often thought she'd have made a good detective herself.

'Even worse than it was.' She took a look along the corridor, as if to check that no-one was listening. 'I don't know how your brain works and I don't know what this has to do with poor old Edwin, but I'll bite.'

'I'll tell you,' he said, cheerfully. Honesty was often rewarded with honesty, and it was refreshing when that happened. 'The paperwork relating to Edwin's period of residence here is either missing or destroyed and I was trying to work out which is most likely.'

'Not destroyed, I'd say,' she said, after a moment. 'Not by Cindy, anyway. She's new, she'd have no idea, and if it's a problem it's not hers.'

'Record keeping's not currently an issue, then.'

'That's the thing, isn't it? I imagine that's why you're asking about management. The truth of it is, this place has been in a death spiral since that mess with poor old Violet Ross. You know that.'

'What do you mean, exactly?'

'It was struggling a bit to begin with. You may know we were part of a very small, luxury chain of residential care homes, but two years ago we got bought over by a much bigger national chain. I wouldn't say they neglect this place, but they took one look at the cost and stopped paying for extras. Still charged the same fees, mind, but the punters aren't that stupid. This is lovely, or it once was, and I'd say it's still better than many in terms of rooms and so on, but why would you pay that money? We aren't full. We can't get the staff. When they come they're paid shockingly and they don't stay. Turnover's rapid. Times have overtaken us. I'd say the days of this place are numbered. Our owners shunt the people over here to manage us who are either rookies like Cindy or just not good enough to manage anything that's under scrutiny. The place is in chaos and I wouldn't be at all surprised to find that whole loads of files and papers just got lost along the way. You wouldn't believe how hard I tried to keep everything going but the minute I turned my back… I went on holiday for two weeks and when I came back there were gaps in the drugs record. It would never have happened on my watch.' She gave him a sidelong look, as though she was measuring up what to tell him. 'This place is finished as a nursing home. We'll be a private home or a hotel before you know it.' She sat back, almost breathless after delivering that monologue.

He nodded. It seemed entirely plausible, if the extent of the problems at Eden's End was as great as it seemed, that whoever had impersonated Connie would have had no problem slipping into the office and removing any paperwork that might later prove incriminating, or which could be used to trace and identify her. With no manager in place it was unlikely that anyone had noticed. If Edwin's records were the only ones missing, that would be the most likely explanation. 'You'll have known Edwin pretty well, then.'

'He was here for a couple of years, so yes. In so far as you ever do get to know these older people.'

'And of everyone here, you're the only one who was here when he was?'

'When you put it like that I realise what kind of disaster this place is turning into.' She shook her head. 'Lovely. That means I'm your key witness. Did Cindy tell you about what happened to him?'

'No.'

'I told her about it yesterday when I called her, but I don't blame her for leaving it to someone else to tell you about. Edwin died from an allergic reaction to a dose of penicillin.'

'That's your department,' said Jude with care, 'isn't it?'

'It is, but I wasn't in. I was on a period of extended leave at the time, as my own father was dying. There was an agency nurse in and she was struggling to get on top of who was who and all the rest of it. No-one's quite sure whether she mixed up the drugs or whether Edwin found some lying around somewhere and helped himself. There's no evidence of the first so it might have been the second. He was fully mobile and used to wander about the place quite the thing.'

'There was an inquiry?'

'Of course, and it was an accident.'

Accident. A sudden death preceding a major fraud. It was a very convenient accident. 'Where was his daughter?'

'I don't know. Not here, for sure, or you people would have been all over it.'

'Weren't we?' said Jude, annoyed by having no recollection of any such incident.

'Up to a point, you were. Someone came in and spoke to everyone involved and the man from the inspectorate had a meltdown and read Karen the Riot Act, though I'm pretty certain that only made matters worse for the poor lamb. It was awkward at the time, and embarrassing, and

I'm glad I was nowhere near it, though it probably wouldn't have happened if I had been. But it did make me think, when the real daughter arrived yesterday. And I bet I'm not half as suspicious as you are.'

She was right. Alarm bells had already begun to ring. There would be no need for Jude to justify his visit to Faye now. 'I'm sure. You say it was an accident?'

'That's what they said. But now I'm wondering.'

Understandably. 'And you're the only one who will have seen the woman calling herself Connie Sheldon and pretending to be Edwin's daughter. I know it's a while ago, but I don't suppose you remember what she was like?'

She considered for a moment, head to one side and a slight frown creasing her forehead. 'When did he come here?'

He handed her the printed sheet Cindy had given him and she scanned it. 'Okay. I'd just started, then, but I don't remember him arriving. If I ever saw the Connie who came in yesterday, I don't remember. But I do remember the woman who visited and said she was his daughter. She was quietly spoken and always seemed in a hurry to see him and to leave, though she spent enough time with him when she was here. She would stay for about an hour, certainly every time I remember, and it always seemed to me she couldn't do enough for him. Brought him flowers, his favourite sweeties, read to him. All that sort of thing.'

At last, a lead. Jude leaned forward with interest. 'What did she look like?'

'Not at all like the other Connie, for sure.' Ellie tapped her fingers on the desk. 'That was the first thing that struck me yesterday. There must be a good twenty years between them, maybe more.'

'Edwin was quite an old father, if I remember.'

'I think that's right. He would have been pushing

ninety, for sure. That's why when I first saw Connie yesterday I thought there was a mistake and she was his granddaughter.'

'She's definitely his daughter.'

'Right. So this woman, Connie Two I'll call her, was neat I would say, maybe five foot four, no more than that. She had grey hair, quite short, and she always dressed very tidily and in muted colours. I never noticed anything distinctive about her at all. Not in the way she looked, or spoke, or acted. She was always polite but never stopped to chat, and I'll be honest, I never encouraged it because back in the day we were full and I was rushed off my feet. Now I look back I wonder if she didn't want people to pay too much attention to her.'

'Very possibly. When did she start visiting him?'

'Again, I can't say for sure. There used to be a visitors' book but now we don't even have that. I'll be gobsmacked if we've kept the old ones, and they were never digitised. I don't know when she first came, but eventually she was a regular, a couple of times a week and more often towards the end. She was hugely diligent, I'll say that for her.'

'There's CCTV?'

'Oh, of course, but you know the way it is. It only ever gets reviewed if there's anything suspicious and it auto-deletes, or gets deleted, after a few months.'

He nodded, unsurprised. 'Did you spend much time with him?' He guessed not. The Edwin he knew had been polite but perfunctory. Connie had said he had few friends and part of that would have been because he had no time for small talk.

She shrugged. 'No. I would come into the room sometimes when the daughter — sorry, supposed daughter — was there and she'd always step outside if I was giving him his drugs or whatever. I wouldn't say Edwin had dementia but he had become very institutionalised, very biddable. He was always pleased to see her.'

'Did he ever say anything to you about her?' Jude asked, interested. A middle-aged woman who did her best to make herself even more invisible than nature and society combined already did? Ellie had described a model fraudster.

'Not much. He'd withdrawn into himself, never talked much, never wanted to come out of his room, though he would occasionally wander about looking for his wife. Poor old soul. But no-one else was visiting him, and we didn't have a full-time events coordinator then, not that we do now, so there was no-one to come in and pull him out of himself. Sometimes I'd be in and say something about how nice it was that his daughter came in and he said yes, she was a lovely girl and he was proud of her.'

'Okay. And did she have power of attorney for him?'

'She took charge of the funeral arrangements and everything, so I would imagine she did, yes. But I never saw it. I never needed to.'

There should have been a copy in the office but, like the rest of the documents pertaining to Edwin Sheldon, Cindy had found no sign of it. Connie had said Edwin had refused to hand over control of his affairs but that didn't mean he had not, at a later date, chosen to hand them over to someone else. 'There are other ways of finding out. Thanks. That's helpful. I'll leave it there. I know you're busy.'

'I'm not as busy as I pretend.' She got up and preceded him along the corridor back towards the door. 'The Violet Ross case and that other one we had here…they scared people off. One woman murdered and a murderer, in a place this size? A few people have come to have a look and asked about that and not come back. We're not full, and if people start thinking of us as dangerous, or even unlucky, we never will be again.'

'If you think of anything else, do feel free to let me know, Mrs Jack,' he said, more formally as they reached the reception area and found Cindy taking delivery of something she was clearly not expecting. 'Goodbye, Ms Rushall, and thank you both for your help.'

SEVEN

'You'll have to forgive me,' Connie said, raising her voice to be heard above the hum of the George Hotel's busy lunchtime bar. 'I'm all over the place just now. My head thinks it's four a.m. and my stomach thinks it's suppertime. But I'll do my best.'

'Jet lag's a beast,' said Ashleigh O'Halloran, sympathetically, watching Connie with an interest that was as much about the woman Jude might have once fancied himself in love with (because at eighteen that was how you thought) as it was about evaluating a victim of crime. 'And that's on top of the shock you must have had. I'm so sorry to hear about your father.'

'Thank you,' said Connie, and reached for the cup in front of her as she stifled a yawn.

Waiting while Connie settled in the deep leather armchair and took a reviving sip of coffee, Ashleigh took in the woman in front of her. After what Connie had endured, both physically and emotionally, over the previous few days it was unsurprising that she wasn't looking her best. Her hair was damp and her face pink in a way that suggested she'd slept late and thrown herself through the shower at pace in order to be down in the hotel lounge in time for this meeting, but there was something about her — the way she seemed so eager to please, perhaps, or the slightly mournful expression on her face — which made Ashleigh feel sorry for her in a way she hadn't expected.

'I'm sorry you've had to go through this,' she said, a gentle reminder to Connie why they were there, 'but we'll get to the bottom of this.'

'Yes, Jude said that. I love the way you're so confident. I wish I was. That Eden's End place is so chaotic, and God help me, it's all my fault for putting Dad in there. I should never have neglected him the way I did, but it wasn't just down to me.' She shook her head. 'He played his part in cutting me off. But in the end, one of you has to be the one to make the extra effort, don't you? If I'd just tried that bit harder he wouldn't have died on his own.'

'You shouldn't punish yourself for it,' said Ashleigh, feeling more like a counsellor than an inquisitor. 'No-one thinks it's your fault.'

'I shouldn't and it isn't, but I will.' Connie stuck her chin forward in defiance.

'I've been briefed about what happened when you arrived yesterday,' said Ashleigh, moving the discussion on, 'and someone has been over at Eden's End this morning, following up. We're also looking into what kind of interactions this woman pretending to be you had with your father's solicitor over the will and the subsequent sale of the property.'

'Of course!' Connie brightened. 'I hadn't really thought that it all had to be registered like that. That's going to make it a bit easier.'

'Clever fraudsters do find ways round it, but yes. It's a lead.'

'When you put it like that I feel more optimistic. She must have thought I'd never come back.' Connie's face crinkled in disgust. 'I wonder if it could be someone I knew? Do you think that's possible?'

'Yes, definitely. And we have an idea of what she looked like.' She repeated the description of the woman they now seemed to be calling Connie Two that Jude had texted through at the conclusion of his visit to Eden's End and watched as Connie frowned and shook her head.

'I mean,' said Connie with a sigh, 'sixty, grey hair, neutral colours? it probably describes three quarters of the women who visit in that fossilised place.'

'It's possible that it's someone who knew your father,' suggested Ashleigh.

'Not in a million years. He wasn't really interested in women after Mum died, and in any case why would she pretend to be me? And more to the point, why would he pretend she was?'

To Ashleigh, the first question was more easily answered than the second. There was money at stake, and if a substantial property up at Fair Hill in Penrith was involved and its rightful inheritor showed no signs of coming home, then impersonating her was worth a gamble. The mystery was how Connie Two had persuaded Edwin to go along with it and how she'd managed to get away with it. 'Can you tell me about your family, Connie?' It might trigger her memory.

'God,' said Connie, pouring herself another coffee from the pot on the table between them and then waving the pot at Ashleigh, who declined. 'I've done nothing but think about it, but I suppose a pair of fresh eyes will help me see things differently. Jude always used to say that, or something like it. It's hardly a surprise he turned out to be a policeman.'

'What about your home life? Could that description fit anyone in your extended family?'

'Possibly. There aren't many and I haven't seen them for so many years I wouldn't even know what they looked like.' Connie's expression creased into one of misery. 'I knew I was a terrible daughter but now I see I was a pretty lousy relative in general. I don't even know if that description fits any of them.'

'It's hard when you're on the other side of the world.'

'But not impossible. Maybe someone was punishing me for behaving so badly towards him. But I can't think of anyone else who cared about him as much as I did, certainly not enough to hurt me because of it.'

'No-one's suggesting you behaved badly to him.' Even if Jude hadn't warned her Ashleigh would have found Connie's assumption of responsibility for her own usurpation intriguing, if only because it showed her vulnerability.

'I don't know. I really loved him, that's the worst of it, but after my mum died I really struggled. He did as well. The problem for me was that he wasn't her, and I suppose it was the same for him. There came a point where we were fighting constantly. It was after I'd been to uni and I found it so difficult to go home where she wasn't and where he was moping around like a lost soul — that's when our relationship really broke down. I suppose neither of us was strong enough to cope for ourselves and we weren't strong enough to offer each other support, either.'

'Wasn't there anyone else?'

'No,' said Connie, frankly. 'He had no family and I was an only child. He never liked Mum's family and they live down south somewhere anyway so we never saw them from one year to the next. There's no way it was one of them. He would have shouted them out of the place.'

It was a puzzle. Nothing Connie had said so far offered any clue to a solution. 'What about his later life? You may find this idea uncomfortable, but is it possible he could have intended to play some kind of trick on you?'

'I wondered that.' Connie set the coffee down, carefully. In the background of the hotel bar someone turned on the music system and Darlene Love boomed out too loud, before the music was swiftly turned down again to background level. 'My life's a complete car crash, and has been ever since I lost Mum. I don't think there's a relationship mistake I haven't made and I don't suppose I'll learn now. I married the first man who was seriously interested in me. He was much older and of course I was looking for a father figure and — of course — it was a terrible mistake. Dad didn't take to my husband and although he did come to the wedding he just sat glowering in the corner the whole time. The marriage barely lasted six months and it was partly because of that. After a few years I came back here because I needed to get away and had nowhere else to go, and met someone else but he was married.' She rolled her eyes. 'He left his wife and that was messy and Dad disapproved of him, too.' She paused for breath. 'That was Matthew, and actually I think he did love me.'

'That's when you went to Australia?' prompted Ashleigh, as Connie's mind seemed to wander down pathways in the past.

'Yes for a fresh start. *Another one*, Dad said, and that annoyed me. He was starting to decline a little by then and he had a fall so I knew he wasn't going to be able to manage on his own. The last time we visited I suggested he should try and move into somewhere more manageable and was surprised when he eventually agreed.' She paused. 'That was the thing, I suppose. He was very hard-headed. He knew he'd end up on his own and he knew there was no way I'd be able to look after him when I was in Australia, even if I wanted to. I had the twins by then. I was even more surprised when he agreed to move into Eden's End. It had a much better reputation then, quite smart, more like a hotel for geriatrics than a care home, but my God, what a shock I had yesterday. It's gone downhill quickly.' She laughed.

'You took him to the care home and signed the paperwork?'

'He signed the paperwork himself. He was fully mentally competent and he made it quite clear that he wasn't about to give me control of his money. I'd assumed if anything became necessary, his solicitor would deal with it.' She shrugged. 'I wonder what he'll have to say about it?'

The Sheldon family solicitor was on Ashleigh's to-do list. It would be interesting to hear how he explained having sold the family property and filled in the probate application for the wrong beneficiary. Immediately, she suspected collusion. 'Were you in contact with the solicitor at any point while you were away?'

She shook her head. 'I never had any reason to be. We don't have much cause for solicitors and when it came to my divorce I used someone else.' She rubbed her eyes, obviously still struggling. 'I don't even know the name of the person he dealt with, only the firm. Jesus, someone must hate me.'

'I don't think so.' Ashleigh's sympathy for Connie was somehow tempered with cynicism and she couldn't tell why. She didn't think the woman was putting on an act and she'd made far too many mistakes of her own to stand in judgement on someone else's relationship failings. 'It's fraud, a scam. In my experience, scammers can't afford to get personal.' It made them take unnecessary risks. To be a successful fraudster you needed to pick your victims with extreme care and know when they were beginning to suspect and it was time to move on and try elsewhere.

'It's a bloody clever one, then.' Connie folded her lips into a narrow scowl.

'It seems that way, and it seems as if it was carefully planned over a long period of time, by someone who knew your family setup pretty well. That's what I'd like you to think about. Is there anyone who knew what you were doing, when you were away, the fact that you weren't on good terms with your father. All that? Because it seems to me that that's the most likely starting point for this.'

'Oh, I see. Right. And I'm going to guess it can't be somebody I know too well, because I'd know if they suddenly came into a small fortune. At least, I assume it's a small fortune. His care cost a lot, of course, but he hadn't had to sell the house to fund it and he had plenty of other assets.'

'They might manage to keep the money concealed, so let's not rule anyone out because they aren't obviously rich, but yes, I think someone a little removed from you would know. And remember, it doesn't have to be a woman.'

'Of course. She could be an accomplice. Okay. The obvious person is my ex-husband. Peter Nash. I'm not sure where he is these days, but I can find out. We aren't in touch but we have plenty of mutuals so he'd know about Dad, if he wanted to. Then there are the cousins. I suppose it's possible for them to have heard about what's going on, and they might actually think they had a right to some of it. Mum had some family money, you see. Then there's my husband's ex. Melanie Trotter.' She laughed as she said the name, not altogether kindly. 'She lived in the same street as us for a while and I think her parents might still be there. She'll definitely know.'

'Any friends?' prompted Ashleigh.

'So-called friends, if it was them.' Connie's expression turned even more sour, if that was possible. 'There's Adam Fleetwood. He always knows everything.'

'He was out of commission at the time.' With his criminal record and his desire for money he couldn't earn Adam Fleetwood, Jude's bête noire, was always a tempting candidate for the culprit, but not only was Adam a petty criminal who was unlikely to have the wherewithal for such a crime, he had been in prison at the time of Edwin Sheldon's death. That said, fraud was a crime that could be years in the planning and could easily be masterminded from a distance.

'I didn't really think it was him, but he did know I never intended to come back from Australia. At least, that was what I said when I went there.' Connie sighed. 'That's it, I'm afraid.'

Thanking her, Ashleigh got to her feet, shook Connie's hand and took her leave. As she reached the door she looked back and saw her dabbing at her eyes with a tissue. For a moment she thought of going back, but she changed her mind and headed back to the office. The best way to comfort Connie was to find out who had stolen her inheritance and restore it to her.

EIGHT

'How did you get on with Connie?' Jude made his way across the open plan office to where Ashleigh was sitting with a notepad in front of her and what he thought was a rather quizzical expression on her face. 'And did you get a chance to speak to the solicitor?'

She pushed the notebook away and the expression shifted to one of faint dissatisfaction. 'I did, yes, though without much joy. As for how I got on with Connie, it's kind of difficult to say, really. The poor woman was all over the place, so I don't imagine I saw the best of her.'

The quizzical look, he now understood, had been aimed at him. His teenage relationship with Connie might be many years in the past and his almost-romance with Ashleigh only very recently deceased, but the two of them were cut from the same cloth and would always be more than friends. As a result, Ashleigh's interest in Connie was more personal than that of an investigating officer in a victim of crime. Connie was another piece of the jigsaw of his life to which Ashleigh was now privy. In life it was rare that any one individual saw another completely. He understood her interest, even as he acknowledged a slight resentment towards it. 'Do you want to compare notes just now?'

'Yes, let's, if you've time. I've become very absorbed in this case, I have to say.' That look again. 'It's a proper puzzle. Though having said that, given I've only been on it a few hours I've managed to cover a remarkable amount of ground and acquire a lot of information.'

'Is it any use?' he asked, and grinned. He'd spent many long hours as a junior detective sifting through endless data only for someone else to come up with the key piece of information.

'I expect it will be, when we've had time to look at it and see how it fits together.'

He pulled up a chair and sat down. As he did so the door swung open with more than usual force, heralding the arrival of Detective Superintendent Faye Scanlon. As usual when Faye erupted into an office, every head in the incident room turned towards her to see which of them was the focus of her attention. On this occasion after her cursory scan of the room she made a beeline for Jude and Ashleigh.

'Excellent,' she said, 'two birds with one stone. What's this I've been hearing about yet another crime at that cursed nursing home?'

Jude got up and pulled up a chair for her. Briefing Faye had been the next item on his to-do list. It never ceased to amaze him how she always knew things before she was officially notified. 'It's an interesting one.'

'So I believe. Tell me all about it. It's exactly the kind of case I joined the force to solve. A nice clean fraud without any violence and no risk to life. Assuming that's what it is and there's no suggestion of murder?'

Jude was never quite sure when Faye was joking, and

he sensed that she liked it like that, that keeping her junior officers guessing was vital to her management strategy. With a gesture, he delegated the question to Ashleigh.

'None,' she said, 'as far as I can tell. Edwin Sheldon was eighty seven and in a nursing home. I spoke to his GP, who told me he was in increasingly poor health and I have the impression he'd rather given up. He died as a result of an allergic reaction to penicillin.'

'What?' said Faye, sitting up.

'Yes. There was a full investigation and nothing was conclusive. He was in the habit of wandering about and he may have picked up medication that was left for someone else. The matter was investigated by the authorities at the time and deemed an accident. He was relatively young by some standards but his death wasn't unexpected.'

'Let's hear the details.' She stared at Jude. 'You've been out at the nursing home, I hear. That either means you've nothing else to do or you think it's serious.'

He was never sure how she knew these things, but although their working relationship was sometimes strained, he had to admire her fierce and phenomenal grasp of detail. 'It's a major fraud, so yes, I think it's serious. I was going to come up and talk to you about it a bit later, because it's something you'll want to be involved in and it's going to need a lot of time and resources.'

'They all do,' she said with a shrug. 'Eden's End does seem to attract them, doesn't it? I sometimes wonder if I should just make that place a cost centre in its own right.'

'It seems so.' Briefly, he outlined the result of his visit to Eden's End. 'I didn't get much from the manager. She's new. Karen Grant was in charge at the time that Edwin Sheldon was admitted and obviously we can't speak to her.'

'Why not? Is she dead?'

'Yes.' Faye hadn't been in Cumbria the first time murder had visited Eden's End. 'It was unfortunate. She embezzled a considerable sum of money from the business.'

'I'm not sure *unfortunate* is the word I would use.'

'She drowned in the Eden,' said Jude, thinking more sympathetically than Faye of Karen Grant. 'The verdict was suicide, though I'm not sure she intended to kill herself. She had a lot of personal issues and no support network. It's entirely plausible to me that the paperwork from that period is in chaos, even years after those events. The home's a small part of a larger operation and never a priority to sort out. According to Ellie Jack the place has been on a downhill slide since she died, and probably before. If someone knew that—'

'Would they know it?' demanded Faye.

'I think so. It's pretty much an open secret locally. That being the case, there's every chance someone spotted an opportunity to slide in and pretend to be Connie, knowing there's a good chance of getting away with it. The real mystery, I think, is the part that Edwin played. He told the staff the woman was his daughter Connie.'

'Could he have been making mischief?' hazarded Faye. 'It's unlikely, I know, but stranger things happen.'

'Possibly. I don't think so, though.'

'You don't? Because naturally you knew him.'

It was always sweet when he could meet Faye's sarcasm head on. 'Yes, I did. I used to date Connie about twenty years back. Briefly, but long enough to go round to her house quite often.' He thought of Edwin Sheldon as he'd known him. Edwin had been a man characterised by a suppressed anger at the injustice of the world, but he'd had no obvious sense of humour and had never seemed malicious.

'Hmm,' said Faye. 'I doubt that counts as a conflict of interest. I see why you're keen to help, though. Fair enough. What else?'

At this, they both turned back to Ashleigh, who had jotted down a note of headings while Jude had been speaking.

'I've touched enough bases this morning to conclude that there's serious fraud here,' she said. 'I've checked with the Office of the Public Guardian. A Power of Attorney was registered by Edwin Sheldon, naming Connie as his attorney and giving his home address as a contact for her. She was using it as a postal address at the time, as her life was in a particular state of turmoil.'

Jude nodded. Clearly Connie and Edwin's relationship hadn't, at bottom, been that bad and it had certainly not been broken beyond repair, but he could see that both of them would have relished the fight. 'She said he'd refused to name her as his attorney.'

'That might just mean he didn't tell her he'd done it.' Faye was by now extremely interested. 'I'm beginning to see how this happened. Disarray at the nursing home. Edwin may have given them a copy of the PoA document, or at least told them about it, but I doubt if we'll ever know for sure. If someone knew — if this woman came to visit, perhaps, if she's someone he knows, perhaps she was able to persuade him. She could intercept the mail at the house — maybe took a key somehow — and produce an alternative identity.'

'According to Ellie Jack this woman was twenty years older than Connie, at least,' pointed out Jude.

'There's make up. And why would anyone suspect, especially if they didn't know Connie and had no idea what she looked like? Though I grant you, the solicitors should have done their due diligence rather better than looks to have been the case, but even then the documents might have been forged.'

'The matter of the will,' said Ashleigh, tapping the next point on her list with her forefinger, 'was dealt with by Andrew Richards, a junior solicitor, straight out of law school. He's still at the practice and I've spoken to him. He says that all the required documents were presented to him when the matter of probate was being dealt with, but that he only met Connie Armstrong, as her name then was and as he believed this woman to be, once, very briefly. He's sending me copies of the relevant documentation.'

'How much money is involved?'

'With the house, and with money left to him by his wife, and with his own assets, Edwin's estate amounted to a fairly tidy sum, somewhere around four hundred thousand pounds.'

It was a lot of money for a relatively small-time criminal but nevertheless Jude thought that if he'd been tempted to turn to crime he might have wanted rather more return for the effort he'd put in and the risk involved. 'I want to say it sounds opportunistic but if it is, it's a very specific opportunity. Either someone put a lot of thought into it, or they gambled a lot and got lucky every time.'

'So what happened to the money?' asked Faye. 'That's the obvious place to start. Follow the money. Always. If it's fraud, that's the motive.'

'The money was paid into a local building society. Connie Two opened an account especially for it. I haven't had time to check but I'll be astonished if that account wasn't closed pretty much immediately, and the money transferred elsewhere.'

'In which case we'll probably be able to trace it, given time.' This was Jude's first spark of optimism. If Connie Two was an opportunist rather than a career criminal, then her attempts at money laundering might prove inadequate. 'Good. It'll take a bit of effort, but…'

He left it trailing deliberately and looked surreptitiously at Faye. His early mention of resources had received no response and for once Faye had ignored the delicate subject of the cost that inevitably went with the effort. She was notoriously stingy when it came to allocating resources whereas he was naturally inclined the other way, to spend as much as the job in hand required. As the senior officer, Faye had the final say and while there was no question in his mind that she'd approve a significant spend on this problem, he also knew her accommodation would have its limits.

She surprised him, waving a hand. 'This is major fraud and the woman might try and do it again. We can get the forensic accountants onto it.'

'Right,' said Ashleigh, the slight lift of her eyebrows signifying to Jude that she was as taken aback by this as he was. 'So that brings us to who might have done it. I wonder if the woman posing as Connie might have been an accomplice, someone recruited specifically for the purpose rather than with any direct connection to the family. That would explain why no-one recognised her. I'd guess she may initially have introduced herself as her real self, or perhaps a distant relative, and over the course of her visits gaslit Edwin, as he became more institutionalised and began to lose his memory and slip into dementia, into believing she was actually his daughter.'

They digested this. 'It's not impossible, of course,' said Faye, 'but is it realistic?'

'I don't see why not. If his memory was starting to go she could easily have done something to convince him. She could Photoshop herself into pictures with him and switch them for any photos he might already have had, for example. We don't know what he had with him in the home but I'd be astonished if he didn't take family photographs, for example. I can check with Connie and see if she knows.'

If that were true, it would be the cruellest deception. Until that moment Jude had been inclined to see Connie as the only real victim; now he saw that Edwin Sheldon's last years might also have been subverted by the plot to obtain his estate after his death. He felt his mouth twist with disgust. 'Good point, especially if it was someone he did vaguely know.'

'Did you ask Ms Sheldon about who might have been in any position to do this?' asked Faye, leaning forward to rest her elbows on the table and place her chin on her hands, focusing on Ashleigh like a retriever about to set off after a rabbit.

'Yes. You'll be amused to hear, Jude,' she said, turning to him with a wry smile, 'that the person who knew everything was a friend of yours. Adam Fleetwood.'

'Adam Fleetwood?' Faye pounced. 'Why does everything keep coming back to your private life?' She turned to Jude, now, this time accusingly.

It was hardly a surprise: Jude made a point of knowing people and he'd lived in this area all his life. The same applied to Adam. It was inevitable that their paths frequently crossed. 'As I said, I was at school with Connie. So was Adam. We were all part of the same friendship group all the way through secondary school. After that we went our separate ways, as you do, but I believe Connie and Adam kept in touch throughout.'

'He was in prison when all this took place,' said Ashleigh, 'and on that basis we can pretty much rule him out. Wouldn't you agree?'

Jude nodded. It was the kind of thing Adam might very well wish he'd have come up with but he thought it unlikely his former friend would have had the patience to construct and carry out such a devious plot, even if it hadn't meant defrauding a close friend. But then again, friendship had never meant that much to Adam. 'Yes.'

'There are other friends. There are other family members.' Faye's mouth was set in a stubborn line. 'I know I said it was a nice clean fraud, but I find myself disliking this particular perpetrator more and more every time I think about it. I shall take a positive pleasure in bringing her to justice.'

NINE

Two days had passed in a whirl of windy weather and a kaleidoscope of pre-Christmas cheer, a haze of skipped meals, sleepless nights and soothing glasses of wine, before Connie had recovered from the effects of her journey halfway round the world. It was then that the ramifications of what had happened became properly clear to her. When she was at last able to process what had happened, what that struck her most was the void that had suddenly appeared at the heart of her life. The plans she had made before leaving had vanished like frost in the sun. She'd expected to live in the family home, where she would have no need to worry about rent and she would have had a grace period in which she could live in comfortable silence. She would have spent weeks — longer if necessary — visiting her father and mending long-broken fences while she decided what she would do, whether she would stay in England or go back, whether there was any chance in fighting for her boys to join her if she did. True, it hadn't been much of a future but it had

had a form, and outcomes (for good or bad) and now even that was taken away from her.

Finally, she remembered resilience. There was no point in mithering about it. She was where she was, and now she was able to look at matters with a cooler head it was time to be realistic about how desperate her situation was. Tiring of the slightly stuffy comfort of her hotel, not to mention its slightly forced Friday-night jollity and the wail of Mariah Carey coming through the speakers in the bar, she wandered down through the town, trying to recapture a flavour of her childhood and adolescence. In some ways nothing had changed; in others, the difference was marked. The big retail development that had been being built when she went to university was now an integral part of the town. A number of small businesses had gone, and new ones had sprung up in their place; others had changed hands. There was now an M&S food hall in the town centre (she noted that with approval).

Once her walk had satisfied her that not everything had changed, she identified a cool and sophisticated wine bar which was very much a positive addition to the town of her adolescence, and settled in the window with a large glass of Australian Shiraz. The place was busy with December drinkers coming in after work, their hair glistening with the drizzle that seemed to make the air hang thick and grey in the streetlights. Every now and again a middle-aged woman would pass by, under an umbrella or a thick woollen hat, or with a hood up against the rain. She took a second look at every one of them, struck by how many of them there were, how indistinguishable one was from another. Was this what happened when women passed fifty? Did they become alike, swarming like bees everywhere you looked, never meeting your eye?

Her mother had not lived to fifty. She shrugged the unwelcome memory aside. There were more immediate things to consider than an old bereavement. The first thing was to find somewhere to live. She couldn't afford to stay at the hotel for ever and nor, tiring already of its old English comfort, did she want to. She'd have to find somewhere to rent or even seek out an old friend to stay with, trading on their goodwill. She was self-aware enough to know that it was better not to go down that route after so long, though if she was absolutely desperate she might have to. It was a mistake, she now saw, to have taken so much delight in dropping almost everyone to embark on her new life.

That life seemed years away. Later that evening, when the time in Australia was more respectable, she'd do what she dreaded and call home. She loved her sons and they loved her, and in the natural order of things she would have brought them home with her but Matthew was adamant that he didn't want to move from Australia for both professional and personal reasons and Connie herself was so tired of the place that she thought living there any longer would kill her, so they'd reached an impasse. Their interaction would be brief. The boys would tell her about their school and she would tell them she loved them. At some point shortly thereafter Matthew would take the phone and tell her they had to hurry away to cricket practice or whatever, and she would tell him there was something they really had to talk about. Then, much later, she would have to tell him what had happened to her and hope he was sufficiently over his bitterness at her abandonment to be kind to her.

The thought depressed her. That her father had died without her at his side was hardly her fault, except at the margins, but the breakup with Matthew could be laid at no-one's door but her own. It was entirely foreseeable that the twins, born and bred in Australia, had no desire to follow her to a strange and distant mother country of which they knew nothing.

It is what it is, she repeated to herself, picking up her half-empty glass and turning it so that it picked up the sparkling lights from outdoors and in, until it was like holding a microcosm of the glittering universe in her hand. Emboldened, she was brave enough, or foolish enough, to do what she'd been trying not to do for the last few days and call Jude. She reached for her phone.

Jude picked up her call straight away, his voice clear against a background of laughter which implied that he, too, was in some pub somewhere, with friends or colleagues, drinking to the end of another working week. Wherever it was, Mariah bloody Carey was playing there, too.

'Sorry to have bothered you,' she said, and found herself smoothing down her hair as if he could see her. 'I suppose you're busy.'

'Not what I'd normally call busy. A few of the team are out for a few drinks on the way home from work. Is everything okay?' He sounded warmly interested, she thought, or maybe that was just wishful thinking on her part.

'Yes. I was just feeling bit sorry for myself. I'll struggle to do anything else until this is all sorted, so I thought I'd phone you and see if you have any update.'

'I was going to check in with you tomorrow, but now's as good a time as any. In short, it's all about tracing the money. It's major fraud and we're treating it seriously.'

She listened, sipping at the smooth Shiraz, as he went over the details of how much effort they were taking over her problems. The solicitor, the care home, the banks, nothing firm yet but a quiet confidence that the impostor would be uncovered, sooner or later.

'The will is a little more complicated,' he said, with a note of caution creeping in to his tone. 'As it's been legally settled and registered, it will be up to you to challenge it in court.'

'Will that be a problem?' Her heart sank.

'I wouldn't imagine so, but it'll be a chore. Assuming we get a conviction you'll have a solid case.'

'Will it take long?'

'These things always do, especially when you get into the realms of forensic accounting. But I have a hunch that the alternative you isn't exactly part of a complex international crime syndicate and if that's the case she may be more than happy to tell us everything, once we find her.'

'I hope you're right.' Of course she hadn't expected she'd get the house back straight away, but it was another reminder that she had nowhere to go. She picked up the glass again.

'I might not be, but in my experience there's a certain type of person for whom crime seems like a good idea until they do it and realise they're going to spend all their lives waiting for a knock at the door. Then they just want to tell you everything and get the weight off their conscience. This has to be traceable, and she must know it.'

Alternatively the woman might have spent the money already and taken off to the other side of the world. What was the use in being owed money by a fraudster who couldn't pay? 'I'm so glad you're dealing with it. I feel such a fool. I don't even know where she's buried him.'

'I can tell you that. It's all recorded up at the solicitor's. He's in the cemetery at Penrith, next to your mother.'

'Next to, not in with?' she asked, flooded by a sudden tide of anxiety. 'Separate headstones?'

'I don't know, but I imagine so.'

That made it a little better. She didn't think she could have borne it if this woman, whom she was increasingly finding she hated, had appropriated her mother as well. 'I'll go up. I was going to go and take flowers to Mum but I haven't got round to it.' Just as well. It would have been another shock to stumble upon another unexpected reminder of her father, of her neglect of him, of the fact that someone else had at least been there for him when he died, however venal their reason might be. That was what hurt most. Someone had helped her father and he would have been grateful to her for it. 'May I ask you a favour?'

'Yes, of course.'

'As I said, I'd like to go up and visit his grave. Both of their graves.' She swallowed. 'On Sunday. It would have been his birthday.' He would have been ninety, and that was one of the reasons she'd come home so precipitately — so that she would be able to spend it with him. 'Would you come with me?'

He hesitated for a moment, and she hoped that was because he was mentally checking whether he was free and if not whether he could rearrange things to accommodate her, rather than because he was trying frantically to produce a suitable excuse.

'Sunday?' he said, sounding brisk. 'Yes, I think so. Tomorrow would have been trickier, and if you could possibly make it the morning that would suit me better, but yes.'

'Thank you. I wouldn't ask, but…' She squeezed her eyes tight to suppress the tears. 'This is all so bloody difficult!'

'I understand. Do you want to knock on my door at the back of ten? We can walk up.'

'Of course. Thank you so much,' said Connie, again, overwhelmed with gratitude.

'See you Sunday,' he said, and rang off.

She laid down her phone, feeling a little better about matters. Her head was still full of confusion and every time she started to get a grip on the practical side of things she found herself emotional, but she'd get over that soon enough. She went to the bar and ordered herself another glass, taking it back to the table and sitting watching the passers-by. When she had somewhere to live she would get a job, as a matter of urgency. She had no idea about either the property market or the job market locally but there had been a sign in the window of the wine bar advertising for a part-time employee, so if all else failed she could do that until something better came up. Thank God she'd never been afraid of hard work.

Then what? Her optimism ran thin. Eventually she and Matthew would settle on a divorce and the house would be sold, but that wouldn't happen overnight. Until then she was on her own.

She picked up her phone to check for non-existent messages, and as she did so her eye was caught by a group of women walking along the street. She watched them with a fatal fascination. It was inevitable. The way her life was going she was bound to bump into the one person who had the most reason to dislike her, and here she was — Melanie Trotter, Matt's first wife, walking ahead of a group of women all dressed up in red and gold and tinsel . It looked like a girls' night out, which would make it even worse because they would all have Melanie's side of the story and all be sympathetic.

Inevitably (because they'd hardly be heading for the

Sainsbury's café, if it even had one) they stopped in a giggle and a gaggle at the door to wait for a few stragglers, teetering on high heels. This gave Connie a precious few minutes to turn away, to pretend to be looking for something in her handbag, to drop something on the floor and bend down to look for it, but she passed up the opportunity. If she was going to stay in Penrith she'd encounter her predecessor as Matt's wife sooner rather than later. It was unfortunate that Melanie, like Connie, had probably had a drink and that she was surrounded by her friends but even then, Connie was no coward. It was much better to get this confrontation over with. She sat back and looked steadily at the group as they came in and scanned the room, presumably for a reserved table, and then her eyes met Melanie's and the deed was done. They stared at one another for a second, then Melanie turned away and followed her friends to the other side of the wine bar.

Connie's sense of relief was short-lived. With much crashing of chairs the group finally settled and sent in their drinks order, but it was a matter of moments before she saw, in the plate glass windows, the reflection of Nemesis approaching. She turned in her chair and smiled. Melanie was even more mercurial than Connie herself (Matthew, it turned out, was attracted to that type of woman while proving totally unable to cope with them) and could choose either to go fully confrontational or merely purr like a cat plotting an assassination.

She opted for the first, perching on the upholstered arm of the empty chair at the table so that she could loom over Connie. 'Goodness me, Connie Sheldon. It is you! I didn't recognise you at first. You look very old, darling. Is it all that sun?'

'Sun's so healthy.' Connie picked up her glass. If the truth were told, Melanie wasn't looking that great herself.

'Much better than the lack of Vitamin D that makes everyone around here look so dull and pale.'

'A little bird told me you've split up with Matthew.' There was a smug satisfaction in her voice.

Had he told her? Connie shrugged. 'It happens. As you know.'

'I'd love to say I'm sorry it didn't work out for you, but you know what? I'm not. I hope it hurts. I hope it hurts like hell for ever.'

Connie stared into the street. The wine was making her light-headed, but she took another sip, for comfort.

'That's not all I hear. You've been the talk of the town. Though, now I know what you're like perhaps it's no surprise your dad took up with someone else—'

Took up with someone else? 'If I were you, Mel, I'd be sorry for someone who's been through what I've been through.'

'I doubt it. And anyway, you deserve it. You do, Connie, because you're a bitch and a marriage wrecker and everyone knows it. Don't think any of your old friends want you back. Every woman knows you'll be after her man.'

Connie had genuinely loved Matthew and thought she still did, and that he still cared about her, too. It was just that love, and distance, had been untenable. 'Don't worry, Mel. If I see you coming I won't waste my time on you.'

'You're a bitch,' repeated Melanie, her voice pitched a little higher so that a woman at the next table turned and looked at her with a raised eyebrow and then, sensing the temperature rising, turned swiftly away. 'A prize-winning bitch. I wouldn't stay here if I were you. You'll have no friends. We know what you are. I'm going to make your life hell. God, that's going to be fun.'

Even more hell. In an effort not to respond, Connie

instead reacted to a message notification on her phone, ignoring Melanie in order to read a detailed offer of a new, up-to-the-minute mobile phone from the provider she'd signed up with just weeks earlier. Then she put the phone back in her pocket, turned slightly away to give the other woman the cold shoulder, and after a moment was hugely relieved to feel the looming shadow slide away and leave her in peace, to finish her drink and get the hell out of there.

TEN

'Do you know the worst of it?' asked Connie, as she and Jude scaled the steep slope of Wordsworth Street towards the cemetery that spread across the hillside above Beacon Edge. She was clutching a large bunch of chrysanthemums in various shades of red, gold spray shimmering on the foliage and greenery that bulked it out. 'It's that I see this woman everywhere. Every inoffensive, dull, dumpy woman in her fifties who walks by. *What if it's her?* But do you know what? When you stop and look, there are hundreds of them. They all have the same hairstyle and the same frumpy clothes and they sidle along pavements and slink out of the way as if they're afraid. Everywhere. And somehow I never noticed them before. Like when you have toothache and are trying to ignore it and somehow every second building is a dental surgery.'

He laughed. He'd always been fond of Connie, and even this, which she had delivered as if it were a plea for help, amused him more than usual because he knew exactly what it was that made her say it. Connie's wit was always dry and more than a little self-deprecating. 'That's only because you don't usually pay attention to them. It's the same with any group. Think of teenagers. They all dress the same, or pretty nearly, and if you don't know you might lump them all together. But every one is different, if you look.'

'I suppose I've never had much cause to look at old people,' she conceded. 'But now I do, they're everywhere.'

'Yes, because now you're looking.'

'I keep thinking. Every single one I see in the street. *Maybe it's her.*'

'One of them might be,' he said, cheerfully, 'and even if not we'll find her.' He'd normally be wary of such a bold assertion but today he was buoyantly optimistic. Faye's surprising enthusiasm for fighting Connie's corner would prevent a potentially long investigation from stalling, and his instinct told him that the perpetrator was an amateur and would betray herself through her mistakes.

They'd reached the top of the road by now, where Wordsworth Street met the broad avenue that ran along the side of Beacon Hill. The cemetery sat at the northern end of it, up on the hill where the dead and their mourners could look out over the Ullswater trough and the northern fells, where the cool curve of Blencathra stood in splendid isolation to one side with the rugged profile of the Helvellyn range away to the south. Like a magician flourishing a rabbit pulled from a hat, the previously dispiriting month of December had produced, out of nowhere, a beautiful day. The morning was fresh and bright and the duck-egg blue sky so clear and icy that it looked as if you might throw a stone up into it and it would crack.

'My point,' went on Connie, tucking the stray flap of a bright green scarf into her coat with her free hand, 'is that I'd never really thought about old women before. Of course, Dad was rather older, if you remember, but that was different. When I went into Eden's End there was a middle-aged woman just getting into her car. There was another one when I was leaving, and one at the solicitor's. It's like they're haunting me. I expect the graveyard is full of them. And so, of course, I start getting mawkish and worrying about how one day I'll be one of them.'

'We're none of us getting younger,' he said, as they crossed the road. Connie had tried to explain her point but he was no nearer getting it. What he did think was that she was lonely, prone to melancholy, and blaming herself for what had happened. Knowing what he knew of Connie's character and of her life story he could see how other people might judge her, but he was less inclined to do so. She'd had plenty of trouble in her life and he knew the sudden loss of her mother had scarred her. It didn't remotely surprise him that she'd chased after commitment and then, when she'd found it, run away. Nor was he surprised that she was back here in such a state, throwing herself at a problem without thought. Connie had made mistakes like everyone did, and she should probably try harder to forgive herself, but this wasn't the time or the place for that conversation. It could wait until she had begun to heal.

'It's ridiculous that I'm being haunted by old ladies, isn't it?' she said, cheerfully. 'Still, I've always been a bit of an idiot, so I don't suppose I'll stop now. Or maybe I just feel everyone's out to get me. Did I tell you I ran into Melanie?'

'I don't think I know who you mean.'

'My husband's first wife. It was just after I called you on Friday. She was quite...well, unpleasant, I suppose. I understand that she feels bad, though I'm actually not a marriage wrecker. It was on the rocks before I came along, but Matt said she flat-out refused to accept it. I suppose it's always easier to have someone else to blame for your own mistakes. Anyway, she made me feel incredibly unwelcome, so perhaps it's women my own age I should be looking out for, not the older ones.' She laughed, a thin, brittle laugh that didn't convince Jude and almost certainly didn't even convince Connie herself. 'That's not why we're here. Let's get on.'

They walked the few hundred yards to the cemetery gates in silence. The previous day's rain had frozen and was beginning to thaw in the weak winter sun, making the ungritted pavement treacherous underfoot. At the gate, Connie stopped and squinted up the hill. 'Is it ridiculous to say I'm a little nervous?'

'Not at all.' For a second Jude wondered if her hesitation was down to the fact that she couldn't quite remember where her mother's grave was. He was toying with how to ask without sounding insulting when she took off and charged up the narrow gravel path towards the top of the hill, the ends of her scarf flapping behind her in the breeze. Wary of imposing on what was both intense and private grief he followed, keeping a respectable distance, and yet being available for support if she should need it.

On a crossing point in the path she paused for a while and waited for him to catch up. 'Nearly there.' Her face was pink with exertion and, he suspected, emotion. 'It's just along here. I haven't been up for such a long time, not even when I came back to settle Dad in at Eden's End. It was raining and I was so emotional about everything I made it an excuse. I feel terrible about it now. Do you think she'll forgive me?'

'Of course.' Jude suppressed his smile. Connie had always been flamboyantly emotional about everything and never attempted to hide it. When they were much younger it had been one of the things that had attracted him to her. He'd been captured by her passion for everything and her disregard for the consequences; his mother had once sagely observed that Connie had probably been in awe of his calm and measured approach. Opposites attracted, after all, or they had done back then. 'Why wouldn't she?'

'Oh, you know. Because it might seem like she was out of sight and out of mind. But I do think of her often. I mean, every single day, and just now I think of her more than ever.' She turned away from him but not before he saw the brightness in her eyes that suggested she might be about to cry. 'Anyway, why worry? I can pop along and ask her.' A few yards along the path, she stopped. 'It's this one.'

There were two headstones, side by side and set a little closer together than those around them, and he noticed that she was fixing her eyes very firmly upon the more weathered of the two rather than the one next to it. He did the same. *In loving memory of Mary Sheldon, beloved wife of Edwin, mother of Connie.* It was made of Lakeland granite, large pink crystals on a fine-grained grey background, and there was an empty metal flower vase in front of it.

Still refusing to look anywhere else, Connie produced a bottle of water from her bag, splashed half of it into the metal vase and begin pulling some of the stems out of the bunch of flowers she'd bought. 'They can share the flowers. Do you think they'll mind?'

'Why would they?'

'You don't, do you Mum?' Connie bent and began to thrust the some of the stems haphazardly into the vase. 'I'll bring you some others later.' Her voice dropped to a whisper. 'I'm sorry. You know that?'

He stepped out of earshot and left her some space, turning his attention to the adjacent plot. The gravestone was of the same decorative local stone but the inscription cut Connie's father starkly off from the wife next to whom he lay. *Edwin Sheldon, beloved father*. Someone had left flowers there, but not recently; they were brown and scattered across the turf. He recognised the remains of chrysanthemums like those that Connie had brought, shrivelled by the recent frost and with their colour unrecognisable.

'Now you, Dad,' said Connie, turning from one parent to another. 'Happy birthday What a great age ninety is. Can we talk? I think I need to say sorry, and actually I think you have some explaining to do, too.'

Curiously moved by the scene Jude turned away, again leaving Connie to attempt to repair the irreparable. The ice-blue sky brought an ice-blue easterly wind with it, cutting like a blade, and he turned his back on it, facing west to the hills and the motorway with its constant stream of noise and traffic, a long queue of cars and lorries stationary in the roadworks. On the lower slopes other people moved among the neat rows of graves, stopping to stand in silence, leaving their bunches of flowers and moving on. He was amused to notice that Connie's theory was correct and that there was a disproportionate number of women, middle-aged and older. And why not? Women tended to outlive their husbands and were more likely to be the carers for their parents. It followed that they were more likely to tend their graves.

Closest to them, a woman was walking up the hill, her head down against the strengthening wind. She was wearing a long, beige puffa coat and sensible boots, the vanilla look brightened by the addition of a rainbow-coloured knitted hat. He watched keenly as she approached, looking up the slope towards them. For a moment he thought she was going to come up to them, but she stopped abruptly a couple of rows below, scanned a row of headstones as if she wasn't sure exactly what she was looking for and then stepped towards one of them, where she bent to lay the small Christmas wreath she'd been carrying, before standing in front of it for a moment with her head bowed.

'Someone's left flowers,' said Connie, in a voice that trembled between anger and shame. Her conversation with her parents had obviously concluded. 'How dare she? It's bad enough that she stole him, but now she's coming back to look after his grave as well. He's my dad, not hers.' She bent and rummaged among the dead chrysanthemums, picking up the remnants of a card, which she handed to him. 'Look.' And then, with sudden concern: 'Do you think she's mad?'

The card was unreadable, a sodden lump on the verge of disintegration, held together only by some kind of micro-plastic in its manufacture. Jude turned it over in gloved fingers. 'It has to be a possibility.'

'Mad doesn't mean dangerous, does it?' she said, anxiously.

'I doubt it.' Until they found the impostor, they wouldn't know. It was harmless enough to adopt an old man who had no-one else to care for him and he could see why someone might think they deserved something for their trouble. 'There are lots of forms of mental instability and most of them only harm the person who suffers from them.'

'Good. But actually, it's not her I'm worried about. It's Melanie Trotter who's going to make my life difficult.' Connie sighed and turned away. 'Let's go. I know I've dragged you up here for less than ten minutes, and I know I should probably stay and do a lot more public grieving so I look like I'm a better daughter than I am, but that was way more overwhelming that it should have been.'

'It got me out of the house on a Sunday,' he said cheerfully, 'and that's always a good thing.'

'You don't have some woman to make your Sundays worthwhile, then?' She gave him a sidelong look.

'Unless you count my mum, no,' he said, as they passed the grave where the other woman, one of that legion of the middle-aged who had so terrified Connie, had laid the Christmas wreath.

'You're way too good to stay single. You never told me about that lovely blonde detective.'

Been there, done that. He didn't say it but, looking for distraction, took the opportunity to bend down and inspect the label on the wreath. There had been something about the woman, the way she'd looked twice at them before placing the wreath in such a perfunctory manner, that had caught his attention. Most people didn't leave cards among the flowers they placed on old graves and this headstone had been there for decades. *William Wells, died 1948.* He dug his fingers among the greenery and turned the card upwards so he could read it before the wind and sleet stole it away.

To my darling Dad on your ninetieth birthday. Love, Connie.

He tweaked the card free and looked down the hill. 'Connie, did you recognise that woman?'

'What woman?'

'The one who was at this grave.'

'I didn't notice her. Should I have done?'

He looked down the hill and saw the flash of that bright rainbow hat. The woman hadn't left, as he'd thought, but had disappeared from his sight for a moment between the yew trees and the memorial chapel near the gate.

'Back in a second.' He ran off down the hill, cursing

the steepness of it, not daring to go full tilt in case he went sprawling and lost her altogether.

'Where are you going?' called Connie, plaintively.

He speeded up. The woman was past the chapel and approaching the gate. He didn't think she'd seen him and was unlikely to cut and run, but he was a long way behind. If she'd walked here, he'd catch up with her somewhere out on the street and if nothing else he would get a good look at her. Even better: he might get a chance to speak to her.

But she hadn't walked. On the roadside in front of the cemetery there was a line of parked cars; she flourished what must have been her car key and the lights flashed on the first of them, a white Citroën saloon. She moved swiftly to the driver's side and barely before the door closed, the car was pulling away.

He'd never catch it, but he wasn't beaten. He snatched for his phone and opened the camera, zoomed it in and snapped, snapped, snapped in the hope that at least one image would be clear enough and then, seeing the car turn down towards the town, realised that he'd done all he could.

'What on earth was that about?' said Connie, arriving at his side. 'Surely you're not that desperate for a woman that you need to go chasing after—' She stopped.

'After a middle-aged woman?' he said. 'Exactly.'

'Do you think that was her?' she said, suddenly anxious. 'Why?'

He fished the card out of the pocket where he'd thrust it and showed it to her. 'I think she was coming up to leave flowers for your dad.' It was Edwin's birthday, a significant one, and there were limited hours of daylight. The chances of running into her had been relatively high. 'She saw us and she left them on the nearest grave and high-tailed it. I don't know, but that's what I think.'

'Right. And now you can find her?'

He looked down at his phone again. Yes, he could just pick out the number plate for the car. He tapped it into the app he had on his phone. The car was registered to a Stephen Warrington, with an address just outside Carlisle. Was the woman Stephen's partner, or his mother? He'd find out. 'Yes. I know who the car belongs to.'

'Well, my God,' said Connie, staring in the direction the car had disappeared. 'Aren't you smart? Now what? Do you drive off, blue lights flashing and slap her in handcuffs?'

He took a movement to think. It would be easy enough to get the car stopped, although the tailback on the motorway and the police car he could see moving along the hard shoulder suggested there might be more important things to do on that particular day. 'I or one of my colleagues will turn up to speak to a Mr Warrington, who is the registered owner, and find out if a woman had permission to drive his car and if so, who she was. And when we know that, we'll have a little chat with her.'

'And when's that likely to be?'

'Tomorrow morning, I expect,' said Jude, rapidly firing off a text to Ashleigh. *I think we've found Connie Two. We need to talk.* 'I doubt she'll run.'

ELEVEN

'Who comes to the door at this time on a Monday morning,' grumbled Stephen Warrington, emerging from the downstairs cloakroom with his coat over his arm. 'Don't they know some of us have work to go to?'

Vivien had been rinsing the coffee mugs, in a leisurely manner, but she took a look out of the window to where a smart car (she wasn't good on cars but it was big and looked expensive) had pulled up on the grass verge outside. When she had come into money she had retired from the country vet practice where she'd worked for decades as office manager though Stephen, rather to her surprise, had opted to keep working. But perhaps, on reflection, it wasn't a surprise. She had considerably understated the amount of her inheritance, for a start, and though he'd never claimed he liked working as a plumber until she'd offered him the option of giving it up, he had since discovered a passion for the job. Vivien wasn't fooled by his sudden realisation of his vocation. There was passion, all right, but it was reserved for his boss Janice, who had taken on her father's business and ran it with a firm hand.

Janice was also rich, though most of her money would be sunk in the business so she was possibly not as wealthy as Vivien in terms of disposable income. Part of her wondered if things would have been different if she'd told him the extent of her legacy, but the greater part was intrigued by watching him stringing along two women until he would have to decide which way to jump, not knowing she knew. If she'd told him the whole story he would have let it slip and discovery would have been a certainty, rather than the inevitable, draining sense of anxiety at the back of her mind, the fear of discovery and accountability. Now she sensed that moment had come, and was surprised to find she was ready for it.

'Can you get the door?' she called, opening the dishwasher and sliding the two mugs into it. Listening, listening, as if there was something more she could do in the seconds before the door opened.

'Coming!' called Stephen as the doorbell shrilled again. 'Seven in the morning. You aren't expecting a parcel, are you?'

'I'm not expecting anything,' she said, though it wasn't exactly true, and she closed the dishwasher and stood facing the hallway, tense as a greyhound waiting in the traps.

'Mr Warrington?' said a male voice. A blast of icy air followed his words into the house. 'I'm Detective Chief Inspector Jude Satterthwaite, and this is my colleague Detective Sergeant Ashleigh O'Halloran. Is your wife in?'

'Yes, but—' Stephen's voice faltered. If the police came at seven o'clock on a Monday morning you naturally assumed bad news, but they had no family left whose death would require this kind of attention, and anyway there was the rank. Detectives, two of them, and one senior. For deaths they sent your average bobby. Retribution required a detective. 'She's in the kitchen. Viv, it's the police. They want to talk to you.'

Vivien closed the dishwasher and went out into the narrow hallway. The two police officers were on the doorstep and it occurred to her, briefly, that she didn't have to let them across the threshold, but Stephen was already waving them in, a blonde woman and a dark man, like yin and yang.

'Good morning,' she said, arranging her expression into one of careful concern, though she knew the moment she saw them that it was pointless to dissemble. The man was the one she'd seen with Connie Sheldon in the cemetery. That explained everything. She wished she hadn't worn that rainbow hat, but she'd felt foolishly Christmassy. Mistakes, so small. They were how you got caught.

'Vivien Warrington?' he said, briskly, and at her nod, he produced his warrant card. 'My name's DCI Satterthwaite. I'm leading an investigation into certain financial irregularities that have recently been reported to us.'

What a roundabout way of saying *fraud*. Did he think words scared her? 'I'm delighted to meet you, Chief Inspector, Sergeant. I hope I'll be able to help you. Shall we go into the kitchen?'

Stephen's mouth had dropped open, now, and his look of puzzlement had been overtaken by one of concern, as well he might. He was good at pretending not to see things and not asking the wrong (or did she mean the right?) questions. Now even he might have to start wondering.

'You head off to work, love,' she said to him. 'It'll just be routine.'

'Well,' he said uncertainly.

'We'd like to have a word with you, too, Mr Warrington,' said the woman, 'once we've spoken to your wife. I'm sure your employers will understand.'

'I'm not sure they will. I said to Janice I'd open up the depot.'

Open up the depot. That was one expression for it. If one good thing came out of this it would be that Stephen and his mistress would miss out on their opportunity for a bit of pre-work friskiness.

'I'm sure it won't take long, love,' she said to him, with a reassuring smile.

'Hopefully not,' said the woman, brightly.

Leaving Stephen already picking at his phone to relay the news of his lateness, she led the two detectives into the living room. 'Do sit down.'

'The three of them sat and the woman — Sergeant O'Halloran, was it? — took out her phone. 'I'd like to record this interview, Mrs Warrington, if I may.'

'Of course.' As if she had any choice.

She waited while the woman reeled off a string of information into the phone — the time, the date, her name, the man's. 'And can I confirm that you are Mrs Vivien Warrington, of this address?'

Vivien took a deep breath. 'Yes, that's correct. I'm sorry — I should have offered you coffee.'

They declined, clearly intending to show they meant business. Vivien kept a careful eye on the phone, which the woman had placed with apparent carelessness on a side table. It would be easy to forget it was there, even though she was clear enough about the purpose of the interview and the risk of incriminating herself.

'Do you know why we're here, Mrs Warrington?' asked DCI Satterthwaite. He had a severe look to him, like an avuncular teacher whose best pupil had disappointed him.

'Yes, I think so.' She waited.

The severity deepened. He obviously wasn't used to witnesses meeting him with such a blank politeness. 'Okay. Would you like to tell us where you were yesterday morning at about half past ten?'

She drew in a long breath. 'You know that, I think. You were there.'

'In your own words, Mrs Warrington,' he said, with a nod.

'I had breakfast with my husband here. Then he went to his allotment to collect some sprouts.' Let them ask him to verify it. She very much doubted that was what he'd done. 'I went to the cemetery in Penrith.'

'Why did you do that?'

'I went to lay a wreath,' said Vivien, choosing her words with extreme care, 'which I did. You saw me.'

'Whose grave did you visit?' asked the woman.

Vivien looked at her in the hope that she'd be less severe, if not sympathetic, but there was no good cop. The woman's face was just as set, her expression the same as her boss's, her gestures brisk and clinical, her questions factual. Seeing no help, she remained silent.

After a pause, the man produced a slip of card from his pocket and placed it on the table. 'Do you recognise this?'

'Yes.'

'This,' he said, presumably for the purpose of the recording, 'is a card I removed from the wreath you left at a grave in the cemetery yesterday morning. The card reads *To my darling Dad on your ninetieth birthday. Love, Connie.*'

'That's correct. I went to visit my father's grave.'

'The grave on which you left this wreath,' he pointed out, 'was that of a man who died in 1948 and who, if it was his birthday yesterday, would have been well over a hundred years old, not ninety. Are you saying he was your father?'

Vivien narrowed her eyes at him. She detested playing games like this, being made to tell them things they already knew, in the hope she'd let slip something they didn't. 'No.'

'Whose grave did you intend to visit?'

He must know. 'Edwin Sheldon.'

'You went to leave a wreath purporting to be from someone other than yourself on Mr Sheldon's grave?' asked the woman, making the idea sound ridiculous when in fact it made perfect sense, if you knew. If you understood.

'Connie Sheldon never visited,' she said, in her own defence. 'Edwin had no-one else.'

'Okay,' said the blonde, serenely, and for the first time there was a softness about her, a half-smile. 'Why don't you tell us about your relationship with Mr Sheldon?'

Thinking about Edwin was for a cosy setting, not this interview with its chill formality. She wished she'd made herself another cup of coffee, thought about interrupting the interview to ask, decided against it. 'He was a friend of my mother's, way back. I don't know where they met. They would exchange Christmas cards every year, though I don't think they ever met up in between times. My mother died some years back and when she was in her final illness, she talked a lot about old friends. Edwin was one of them.' Truth, lies — did it matter which, after all this time? 'After her death I wrote to tell him and he wrote back, a very kind letter saying how sorry he was and that he would love to come to the funeral but because of his own failing health he was unable to attend. He told me he would be going into a nursing home and that it would be nice if I could visit. He said he didn't expect to get any visitors once he was there and that his daughter was in Australia and unlikely ever to come back.'

Edwin had said much more than that about Connie,

and most of it had been pretty much toxic, but she wasn't so deluded as to think that he meant it, or not all of it. She fought to subdue her disapproval. The occasional letters from Connie that she'd read — short and to the point, all about *stuff* and never anything about *emotion* — had testified to the way the relationship had festered. Connie had been too busy asserting her independence to learn to handle someone as fragile as Edwin and, to her surprise, Vivien had found him straightforward. All he'd wanted was someone to listen to him and soothe his fragile ego. He was old and lonely and it cost her nothing to go along with that.

'Did you keep the letter?' asked Sergeant O'Halloran.

'I didn't, I'm afraid. Nor the Christmas cards. I couldn't imagine why anyone would need them.' Vivien lowered her eyes demurely.

'Are you a regular visitor to your parents' friends in nursing homes?'

The chief inspector, this time. She turned once more from one to the other, sure they were doing this deliberately to keep her on her toes. Feeling a little more confident, she took a moment to assess him but he was giving nothing away, sitting there like a mannequin in a sharp suit, devoid of any emotion.

'I know it seems unusual,' she said.

'I believe you visited every week. Sometimes more.'

'Yes, I think I did.'

'How did you introduce yourself when you visited?'

'I don't recall ever introducing myself by name. It was informal. I'd call and someone would answer the door — they were always in such a hurry there — and sign in the visitors' book and then go down to see Edwin.' She'd made a deliberate scrawl of it every time, so that if the books were kept, which she thought unlikely given the spiral of confusion which had reigned throughout the period when she had visited, no-one would have been able to make it out. But they'd found her here, so there was no harm in admitting to her visits.

'Okay. You could hardly be unaware that the staff were under the impression you were Connie Sheldon. Mr Sheldon's daughter.'

'Wasn't her name Armstrong? I'm sure he said she was married. She and I never met. But if you think about it, though I didn't at the time, it was a perfectly natural assumption for them to make.'

'Do you think so?'

He was looking at her, thoughtfully, as if he was measuring everything she said and sifting the truth from the lies. Of course; that was his job. She had better, therefore, stick as closely as possible to the truth. 'Yes. Edwin missed his daughter very much and after he went into Eden's End his mental and emotional state deteriorated rapidly. He became fixated on the fact that Connie never visited. To begin with I tried to explain where she was. I read him her letters, though they just made him angry and eventually they stopped coming. By that time he'd begun to confuse me with Connie, though I'm obviously much older and we don't look remotely alike.'

'You went along with this?' asked the woman.

'Yes, of course. After a while the truth became distressing for him. He couldn't bear to be told I was Vivien. He insisted on calling me Connie. There was no harm in indulging him.'

'You thought not?'

'He was an old man!' she said, indignantly. 'I know you people have an obsession with the truth, but sometimes truth causes pain. It wasn't his fault. It wasn't mine.' It was

Connie Sheldon's. 'It was a matter of basic humanity and it hurt no-one.'

'You didn't tell the staff?'

'I barely interacted with them and when I did he was there, so it was impossible to correct them. He referred to me as his daughter. He called me Connie. In the beginning I thought it was clear what our relationship was but there was such a high turnover of staff there that it just became…I don't know…assumed that I was his daughter.'

The two detectives looked at one another and Vivien, feeling herself going pink, pretended to look away. At one level this was easier than she'd expected because he wasn't pressing her or challenging her, just letting her tell the story she'd prepared with nothing but the slightest prompt. At another level it was troubling because she sensed they were listening for things she wasn't saying as much as for the truth she was telling them. There would come a point, for sure, when the questions came at her with the whip and the sting of flying ants, but she would be ready.

'Okay,' he said, more agreeably. 'I understand that, and I can see that you might think it was the humane thing to do. But didn't you think his daughter had a right to know? She might have been glad that someone was visiting.'

She might. Indeed, she would almost certainly have been delighted that someone else was taking on the burden. 'As far as I knew she was in Australia. If she wasn't, she hadn't made any effort to come and see him, or get in contact. The people at the home would have made her his point of contact and if he'd been ill they would have called her, not me. She might not have got there in time. He would have died alone. Or if she'd made it he might not have recognised her and that would have upset him even more, and he would have died in distress. I didn't want either of those things to happen, so it was easier just to stay quiet.'

He was silent for a moment. She noticed that he'd assumed control of the questions and his colleague was listening intently. 'Did it ever occur to you that neither of things might have happened? That he might have had a deathbed reconciliation with his daughter and that might have been better for both of them?'

It was too late to put that right for Edwin now, and if she was honest Vivien thought Connie deserved every moment of bitter regret that came her way. 'I see now that that was a mistake but I'd become very fond of Edwin. I genuinely thought it was the kindest thing.'

He let that pass with a brisk nod of his head. 'He died very suddenly, and unexpectedly, I believe.'

She looked him straight in the eye. 'That's correct.'

'He had an allergic reaction to penicillin. Where were you when he died?'

'Stephen and I were in Majorca. It was our fortieth wedding anniversary.' They had married far too young and grown apart, but they both kept up the pretence. 'The home called me and told me what had happened. They were so apologetic. I could only be sorry for them. How could they have known he had an allergy? It should have been in his medical records, of course, but I can imagine… anyway. I didn't want to make trouble, but I was distraught. Because, after all, when they did call me I couldn't come and so he did die alone after all.'

She had been fond of Edwin, genuinely so. He had been a cantankerous old man but they had been comfortable together. She sniffed.

'And after his death? The care home assumed you were who you had been claiming to be?'

'I'm afraid the manager…' she said, and left the

sentence trailing. Karen Grant, who had been the manager of Eden's End at the time, had been a disaster. She had been a drinker and a manic depressive, under whose rule the home had descended into chaos and sustained reputational damage from which it would probably never recover. Furthermore, Karen was dead and could freely be slandered. 'She could be confused. Yes, she assumed I was his next of kin?'

'And you did nothing to enlighten her?'

'Of course I did. I told Ms Grant, several times, but she insisted that it was appropriate for me to undertake the paperwork. If I'm honest she seemed very much as if she didn't want the trouble of tracking down a next of kin who might not want to be involved. It was kinder of me to help her out.'

His lips twisted into an ironic smile. 'I have a nasty feeling your good nature has led you into a very awkward place, Mrs Warrington. I don't think I've ever heard of anyone committing fraud by accident, but you seem to be telling me that's what happened.'

It was the first time he had implied she was being questioned over a criminal offence. Of course she knew it, but it was only now that she realised how their failure to mention it had unaccountably lulled her into telling her story too easily. 'I did what I thought best.'

'You allowed the home to think you were Connie Sheldon. You failed to inform Connie, or ask anyone else to inform her, that her father was dead.'

'That isn't a crime,' said Vivien, with spirit, though she accepted it was morally reprehensible.

'Edwin's funeral, arranged by you, was a small affair,' he remarked, letting that go.

'You were there?' she asked, impudently. 'How come I didn't see you, if it was small?'

He smiled. 'We know who was there. There was yourself and two representatives from the home. Not even your husband?'

'Edwin had no relatives apart from Connie and I don't know if he had any friends. Stephen was away on a football weekend at the time.'

'I see. You'll correct me if I'm wrong, Mrs Warrington, but it looks to me as if this funeral was kept extremely quiet, perhaps with the intention of concealing matters from Connie, Edwin's actual daughter. I've been asking myself why this might be, and there's an obvious answer.'

There was, but she wasn't going to give it to him. She looked at him.

'After Edwin's death,' he went on, 'someone approached his solicitors to inform them of his death. Was that you?'

'Yes.'

'And wasn't this the point at which you realised that this…misunderstanding…had gone on long enough? Didn't you stop to think that you had to be honest with the solicitor? With Connie Sheldon — who, I shouldn't have to remind you, is actually Edwin's daughter? Because this is the point at which any…errors…on your part start to look less like a genuine mistake and much more like a serious effort to assume Connie Sheldon's identity.'

He stopped and the blonde moved swiftly into the silence. 'What did you say to the solicitor?'

'I'm afraid I don't remember.'

'No,' said DCI Satterthwaite, 'because at this point, if I understand it correctly, you misled the solicitor into believing you were Connie Sheldon, which given the paperwork required I struggle to believe was an *accident*,' (the emphasis was definitely sarcastic) 'and were successful enough to continue the deception through the entire probate process, and in the end you benefited from the entirety of Edwin Sheldon's estate. Am I right?'

She looked up to meet his gaze and found him thoughtful and confident. He thought he had her checkmated. She took a deep breath. 'I'm afraid I wasn't entirely honest with you, Chief Inspector.'

'I didn't think you were,' he said, without missing a beat.

'I have something I'd like to show you, if I may.'

'Go ahead.'

Vivien got up and crossed the room, feeling their gaze upon her, and opened the drawer in the side unit where she and Stephen were in the habit of placing anything — letters, memos, pens, cables, keys — which had no place elsewhere. From there she withdrew a brown A4 envelope which she had placed there for this very moment, and handed it to him.

He raised an eyebrow as he opened it and withdrew the two sheets of paper it contained, and that was the most response she'd got out of him throughout the whole interview.

'I was baptised Constance Sheldon,' said Vivien, 'though when I became an adult I changed my name. The top document is my birth certificate. The other one is a legal paper signed and registered by Edwin Sheldon shortly after my birth, in which he acknowledges that he is my father and that he paid a sum of a thousand pounds to my mother immediately, in order to discharge any future responsibility for my keep. I haven't committed any crime. These documents are proof of my parentage. Edwin left his money to his daughter, Connie Sheldon. That's me. I have more right to the money than the daughter who neglected him.'

TWELVE

'It was a performance,' Jude said. 'There's no other word for it.' He shook his head. Part of him was fuming about Vivien's nonchalance, the way she'd so obviously taken pleasure in leading him up the garden path, the triumph as she'd played her trump card. *I'm Connie Sheldon and I claim my four hundred thousand pounds.* It rankled: nobody liked to be made a fool of. Nevertheless, part of him admired her for it. He looked to Ashleigh for confirmation. 'Do you agree?'

They were in the incident room where Faye, who had become deeply invested in the case of the two Connies, had been waiting for them to come back up from speaking to Vivien. He'd hoped to have a few minutes to collect his thoughts and formulate a plan before he spoke to her, but he wasn't about to try and dampen her enthusiasm.

'I do,' said Ashleigh, fidgeting with her pen and, he thought, still as irritated by the way the interview had played out as he was. 'But it isn't the slam-dunk she thinks it is and I'm pretty sure she knows it. She loved delivering that gotcha moment. But when it came to the nuts and bolts of it, there are a lot of questions she still has to answer.'

'It's a pity we can't check with that woman at the nursing home about whether she really did insist on dealing with this Warrington woman, even though she had no authority,' said Faye, a trifle irritated, 'and though I hate to say it, it does sound credible that everyone else at the place just got used to thinking she was his daughter. But there are procedures, for God's sake. Most of these places are throttled by paperwork. This is exactly the sort of situation it's meant to prevent.'

'I'm afraid it's entirely plausible that Karen Grant did the easy thing,' said Ashleigh, with a shrug. 'She was an unhappy woman with huge issues. I can see why the effort of finding the real Connie would be too much for her.'

'If the home where my mother—' Faye, who was notoriously fierce about her privacy, stopped herself. 'Never mind. Let's just say they'd never hear the last of it from me.'

'I don't imagine it was cynical,' said Ashleigh. 'Just too difficult.' She had always had more sympathy for the hapless Karen Grant than anyone else.

'I believe it, too.' Jude frowned. Vivien had been adamant that she was entitled to the money and the settlement of the will had given her legal possession of it, but even if Connie tried and failed to challenge her, there were claims of criminality still to be investigated. 'Especially if Edwin confirmed her story. We don't know what passed between Vivien and her father, assuming he is her father, but I'm willing to bet that there was at the very least a degree of coercion going on. Karen may have found it easier to ignore it.'

'If that's the case, it'll be difficult to prove anything.' Faye, it was clear, shared his dissatisfaction. 'We're going to have to look at this one extremely closely. You say, assuming he's her father. Is there any doubt?'

'My gut feeling is that there isn't. Chris Marshall is checking the documents she gave us, but I've no reason to believe they're fake, and the story she provided to back them up sounds entirely possible. Her version is that Edwin had an affair with her mother as a young man and didn't want to marry her. He acknowledged the child but paid the mother off. The mother named her daughter Connie, after Edwin's mother.'

'When he'd refused to marry her? That sounds like a micro-aggression to me,' said Faye, making a note.

'Agreed. When she discovered that Edwin had a daughter with his wife, and that she was also called Connie, Vivien changed her name.'

'Did she say why?'

'Yes. Apparently she'd always hoped she'd find her father and when her mother finally told her who he was and she made inquiries, she learned that he was recently married and had a new baby. She abandoned any idea of a meeting at that point, but she kept an eye on him and his family through various means and through social media when it came in.'

'Basically, she's been stalking Connie for years.' Ashleigh shook her head. 'I'm not sure that looks good.'

It might not be a crime in itself, but it was another thread of evidence that might help towards a prosecution and conviction. 'Stalking is maybe overstating it, but I agree. Yes. Her version of events stacks up. Obviously if the documents turn out to be fake that changes matters, but DNA will tell us whether she's his daughter or not. If I had to put my house on it, I'd say yes. She's his daughter and her original name is Connie Sheldon.' Jude shrugged.

'So far no crime in claiming to be his daughter,' said

Faye, replicating the shrug, 'but there's a lot more to it than that. She knowingly misrepresented herself to the undertaker and the solicitor as Connie Sheldon—'

What Vivien had said to whom, who she'd claimed to be at what point, reminded Jude of a tangled rope of Christmas tree lights and would require the same kind of patience to unravel it. 'And to other people, too.'

'The Power of Attorney, though.' Ashleigh sipped the cup of coffee she'd brought with her to the meeting. 'What about that?'

The minute they'd left Vivien, smug but (he hoped) with her head ringing with warnings, Jude had been on the phone to Edwin Sheldon's solicitor, even before Ashleigh had started the car engine. The senior partner he'd spoken to had been as baffled and outraged as Jude himself and had promised to get to the bottom of the matter as soon as possible. 'It was made out in the name of Connie Sheldon.'

'There must have been an address on it,' pointed out Faye.

'At the time it was made, the real Connie was using her father's address. She'd left her husband and was renting while she sorted out her new life and before she moved in with her new man. Connie Two — Vivien — must somehow have found out about that. Maybe Edwin told her, when he was more lucid. I expect she obtained his keys, let herself into the house, helped herself to anything she could find with Connie's name and address and either presented those as evidence of her identity or used them to procure something.'

'Really?' said Faye, with deep scepticism. 'Are you telling me that passed muster?'

'She had her birth certificate, which I presume is genuine. I agree that someone at the solicitor's should have looked a little more closely but perhaps for some reason they didn't. I sometimes think we aren't suspicious enough of women in their sixties. Nobody notices them but they can be bloody smart. The senior partner I spoke to knew of Edwin but had never dealt with him. The likes of a PoA would have been handled by someone more junior. That person might have been more easily convinced.'

'In a bit of a hurry, everything apparently okay,' said Faye. 'I know. Excuses from Mrs Warrington. *Passport in for renewal and not back, sorry, no driving licence, I don't drive, will these be enough?* That sort of thing.'

'Exactly this.' But just because someone failed to spot a scam didn't mean the scammer should get away with it. 'It's going to take time and effort to go back through this paper trail and find out exactly where Vivien's actions cross over from the true to the fake. Despite what she says, and even if she really was registered as Connie Sheldon at birth, it's clear that at some point she deliberately adopted her younger half-sister's identity. My guess it was when she accessed the house, assuming she did so.'

'That's a lead,' said Faye with a degree of satisfaction. 'I bet she can't produce any evidence that she actually lived there. We'll talk to the neighbours.'

'That's in hand.'

'When was the will made?' asked Ashleigh, interested.

'At the same time as the Power of Attorney was registered. It also gives Connie's address as being care of Edwin's address. Vivien must have had enough information from the house to satisfy the solicitor of a change of address.'

'And the money?' asked Faye, with a steely glint in her eye. 'That's what it's all about.'

'On completion of probate the money was deposited in an account which Vivien set up specifically and which she emptied shortly afterwards. She was open about that. She said she didn't want that amount of money in one account. She's furnished us with details and we'll be able to look at where it went.' He'd been surprised at how readily she'd provided the information.

'Does she think she's got away with it?' asked Faye. 'That approach seems very brazen.'

He shrugged. 'Maybe. It may not all be accountable for. Some might have been hidden away. I don't imagine for one moment that it's all sitting there waiting for Connie to claim it.'

'I imagine she was hoping Connie wouldn't come back,' said Ashleigh. 'It could have gone on for years and she might have moved on and proved difficult to find.'

'Yes,' said Faye, looking at Jude, 'you had a stroke of luck there.'

He smiled at her. Personally he was proud of making the connection between Connie and Vivien, but Faye was always grudging with her praise. 'Yes. And so, when she was questioned, she fell back on Plan B. That it was meant for her and she's entitled to it.'

'That's the claim. *I'm Connie Sheldon, I'm Edwin's daughter, he left his money to his daughter Connie Sheldon, therefore it's my money*. Ballsy,' said Faye, admiringly, 'especially because it's up to Connie to get it back. I don't suppose we have an independent opinion on Edwin's attentions?'

'Only that the solicitor vaguely remembered drawing up the will and he was quite clear that Edwin intended to leave everything to his only daughter.'

'That's odd, because he'd previously signed the document acknowledging he was Vivien's father. So either he forgot about her, which is surely unlikely, or he just ignored her and assumed she didn't know about him so the matter would never arise.' Faye rubbed her chin. 'Maybe we need to think outside the box here. Is it conceivable that your Connie Sheldon isn't his daughter?'

Jude shook his head. Technically it was possible, and a DNA test would clarify it, but he couldn't see it. 'I did know Edwin, remember, though only briefly. There's a definite family resemblance. I'd be astonished if she wasn't. And she's definitely no impostor.'

'What was their relationship like?' asked Faye, curiously. 'I'd forgotten you said you knew her. I should probably have asked you before.'

He thought about it. 'I don't know for certain anything that happened between them over the last twenty years. I know their relationship was difficult, but I only have Connie's explanation for that. They fought a lot but they were very close. Looking back I wonder if he wanted the best for her but just wasn't equipped to deal with a teenage girl, while also mourning the sudden death of his much younger wife, who he would reasonably have expected to outlive him. I would definitely say he cared for Connie, maybe too much. He was extremely protective. I'd be very surprised if it turned out he was cutting her out of the will in favour of her half-sister.'

'You'd tell someone if you were doing that, wouldn't you?' asked Ashleigh. 'Otherwise, what's the point? If you're going to be that cruel I'd imagine you want to see someone suffer.'

'You'd have thought so,' he said, wondering what Connie would have to say and how she would take the news, not only that she had a sister but that that sister had attempted to defraud her of her inheritance.

'And what about Mr Warrington?' asked Faye. 'You surely aren't going to tell me the enterprising Mrs Warrington was flying solo?'

'She says so, and so does he.'

'And did either of you believe that?'

They had been so busy on the way back to the office discussing Vivien's statement that they hadn't had time to share their views on Stephen. Not a man to jump to instant conclusions, Jude nodded that one over to Ashleigh, whose instant judgements on human nature were generally more accurate than his.

'I'm not sure. It's possible. He says she told him she was visiting her father and had inherited and he believed it was legit.'

'Seriously? He must know about the money.' Faye snorted in disbelief. 'They got their story straight to keep him out of it. I'll bet she squeals when she realises what trouble she's in. She won't go down alone.'

Vivien had probably thought she'd get away with it. They'd been tougher in their questioning of Stephen than they had with Vivien, largely because of his blanket denials, but the story that had come out had been the same from both of them. 'She says she told him she was visiting her father. She says she told him he'd left her a comfortable sum of money. He claims he never read the will or saw any of the paperwork.'

'And he never visited?' said Faye, sceptically.

'Once or twice, I believe, latterly.' By which time Edwin had apparently believed that Vivien was Connie. And actually Stephen Warrington had struck him as very smart, in a self-preserving way. He was the type of man who turned his back when there was something he thought he ought not to see, who would buy something from a man in a pub and take care not to ask its provenance, in case it turned out to have fallen off the back of a lorry. That way he could reap the rewards and yet keep his hands clean. 'He preferred not to know. And I wouldn't be at all surprised to find that was exactly the way that Vivien preferred it, too.'

THIRTEEN

Jude broke the news to Connie that evening, over a drink and a few bar snacks in one of Penrith's many pubs. It was something that could equally well have been done over the phone but he seemed acutely aware of how difficult she was finding it to return to her home town and discover hardly anyone there but himself who had any time for her. She'd always liked that aspect of his character, the concern for others and their welfare. When he'd called to update her on progress, she had (somewhat optimistically) proposed taking him out for dinner to say thank you, but he'd excused himself with a half-serious remark about professional standards and accepting bribes. This brief interlude seemed an appropriately happy medium, and even an hour or so of good — of sustaining — company was a break in the battle that her life had become.

'Cheers, Jude.' She lifted her glass and smiled at him. He was distinguished rather than handsome these days, but he retained the slight air of aloofness that had always attracted her. Indeed, it was heightened now that he'd matured from a gangly youth into a cool and smart adult. So different from the beach-bum types she had married for their free-thinking hippydom, only to discover that they couldn't handle responsibility.

'How on earth are you still single?' she asked, because she wasn't someone who'd die wondering. 'I was sure someone would have snapped you up years ago.'

'I have impossibly high standards,' he joked. He flourished his own glass in salute, but set it down without drinking. 'Have you seen anything of Adam since you got back?'

'I thought the two of you didn't speak.' Even from the other side of the world Connie had kept up with the low-key soap opera that Adam had made of his fallout with his former best friend.

'We don't, or not much, but I know you do. I was wondering whether you were starting to catch up with any old friends.'

She kept thinking he'd become an enigma and then he gave her glimpses such as this that showed that he hadn't, and that she still understood how his mind went. He didn't particularly care what Adam Fleetwood did or who he saw, but he wasn't above offering her a subtle nudge to indicate that, though her friends in the town were few, he wasn't the only one of them. On another day she might have interpreted that as rejection but today she preferred to see it as a gesture of goodwill.

'I saw him on Saturday, for lunch.' She relaxed back into her leather seat, her fingers curled around the long slender stem of a glass of red wine. When he'd arrived, fifteen minutes or so late and full of apologies, she'd already had an empty glass in front of her and she'd spotted him looking at it, clearly wondering if it might not be the first of the evening. Surely he wouldn't blame Connie for drinking to drown her sorrows? She had enough of them. 'He was full of chat, like he always is, but none of it was what you call serious. All idle gossip. He did give me a full account of all your doings, though.'

'I can guarantee he doesn't know what my doings are,' he said, and laughed, a little bitterly.

The three of them had been close and she, at least, had been sure they'd be friends for ever. Now the relationship between Jude and Adam was fractured beyond repair and there were twenty missing years in which Connie had rebelled and rebelled and rebelled against everything associated with her upbringing. It was time to come home, but slipping back into the comfort of the familiar might not be as easy as she'd thought. 'He said you recently split up with your girlfriend. I'm sorry to hear that.'

'Didn't I tell you that earlier?'

He had; she was testing the water. It occurred to her that if the two of them were both still single after all these years, perhaps they'd been waiting for one another without knowing it. 'Probably, but if I was jet-lagged it would have gone in one ear and out the other. Was she that lovely detective who came to talk to me?'

He grinned. 'She's only lovely if you're one of the good guys.'

'And then there was that girl from the village you lived in, wasn't there? Becca?' There was a whole story there, too, and Adam had filled her in on it. She wasn't so naive as to think he told her the truth, only his version of it, and it would have been embellished until it bore only a nodding acquaintance with reality, but there would remain a kernel of truth at its heart. Of the three of them, perhaps Adam was the one least like his former self. Now that she'd come back and met him face to face, she was no longer sure that she liked him.

'There was, but you know how it goes. Since I last saw

you, you've got through two marriages and I've got through two non-marriages. I'd say that's about evens.'

'Ouch!' she said, not at all perturbed, and raised her glass. 'Point taken. I'm just interested in your life, that's all. We're friends, and I've neglected you.' Just like she'd neglected all the others. 'I was sorry to hear that your parents had split up, and then Adam told me your mum had been ill—'

'She's fine, now.'

'I'm glad. And now you—'

'My life is entirely dull, and at the moment it's largely concentrated on finding out what happened to all your money. Which is the main reason why I'm here.'

He was so amiably off-putting. 'Of course. You'd better bring me up to date.' He'd given her the briefest outline over the phone, but the details were yet to come. 'I've just about got over learning I have a half sister I never knew about, but I'm afraid when I stop to think about it, it isn't too much of shock.'

'Really?'

'Yes. I loved Dad very much, but he was a bit of an old goat. I do remember overhearing a conversation after Mum died, one of the cousins saying that Mum must have been a special person to have tamed him because he'd sown so many wild oats no-one thought he'd ever settle. But that was before he met her, of course. He fell head-over-heels in love, even though she was so much younger.'

'There was me thinking he was just a sober, sensible—'

'He was discreet. I never knew of any other women while Mum was alive, and maybe there weren't any and he was prepared to change his ways while he had her, but there were definitely some affairs after she died. I never met any of the women, thank God. I doubt he really cared much about them and he wasn't about to try and force a stepmother on me.' Or a wife upon himself. It seemed that her father, like herself, had room for only one permanent relationship in his life but he had found his and she hadn't, not yet. 'When I think about it, he and I are very alike.'

'Yes,' he said, after a moment's thought. 'I see that.'

'And do you know what? Now I know I have a half-sister I think I'd like to meet her.'

'Would you?' he asked, in a tone that was equal parts warning and surprise.

'Yes. We're the same flesh and blood. She spent a lot of time with him at the end.'

'I don't know if that's wise. The impression I formed of her that she's actually quite calculating and genuinely believes she's entitled to the money. Obviously it's a long way before we can prove anything, but my gut reaction is that she gaslit your father into thinking you'd abandoned him. I don't think she'd necessarily be as kind to you as you would to her.'

'I'd like to know if he ever asked after me,' she said, setting her lips in a stubborn line.

'If he did I don't know if she'd tell you and if she did it might not be what you want to hear.'

Her father's opinion of her at the end could have been either good or bad. Whatever her half-sister told her, she wouldn't know if it was true. Her anxiety rose. These days it felt as though very few people were kind to her. It was why she treasured spending time with Jude, who could be aloof and hadn't always shared her sense of humour, but who was never unkind. 'Do you really think she gaslit him?'

'I think so. Let me tell you what I know.'

She listened without comment while he outlined his interview with Connie-known-as-Vivien from the moment of her first visit to the home, the paper trail, the visit to the solicitor. How strange, and somehow creepy, to think that her sister had the same name and had assumed her identity so easily. 'That sounds so wild.'

'I've heard worse. There's a lot of detail still to be uncovered — a lot — and it'll take some time. But we know now what happened and how. It's a question of criminality.'

'Is it? Isn't it obvious that it's a crime?' For a moment she was perplexed. She was so low that no body blow could hurt her, or so she thought.

'The issue is the burden of proof. Given the birth certificate and the fact that she has the same name — and the fact that she claims that she has a right to the money — we have to be extremely careful to make the case against her water-tight.'

'I hadn't realised. I thought it was just a matter of—'

'It's unquestionably fraud. She pretended to be you. But there are legal issues. The will is settled and you'll have to go to court to challenge it. I fully expect you'll get your money, unless the system really lets you down, but it'll take a long time.'

The mills of God grind slowly, her mother used to say, *but they grind exceeding small*. She digested the idea of a long legal battle. In the past few days her thinking had been chaotic, but she hadn't really expected to come back to money, whether her father had been alive or dead. What she had been sure of was that she'd have somewhere to live; finding the lights on in the family home, having the door opened to her by a stranger, snatching a shocked glimpse through a familiar door into an unfamiliar interior had been traumatic. She'd think about that, in the small hours. 'I can wait as long as I have to.' She had no choice. 'But it's the house. I was counting on somewhere to lay my head.'

'Will you look for somewhere to rent?'

'I've found somewhere, for the short term at least. A furnished flat in a new block at the back of Castle Hill, on the ground floor. It's small, but I don't expect to stay there long. It could be a lot worse.'

'What about a job?' he asked. Her glass was long empty and she was impatient for another, but that would look desperate.

'I'll have to look for something. The problem is, I've been out of the workplace for so long. I'll find something.'

'You're pretty resourceful,' he agreed, and at last he drained his glass and set it down.

'Would you like another?' She gestured to the bar.

'I'll get them. If I'm honest, I'm ready for something to eat.' And then, quickly, like a chess player who'd saved himself from a huge mistake, he specified. 'I'll get crisps. Salt and vinegar?'

'You remembered.' Of course he had. 'Never change, Jude.'

He laughed and made his way to the bar, leaving Connie to take in the world around her. Against the background of her own troubles, her fellow drinkers seemed excessively jolly, almost overflowing with goodwill. She turned towards the group congregating at the next table, hoping some of their bonhomie would trickle towards her. There must have been a dozen of them, all female, all around their sixties (of course, now you noticed it) and they were there for a birthday, all armed with sparkly parcels. One of them produced a helium ballon emblazoned with 60 in pink and gold and tied it to the back of an empty chair, set in prime position, and at that precise moment a woman came sweeping into the bar, flung her hands to her mouth at what was clearly a surprise, and promptly disappeared under a scrum of ecstatic friends.

What on earth did you have to do to be that person,

clearly adored by a whole group of friends (a couple more, arriving late, were scurrying across the bar)? But Connie knew the answer. You had to have a rare *joie de vivre*, a gift for making people like you. For a second she fell victim to a stab of bitter envy but in a moment their smiles and their laughter enfolded her, too, and she looked over and smiled and mouthed a happy birthday at the group in a way that made her feel both ridiculous and beneficent.

Still watching them as they waved to the bar and a tray of champagne flutes arrived, she sat back and let a feeling of well-being flow over her. It wouldn't last — it never did — but she could enjoy it for a moment. She saw, now, that she would be unhappy if she went back to Australia and that she was better settling in her home town whose long dark winters might be depressing but whose soft springs and summers and vibrant autumns were a thousand times better than the harsh heat she had struggled to become used to. At least here she had her two old friends, Adam who was waspish but connected and therefore useful, and Jude of whom she would always be immensely fond. It would be immeasurably painful being apart from her sons, but less painful than the carnage of them living between two warring parents, and she thought if she stayed it would kill her, and what use would she be to them then?

'You again,' said the voice in her ear. 'I thought I warned you.'

Connie whirled round. The birthday party (now passing around the champagne flutes and preparing for a toast) had absorbed all her attention and she had failed to spot Melanie approaching her. Her good will dissipated. There were people here who hated her as well as those for whom she was a harmless amusement. Maybe Jude had been right and one of them was Vivien, but her predecessor in Matthew's arms was certainly another.

'If you don't want to see me you could go to another pub.' She turned away, her attention still absorbed by the wholesomeness beside her.

'To Gill,' said one of the party, raising a glass in the direction of the birthday girl, 'the best friend anyone could ever have!'

'To Gill!' they chorused.

'Thank you!' said their friend, and flourished her own glass. 'Here's to all of you, and to life! Drink it while it's fizzing!'

'Drink it while it's fizzing!' they chorused.

'I warned you to keep away,' said Melanie, loudly.

Tearing herself away (she'd almost felt herself part of that group, so warmed had she been by their positivity) Connie turned back to the matter in hand. 'Go away, Mel. I'm home now. I've every right to be here.' Melanie had a glass in her hand, something vile and avocado-green with a maraschino cherry on top. *I'm a lot of things*, Connie said to herself, *but at least I'm not a fool for a cheap drink*.

'If you've got any sense you'll go somewhere else.'

'I'm not leaving just because you tell me to.'

'We all know what you're like. All of us are talking about you.'

'And?' said Connie raising her voice to be heard above the chorus of *Happy Birthday* that was starting up a few feet to her right.

'I heard you're after a job but don't think anyone's going to give you one. Unless they need someone to clean out a pigsty.'

Connie looked at her — at the cocktail, the heels, the plunging cleavage. Melanie was only a little younger than she was, well past thirty; dressing like a teenager only made her look ridiculous. 'I'm not sure I'd stoop to the kind of job you have connections with, Mel. I'm not that desperate.' What had Matthew ever seen in this simple, shallow woman?

'You were always a cow, Connie. If I were you I'd get out of town.' Mel drew her hand back and made as if to hurl the drink in her direction. The liquid slopped about in the glass and the foil cocktail umbrella collapsed into it.

'I'm not you, though,' said Connie, 'am I? And thank God for that.'

'Here's your drink, Connie.' Jude put two glasses down on the table, fished two packets of crisps out of his pocket and tossed them beside the glasses, and sat down. His expression was perfectly neutral and he paid no attention to Mel. 'Cheers.'

Confident that the slimy green concoction was now no longer about to land on her head, Connie lifted her glass. 'Thank you.'

'Is everything all right?'

She snatched a glance around the bar. On the one side Melanie's silver-sequinned top was already barely more than a flicker in the throng. On the other, a woman among the birthday party who, she now saw, had been watching her with concern gave her a tentative thumbs up.

'Yes,' said Connie and smiled in return.

'Another old friend?' said Jude, following the smile.

'No, I don't know these people at all.' Though she'd like to. 'Oh, you mean Melanie? Actually yes, she is a friend or was, many years back, but these days she's my ex's ex.'

'I'd call that a comfortably distant relationship,' he said looking past her, no doubt to check that Melanie had gone.

'You'd think so, but no. Some people live off spite,' she said, smiled as brightly as she could, and reached for the crisps. 'You'll be bored of talking shop. Let's talk about something else. What are your plans for Christmas?'

FOURTEEN

'It was pretty awkward,' said Jude to Becca Reid, taking the seat she indicated for him on the sofa, 'as she doesn't have any plans for Christmas. I don't like to think of anyone on their own if they don't choose to be, but it isn't really for me to invite Connie along to my mother's when it's Mum's turn to host the various cousins.'

'Well, quite,' said Becca, with the correct amount of sympathy. 'Your mum said she's expecting a houseful.'

'On the one hand there will be so many that one more won't make any difference, but on the other hand it's not my house. And the last thing I want is people thinking there's something between Connie and me just because we've got previous.'

'How old are you?' she teased. 'Is this what you're here for, to get your side of the story in before the gossips get started? I thought it was because you knew I've got mince pies.'

He laughed. 'I'm down in the village to drop off a few things with Mum, but I'm glad you're in, because if you've got five minutes, I'd like to talk to you about Connie. I think you might be able to help me.'

'I'll be surprised. I barely knew her except vaguely in the distance at school.' Becca was three years younger than he was. 'She'll hardly remember who I am, if she ever knew.'

'She's active on social media, I think. She was telling me about it. And I'm pretty sure you and she have mutuals.' He turned to watch as Becca's cat, Holmes, came trotting in to see what was going on, and stretched a hand down to pay homage. Holmes adored Jude, if a cat could adore anyone, and the feeling was mutual.

'If you think it'll help. Just give me a minute and I'll get us those mince pies and a coffee.'

He made a fuss of Holmes while she busied herself in the kitchen, coming back with a plate of mince pies, still warm, and two mugs of coffee.

'Do you know what?' she said. 'You'd find your life so much easier if you actually stooped to our level and signed up for some of these hell sites.'

That would mean letting people know what he was doing and that would never do. Jude was a very private person. 'I'm way too old for things like that. Old dog, new tricks and all that.'

'What nonsense. Facebook is the place where people like us go. The youngsters are all on TikTok or Instagram or wherever the current sewer of choice is.'

Jude smiled at that. Mikey, his much younger brother, was scathing about old people (by which he meant anyone over thirty) and social media but even Mikey was getting too old to keep up with every new trend. 'I doubt Connie will be on those.'

'Let me get this straight,' she said, offering him the mince pies and a plate. 'You're here because you want me to use my social media to check up on Connie. Is that right?'

'Got it in one.'

'Don't you have other sources you could tap into for that?' she asked, turning to thrust another log on the wood burner. 'I always assumed you had access to all these things at your fingertips.'

He bit into the mince pie and found it crumbly, buttery and delicious, the faintest trace of brandy in the satisfyingly sweet filling. 'I do.' But she had immediately identified his ulterior motive. Connie had committed no crime and was not suspected of one but her background was nevertheless of interest. With a few clicks on the mouse or a quick call to someone in the appropriate department, he could find out everything he wanted without the risk of serious trouble he might have run if she'd been a mere acquaintance. 'A lot of the guys who deal with these things are off on holiday, so I thought I'd do it the amateur way. It's much quicker to ask you than it is to learn to do it myself.'

'It would take you a few minutes,' she said, amused, 'but why not? I'm interested in Connie myself, and when it comes down to it, it's social media. The clue's in the name. It's meant for sharing.' She closed the log burner and went over to the Christmas tree in the corner. One flick of the switch transformed the room and made it cheery and welcoming. That, the fire and Becca's company made him feel he could stay there in comfort all evening. 'I'm sure if you were on there Connie would be among the first to accept your friend requests. What do you want to know that you can't just ask her?'

Connie was unreliable, that was the thing. He was fond of her and had once been more than fond of her, but there was something off and he needed to know what it was. 'I'm worried about her.'

Holmes, attracted by the lights, strolled over to the tree and gave its dangling baubles the benefit of a deeply suspicious glare. His paw twitched.

'No, Holmes,' said Becca, automatically. 'Do you think she won't get her money back, then? That would be terrible.'

'It's not that. I've seen her a couple of times and I just have a funny feeling things aren't right. The first time it might have been jet lag, but she's well over that now. She's drinking a lot and I get the feeling she's not going out of her way to make new friends or look up old ones.'

'That is a bit unusual.'

'She's always had a self-destruct button.'

'I think we all have one of those.' Becca picked up her iPad and came and sat next to him on the sofa, closer than was entirely necessary but not so close that they were touching. He wondered if, like him, she was remembering the time he'd asked her if they could try again together and how she'd turned him down flat without a second thought. At the time he hadn't thought she'd meant it, that it had been a gut reaction, but now there was nothing more he could do or say without crossing the invisible line she had drawn between them. He loved her, he was sure that she loved him, but maybe for Becca love wasn't enough, or she thought it not worth the pain that so often went with it. He didn't suppose he'd ever find out the truth. Friendship was all she'd left on the table and he would rather take it than leave it, and at least enjoy the pleasure of her company.

'Before we get on to that,' he said, as she swiped her finger across the screen and brought up her Facebook profile, 'there was something else I was going to ask you. I wondered whether you'd picked up any chat about Edwin Sheldon when you've been up at Eden's End.'

'I'm not up there much these days,' she said busily typing Connie's name into the search bar, 'though I do see Ellie Jack occasionally if she comes into down into the office for liaison meetings or what have you. Obviously she doesn't work for the NHS but there are always points of contact, and I do still have the occasional call to make up there.'

'I bet she keeps you up to date,' he said, and grinned. There was very little that got past Ellie.

'She does. I like her. I did see her the other day and she told me all about it, but I don't imagine she'll have told me anything she didn't tell you. Or rather, I'm sure she did but all I'll have got that was extra was the embroidered bits from a story going round too many times. She wouldn't dare try that on you. You're way too analytical.' She held up the iPad. 'Look, there you go. There's Connie's feed. I don't know how much you'll get from it.'

He scrolled through it. Connie wasn't shy about sharing her soul. In five minutes he learned more about her than he'd thought possible, not just from her own, inevitably self-serving, posts about her life in Australia, but from the reactions of her friends and acquaintances as the cracks in her marriage began to show. The majority were soothing and supportive. Some were more cautious. *Jeez, Connie*, one friend had written, *you do get yourself into difficult situations*. Others were trenchant. *I can't see you've anyone to blame but yourself*, though they had softened the blow with a caring emoji. And Connie, of course, reacted to every one.

That figured. She had never been one to let a criticism past, and always been ready to stand up for herself.

'Is this how people normally behave on here?' he asked, intrigued.

Becca smiled, presumably at his naivety. 'No, not really. We're mostly very anodyne. When I look at some of these posts I do see someone spoiling for a fight, don't you?'

'Has she always been like that on here, do you think?'

Becca swiped the screen again, back through weeks, months of Connie's posts, stopping occasionally so they could read one or another. There were pictures of beaches and swimming pools and barbecues, shared posts from news media about bush fires and storms, pictures of Connie with husband and two small boys. Several showed her with groups of women, sometimes with men who might be their partners. The comments implied that most were her new friends, the ones she'd now left behind. On one, a picture of Connie and Matthew gazing into each other's eyes on a tropical beach, captioned *Second honeymoon*, he noticed a comment from Melanie Trotter, appearing from cyberspace like the bad fairy at the princess's christening and it wasn't polite. *I haven't forgotten what you did.* Connie's response had been to the point. *Loser.*

'I don't know how she could do it,' said Becca, looking at a photo of Connie with one son on her lap and the other climbing on her back and laughing over her shoulder. 'Leaving those boys behind, I mean. I think if I had two kids as gorgeous as that — if I had two kids of my own, never mind whether they were gorgeous or not — I wouldn't leave them. I couldn't, no matter what.'

Becca had always wanted children. For a long time, when they'd been together, they'd both assumed that they would have them together when the time was right, but his falling out with Adam Fleetwood had put a stop to that. For whatever reason — maybe just because their relationship had run into a period of readjustment and the freshness had gone — Becca had picked a side, and it had been Adam's. He was sure, as he snatched a look at her wistful expression, that she regretted it. For a moment he thought of reaching out to touch her hand, but stopped himself. Any move had to come from her. He sat back and stretched out a hand for a second mince pie, without waiting to be asked. 'These are good.'

'Thank you.' Becca, too, helped herself and pushed the iPad away. 'I'm guessing you didn't find what you wanted.'

'I don't know what I wanted. I just have a sense that there's something very wrong here, above and beyond the obvious fraud, and I don't know what it is.'

'To do with what happened at Eden's End?'

'Not that, though it's an obvious issue in itself. We're on top of that. But I am worried about her.'

'Do you think she'll do something stupid?' Becca, who thought kindly of everyone, looked genuinely concerned.

'I don't know. She might.' To herself, possibly, to someone else, perhaps less likely, but that was always the thing with fiery, feisty Connie, whose actions had always seemed slightly unhinged and alive with possibilities, both good and bad. In all the time he'd known her, he didn't think there had ever been anything he was quite sure she wouldn't do.

'You're fond of her, aren't you?' she asked, not looking at him.

He took a while to answer that one, licking the last of the delicious crumbs of pastry off his fingers while he tried to work out whether the question was loaded and if so in what way. In the end it was simpler just to answer it. 'Yes, I think so. I've known her a long time, and you don't give up on your friends.' Most of them. There were exceptions. Connie had form for doing just that.

'And is she fond of you?'

'I'm sure she is, yes. But we're friends, that's all.' *Are you jealous*, he wanted to ask her, but he didn't dare.

'If you really want an opinion you should probably go and talk to Adam,' she said, after a while, 'but I can quite see that you wouldn't want to do that.'

'He'd take a delight in sending me entirely the wrong direction and then telling her all about it,' he said, and laughed. 'Better not. I think I've done quite enough digging into Connie's background already, given she hasn't given me any cause for it.' Now he thought about it, he regretted it. What business was it of his if Connie opened her heart on social media? Just because that was where she chose to share it, it didn't mean that what she shared was true — knowing Connie, the opposite, a performance with a worldwide audience. That would be why all her posts were open to anyone who wanted to see them. Maybe it was how Vivien Warrington had known she was in Australia; if so, what a shock she would have had when she learned that Connie was coming home.

'I never put anything on here unless I'm prepared for the world to know about it,' said Becca, and laughed. 'Not that I have anything interesting to say anyway. Would you like another coffee?'

The room was warm and cosy, and his own house would be cold and dark, and have the added disadvantage of knowing that Adam, who lived in the flat opposite (a deliberate act of harassment, Jude thought) would be sitting in his living room with the curtains open, waiting to give Jude a cheeky wave on his way home. Adam would definitely be talking about him to Connie, and spreading rumours, too. 'I'd love to, but I've got things to do.'

'Places to go, people to see, eh?' she said, briskly. 'I expect I'll see you over Christmas.'

'I expect so,' he said, and stood up to take his leave.

FIFTEEN

It was as if she'd called up the devil, thought Becca crossly as she answered the brisk tattoo on her front door. Jude had barely been out of her cottage long enough for her to take the mugs and the plate of mince pies through to the kitchen and she hadn't even started thinking about supper, or even feeding Holmes, before there was someone else at the door and of course — of course — it was Adam Fleetwood. She'd dated him once, and his parents lived up the street. Like herself and Jude he'd grown up in the village, and he seemed to think these facts gave him the right to come and go as he pleased, to impose himself on her time whenever it suited him. She knew him better than she liked. He'd grown up to be a sour and bitter man, and one of the very few things that gave him joy was causing trouble for others. Adam was never happier than when his presence irritated someone and Becca, even though she knew this, was unable to do what she knew she should and either decline to answer the door or pretend to be pleased to see him. The end result was that he kept calling and she kept showing her irritation. Every time, the vicious spiral deepened.

'Hola, Chica,' he greeted her. 'I was passing. I thought I'd pop in and say hello.'

'Hello,' said Becca, with considerably less pleasure than she'd felt when she'd opened the door an hour or so before and found Jude standing there. 'I'm sorry Adam, but I'm really busy just now—'

'I saw you just had a visitor. You weren't too busy to see him.'

'The reason I'm too busy to see you,' said Becca, smartly, 'is that I've just spent more time than I can spare talking to him. There are only so many hours in a day.'

'I brought you a present.' He lifted up a foil gift bag. 'A nice red, a Malbec. It's nearly Christmas. We can drink it now or I can come back later in the week and we can share it then.'

She hated to feel churlish. 'Come on in, then. Though if you don't mind, we can drink it some other time.' That meant he'd be back, but if she was smart she'd make sure someone else was there. At least this spared her from spending the rest of the evening drinking wine she didn't want in the company of a man she increasingly disliked.

'I won't stay long,' he assured her, and he didn't take his coat off, though he did go through to the living room uninvited and slump into the most comfortable armchair next to the fire. 'It's cosy in here.'

'Let me feed Holmes.' The cat had appeared, whiskers quivering, when he'd heard someone at the door but Adam didn't like cats and Holmes knew it, so naturally he made a point of rubbing round his legs before retreating to the kitchen in disgust. Following him, Becca rinsed his bowl, spooned fresh food into it and set it down on the floor before going back to the living room. That, at least, gave her the opportunity to gather her thoughts. 'Okay. I'm sorry, Adam, but I really am busy.'

'You always are.'

'Not always, but it's the Brownies' Christmas party tomorrow.'

'You're such a good person.' He made it sound like a bad thing. 'So community spirited.'

'Is this a social call or is there anything I can do for you?'

'No, as I said. I was passing. And you know me, Becca. I can't resist a bit of gossip.'

'You missed your vocation. You should have been a newshound.'

'Or a detective.' He laughed.

'I'm sure you'd have made a very good one,' she said, though she thought exactly the opposite. He was anything but fair and open-minded and had never pretended to be objective.

He made a point of picking cat hair from his trousers. 'I saw our local detective coming out of here. Back on, is it?'

None of your business. But she didn't say it, since it would have left him with the germ of an idea that it was. Silence would have had the same effect. He could frame a question so that he always got an answer. 'Certainly not.'

'Good. Because if it was I'd hate to have to be the person to tell you he's been two-timing you.'

She almost laughed. Jude had many faults, and at the time they'd split she'd decided that some of them were too much for her to live with, but he was always honest and the very idea of him two-timing anyone was ludicrous. 'Yes, it would have been, but he isn't, so your conscience is clear.' Of that, at least.

But now, of course, she was itching to know. Information was one thing, perfectly legitimate, and scurrilous gossip quite another, but when it came to Jude she couldn't help herself. She had been wildly jealous when he'd dated Ashleigh O'Halloran even though she herself had already turned him down not once but twice, and now the very thought that Jude might have another woman was intolerable to her. It was her great character flaw. She hesitated, but only for a second. 'Who?'

He smiled. He knew he had her interest and saw right through her attempt to sound casual. 'Connie Sheldon. You know, the one that came back from Australia and found someone had stolen her inheritance. Smart trick, if you ask me, and she didn't deserve to keep it if she couldn't be bothered to look after her old man on his deathbed, but there you have it. Anyway, it seems she's found herself a white knight in the form of our mutual friend.' He jerked his head towards the door.

Adam was so childish. She'd noticed before that he couldn't bring himself to say Jude's name. And he was playing with her. He knew she knew that he, Jude and Connie had all been friends together. 'Oh, yes. He mentioned her when he was here earlier.'

'He's definitely seeing her, then?' he said, quivering with interest.

'I mean, it's none of my business, or yours either, but for what it's worth, he isn't.' Though would he tell her if he was? 'She doesn't have many friends left in the town—'

'There's a reason for that,' said Adam darkly, 'and that's that she's pretty high-maintenance.'

'—and so naturally Jude's keeping an eye out for her. After all, what happened to her seems to have been traumatic.' She wasn't sure she liked the sound of Connie, who was by all accounts (not just Adam's) needy and selfish and too quick to pursue her own desires at the expense of others. Becca, who was the opposite, spent much of her life balancing that kind of neediness by doing kind things to people she really didn't like and Jude was cut from the same mould. It was why they got on so well.

'What a saint,' he said, watching her with a sly smile. 'I'm pretty sure they've been out a couple of times.'

'Jude can go out with whoever he wants whenever he wants,' she said, rattled by the fact that she cared. 'So can you. So can I, for that matter.'

'You could go out with me.'

'No, Adam.' She knew she was being rude but she didn't sit down. She wanted him out of the house and he was the kind of man who barely needed an invitation to make himself comfortable. 'That ship sailed long ago.'

'No harm in asking. I know you still hold a candle for him — that's fair, isn't it? — but he's definitely been seeing Connie Sheldon and they're not just friends. Unless you count kissing in the street being just friends.'

She really did hate him. She was quite sure that if Jude was dating Connie, he'd have told her but there was always a seed of doubt.

'I don't know Connie very well,' she said, trying to shift the conversation sideways since Adam obviously wasn't going to let it drop.

'I do, and she's a bit of a man-eater. I wouldn't worry. She'll move on from him pretty quickly.'

'I thought you were supposed to be a friend of hers.'

He shrugged. 'I don't know who my friends are any more.'

You had to give friendship to get it. That was what he wasn't good at. 'Thanks for the wine, but I have a million cupcakes to bake and ice tonight.' She lingered in the doorway, not even coming into her own living room, until it seemed she'd finally succeeded in making him uncomfortable.

'A million, eh? That's a lot.' He got to his feet.

Now that he was going she could laugh at herself. 'Okay, I exaggerated. Maybe a hundred thousand.'

'I'll pop back tomorrow and see if there are any left over.'

Just in time she recognised that as a joke. 'You don't know my Brownies. They'll eat the lot.'

'Then you can make me some more.' He headed to the hallway with a show of reluctance.

She was quick to open the door for him, and a blast of cold air swept in. 'If I don't see you before Christmas, have a good one.'

'I'll be back here with my folks as usual, so I expect I'll bump into you.' He lingered on the doorstep. 'Maybe Connie will be invited to the Satterthwaites' for Christmas.'

'Have you ever thought of asking her out yourself?' she asked, irritated. 'I think you'd be the perfect match.'

'Do you? I don't. The woman's an absolute bunny-boiling psycho. I know people who know people, and the way she got her hooks into that second husband of hers was a classic, or so I'm told. She was always a bit crazy but it sounds as though she's completely lost it.'

Yes; they would be perfect for one another. 'Thank you for the wine.'

'We'll drink it over Christmas,' he said, and leaned in to give her a farewell kiss but she was expecting it and swayed back. The manoeuvre amused him and he was laughing as he left.

She closed the door more firmly that was necessary and went into the kitchen to put the oven on. The temptation to call Jude and find out the truth of it was overwhelming but he would be driving. And anyway, if he was dating Connie it was none of her business.

SIXTEEN

It was a cold and depressing day and one on which Stephen wasn't working. Janice must have taken the day off to go Christmas shopping or something, thought Vivien uncharitably, because otherwise no doubt Stephen would have been following his boss (younger, affluent and good looking, as well as having the added cachet of being a successful woman in what was still a man's world) around the office with his tongue hanging out. With Janice unavailable he had decided to stay at home and get under his wife's feet. They would have their coffee and then he had suggested lunch and some Christmas shopping. You had to hand it to him. He was doing his best to keep all his irons in the fire, but one day he would have to decide which way to jump.

She watched the postman plodding up the path, head bent against the wind and rain, and saw a fat pile of letters in his hand. Giving him a cheery wave, which he either didn't see or ignored, she went to collect the post, which comprised a couple of bills, too much junk mail, and three white envelopes.

Christmas cards always gave her a moment of pleasure. These days there were fewer of them because no-one used the post any more (why would you, when even a second-class stamp cost so much?) and next year there would no doubt be even fewer. The matter of her inheritance was already making waves among her friends. If everything went badly, who would send Christmas cards to a convicted fraudster? It would be natural justice if she were to be cleared, or even if no charges were brought, but everyone knew that natural justice wasn't the same as the law of the land. Even Vivien, so sure that right was on her side, wasn't optimistic that she would emerge, even in the best-case scenario, with all her money and with her reputation and friendships intact.

She stuck her jaw out at the injustice of that. What utter nonsense. Marriage had a value (despite his infidelity she was generally comfortable being married to Stephen, since their marriage certificate gave a feeling of solidarity, their public vows a permanence, that merely living together would not have done) but it was undeniably exclusionary in law. It wasn't right that just because she'd been born on the wrong side of the blanket, as her mother would say with a weary sigh, she hadn't had the chances that Edwin's marriage had conferred on Connie.

It wasn't just the money, though that was important, because she felt so strongly that she was entitled to it. She would fight for it and, if necessary, spend the whole lot of it on lawyers so that there was none left and Connie's victory would be worthless. It was everything. It was the fact that she'd been deprived of Edwin as a father when she was growing up. On her eighteenth birthday her mother had finally told her who her father was, and she had spent a lot of time trying to track him down in the hope of building a relationship with him. When she'd finally succeeded, those hopes had been doused by the discovery that the man who had rejected both her mother and herself had, after all, chosen to build a life with someone else. Marriage was bad enough but there had been worse — a new baby, a cuckoo in the nest.

Thrusting the junk mail straight into the recycling bin she went into the kitchen, placed the bills on the table and turned the Christmas cards over in her hand. Dwelling on her father's betrayal was unhealthy but she couldn't stop herself. Resentment had been the background to her life and now that Connie was back and causing trouble, it was all she ever thought about. She had come to love Edwin, as she'd expected she would, but his disregard for her had been such that, even though he knew of her existence, he had chosen to bestow her name upon his second daughter as though she was the only one,. How bitterly Vivien now regretted that she had chosen to change it, rather than remain as the other Connie Sheldon.

The other Connie. She shook her head. What nonsense. She was the original Connie. She should have kept her name, introduced herself to Edwin when first she found him, asserted herself and insisted on her rights. She should have marched in and challenged the naming of this new child. *I was here first. You must call her something else.* What would Edwin have said to that?

'You all right, Viv?'

She put the cards down on the kitchen table unopened, and looked across to where Stephen was looking anxiously at her. Didn't they say you married someone like your father? Stephen was less antagonistic, for sure, but he kept his brains in his boxers, just as her father had done. 'I'm fine.'

'Don't be worried about all this inheritance stuff, eh? Not over Christmas.'

'Can you read my mind?' she asked, trying to make light of it.

'I can tell it's bothering you.'

Anxiety surged within her. The police had spoken to him, too, and it had been a tough interview, but there would be little he could say to incriminate her. She'd been careful to tell him the truth wherever possible, with necessary tweaks and a considerable number of omissions, and he'd been relieved when she'd declared there was no need for him to be burdened with visiting an elderly father-in-law who wouldn't even know who he was, but she'd always been careful to tell him as little as possible. Stephen wasn't academic but he was canny — the way he had proceeded with his affair told her that — and when she'd started talking about visiting her father in the home he'd raised an eyebrow, but no more. He'd swallowed her story about the Power of Attorney and the inheritance, too, or she thought he had. Now she wasn't so sure. Perhaps he'd seen what she was up to all along and was standing ready to benefit from the money, prepared to let her take the rap if it all went wrong. Or perhaps he saw it, as she did, as her personal battle, one that she must fight alone.

'It's not that,' she said, picking the cards up again. 'I don't regret any of it.'

'I worry about you. That's all.'

For sure. If she lost the money so would he. He'd make his decision then, she was sure, and she wouldn't see him for dust. She slit open the first envelope. 'A card from Lyn and Geoff.' Cheery robins in the snow. She set it on the kitchen table. Then the next one. 'This is from Lydia.'

'Lydia?'

He said that every year. She smiled, indulgently. 'An old schoolfriend of mine. I don't think you ever met her.' Lydia had sent a round-robin letter, no doubt dealing largely with her post-retirement travels. She unfolded it, glanced down and set it aside to read later.

The next envelope gave her cause to stop. It was addressed to her, rather than to both of them, and it didn't have the weight to be a Christmas card. It wasn't; it was a letter written on a single sheet of paper headed with the name and crest of a hotel group. *Hi Vivien/Connie. This has been traumatic for both of us, but after all, we are sisters. Can we meet? I really would like to get to know you and hear all about Dad, and how he was when he died. Love, Connie.* And then her phone number.

Love. What nonsense when Connie had had two husbands, abandoned them both, and then run off leaving her two little boys behind — and that was after hightailing it out of the country leaving her elderly father to fend for himself and only coming back when she needed somewhere to live. There was no way Connie Sheldon could know what love was.

'Are you sure you're all right?' said Stephen, standing over the kettle while it fizzed to the boil and snapped off.

She crossed the kitchen and handed him the letter, watching his forehead crease into a deep frown as he read it. 'What the hell? How did she get this address?'

'I don't know.' Though it wouldn't be difficult. Vivien had found Edwin with relative ease, long before the days of digital footprints and internet search engines.

'You're not going to see her?'

'Yes, I think I am.' She put her hand out for the letter and, when he gave it to her, looked at it again. 'Where's the harm?'

'She'll want something.'

'Of course she will. She's not doing this out of the goodness of her soul.' It would be interesting to know exactly what Connie wanted. It might be to satisfy her curiosity, or to unburden herself of her feelings, or something else. 'I won't know until I meet her, will I?'

'Do you want to?' he asked, getting two cups out of the cupboard, spooning instant coffee into them and then splashing in boiling water.

She thought about that until he'd made the coffees and handed one to her, and they stood side by side looking at the letter — not even a letter, just a note, really — where it lay on the counter, as if it were a sleeping snake that might rear and bite them. 'I don't think I do.' She had done, once, but not to make friends. Now she had a lingering desire to know exactly what it was about this woman that had made her father so exclusively devoted to her that he left her everything, even though she treated him so badly. Edwin had left Vivien under no illusions when she'd introduced herself; he had wanted everything to go to Connie, but he should have been more careful with the wording of the will. He had two daughters called Connie Sheldon and there was bound to be ambiguity. She deserved something to compensate for the loss of his love and she would fight for it.

'I'll say it, Viv. I don't think you should. I can't see how it ends well for anyone, but most of all for you.'

She sipped the coffee and looked at the note again, trying to pick up clues. The letters Connie had sent to Edwin had been strangely disjointed, streams of consciousness as if her mind wasn't entirely upon him. She'd talked of people he didn't know or couldn't remember, places he'd never visited as if he knew them well. They had portrayed Connie as someone entirely self-centred, barely capable of an effort. On the strength of those letters alone Vivien had formed a strong dislike of her half-sister and this letter only enforced it.

'Of course I'll go and see her,' she said, after moment. 'She'll be wanting to talk about Dad. What could possibly go wrong?'

SEVENTEEN

'I don't know why,' said DCI Chris Dodd, aka Doddsy, after he'd returned from the bar with a round of drinks, doled them out and taken his seat next to Jude in the corner of the bar, 'but I'm getting the feeling you're not exactly in the mood for Christmas jollity. What's up?'

'Is it that obvious?' Doddsy, who was Jude's best friend as well as his colleague, was correct. The last thing Jude was in the mood for was yet another night socialising (the third or fourth that week, depending on how you defined socialising) but he thought he'd managed to hide it reasonably well. He didn't dislike Christmas but it slowed everything down with its obligations to friends, its staff absences, the reduced hours of the various outside agencies on whom they increasingly depended for data analysis. He had myriad things to do, preferably before Christmas closed in on them, and the slow progress of the case of Connie Sheldon's inheritance, while anything but unexpected and certainly not a priority, was dragging on him.

Until it was solved he would feel a responsibility for Connie's well-being.

'It is to people who know you well. Skulking in a corner like you're hoping for a quick getaway.'

Jude felt a pang of guilt, because that was exactly the way his mind had been going. Over his fifteen years in the police Doddsy had become his closest friend. Until relatively recently they'd made a point of meeting up every week to chew the fat and set the world, both personal and professional, to rights. Latterly these sessions had become rarer as Jude had embarked on that relationship with Ashleigh while Doddsy had found a long-term partner in the young police constable Tyrone Garner, and he keenly felt their loss. It was always beneficial to have a drinking companion who was calm and rational and with whom he was not, as he was with both Ashleigh and Becca and with his brother, Mikey, heavily invested emotionally. Without Doddsy's perspective he found it much harder to clear his head of the things that troubled him.

'I'm busy. That's all,' he said, part defensive, part remorseful. 'And I'm not saying my middle names are *Ebenezer* and *Scrooge*, but I'm getting a bit too old to socialise at the level everyone seems to expect from me at this time of year.' Maybe he should try a bit harder. He was conscious that he was becoming less tolerant as he got older.

'Aye, I know. Tyrone says he can't knock on someone's door without being offered a wee sherry.' Doddsy, who didn't drink, laughed.

Jude checked his watch. It was Friday night, and the team's Christmas night out. They'd been to an Italian restaurant and were now in the pub. He'd paid for a round of drinks and now, approaching nine o'clock, he found himself wondering whether it was too early to head home.

'It's been a busy week. I've got a busy weekend. I'm starting to think I'm too old for this game.' He disliked himself. He usually made more of an effort that that.

'What are you up to, then?' Doddsy sipped at his St Clement's, looking as if he was settled in for the evening.

'I'm going to the football with my Dad tomorrow. And in the evening Ashleigh's having a few friends round for drinks.' No matter how hard he tried, he couldn't make himself enthusiastic about that. She'd been uncharacteristically tight-lipped about the other guests and he was pretty certain that would be because she was hoping her ex-husband would turn up. If he did, and if the two of them weren't already back together, he suspected it wouldn't be long before they were. 'I haven't committed to that. I'll maybe pass on it.' He looked across the room to where Ashleigh was laughing with Chris Marshall, who was telling some story that was almost certainly made more uproarious by drink. He wasn't in the least possessive, but it astonished him how Ashleigh's instinctive understanding of other people's emotions was a blind spot when it came to her own, and how she seemed unable to follow the sound advice she always found for other people.

'You've Sunday to yourself, at least.'

Sunday was a sore point. 'Nope. Connie Sheldon asked me to go and help her to move into her flat and, fool that I am, I said I would.' She was bound to offer to cook for him to thank him for doing very little, since she could hardly have a huge amount of stuff to move in. There would be furniture to shift and odds and ends to mend or assemble but that was it. He wished he'd said no but she'd made it seem such a small request that it had been hard to refuse without sounding churlish.

'Maybe pass on that, too,' suggested Doddsy, and then

allowed himself a very delicate pause. 'I thought you and Connie got on well.'

Your history never let you go. 'I get on fine with Connie, but we're not eighteen any more.' There had been a reason their teenage romance had petered out. They weren't romantically compatible. 'There's nothing in it in that sense, but I feel responsible for her.'

'I don't know why. It's not for you to take on her problems.'

'No. But you know what, Doddsy?' Jude took a long sup of his pint and found himself relaxing. It wasn't the drink, though he'd had more than enough of that. It was that he finally had the chance to get things off his chest. 'I'm worried about her. A lot of her problems may be her own fault—'

'She can hardly be held responsible for someone stealing her inheritance.'

'No, but she knows that if she'd been a bit more attentive, even if she'd phoned the home occasionally when he stopped answering her calls and her letters, this might have been avoided.' He could imagine how Ellie Jack would have relished telling the tale of how Edwin's daughter had phoned from Australia when another woman pretending to be her was in that very room. His lips twitched at the thought, but only for a second. There was no point in smiling at what might have happened when too many people were dealing with the consequences of reality. 'She's not in a good place right now.'

'You're doing what you can to get her money back. You don't need to take responsibility for her personal welfare as well.'

'I know. I know.' Jude set the drink down and leaned forward, lowering his voice. 'But you know what? She doesn't have anyone else. The only other person she's in touch with is Adam Fleetwood, and he's the last person I'd turn to if I needed help.'

Doddsy poked at the ice in his glass. 'It shouldn't be beyond the wit of someone like Connie to go and look for her old friends and reconnect with them, no?'

'I'll be honest with you. I had a look at her social media, or rather Becca did.' There was no point in concealing anything from Doddsy. 'They have friends in common, or friends of friends or whatever. It didn't take much to see she comprehensively alienated most of her friends here when she disappeared off to Australia with another woman's husband. The ones who were in any way sympathetic seem to have lost any fellow feeling for her now she's dumped him and the kids — they're just young, four or five — and come home.'

Doddsy raised an eyebrow. 'She doesn't give much thought to consequences, does she?'

'That's exactly the problem. She burns bridges everywhere she goes. I don't know what went on in her life when she was away but I wouldn't be surprised if she had some kind of breakdown. There may have been domestic abuse. There might have been something else. I just don't know. But as I said, I do worry that she's not in a good place.' Connie always seemed cheerful enough, always tried to be positive, but he realised now that since she'd come back to Penrith the only time he'd seen her without a drink in her hand or spoken to her without hearing a slight slurring in her voice had been when they had gone up to the cemetery to visit her father's grave.

'Right. But that's not your problem.'

'There's literally no-one else to take it on.' And in the background there was Melanie Trotter, stirring up unpleasantness among mutual friends on Facebook (he had Becca to thank for this particular scrap of information) and issuing vague threats of revenge. It turned out that the time he'd seen Melanie approach Connie in the pub wasn't the first time they'd met. Penrith wasn't a small place and it was easy to avoid people there, but it was just as easy to make sure that you could always be in someone's path if you wanted to annoy them. He'd learned that to his own cost. 'Add to that I think she's picked up some unwelcome attention from her husband's ex.'

'Serious attention?'

'Unpleasant, but not enough to make it worth reporting.' Possibly enough to tip her over the edge, though. Could Melanie possibly know that?

'It makes sense she looked you up, then,' said Doddsy, 'given as you're a policeman. Her own personal bodyguard.'

'That's just it. I don't want to be her bodyguard. I'm telling you, Doddsy. I know Connie and I'm pretty sure she has intentions.'

At this admittedly old-fashioned expression, Doddsy laughed out loud. 'What, carnal ones?'

'Probably.' Jude grinned. Connie's neediness had begun to weigh him down but his friend's amusement put it back in perspective. 'I'm caught in a bit of a trap.'

Doddsy considered this for a moment. Jude, who had known him for a long time, couldn't decide whether this consideration was serious or amused. 'Don't take this the wrong way, but I thought you were a bit more ruthless than that.'

'So did I, but it appears I'm not.' It was never great to understand that what you had considered a strength was in fact a weakness. 'I don't need Connie in my life right now. I like her, but she's complicated and she's needy. I don't feel I can leave her struggling with no help at all, but I don't have either the time or the inclination to give her all the help she thinks she needs.' And the rest. Connie didn't just want a man to move furniture for her. It would have been nice if her other contact, Adam, had found his way to do something more practical than sniping from the sidelines.

'Tricky. I don't suppose you want advice from old Uncle Doddsy, but if you do…'

'Right now I'm considering writing in to *Dear Deirdre*. I'll be happy to hear anything you have to say.'

'I think you know the answer. You aren't responsible for her problems, you've done everything you can for her at a personal level and the best help you can give her is by making sure her half-sister faces up to what she's done so that Connie can get some closure, and her money back. You have to draw a line, for your own well-being, and you have to make it clear to her exactly what it is.'

When Doddsy put it like that it was so straightforward, exactly the same life advice Jude himself would have given to Mikey in similar circumstances. Setting boundaries was healthy for everyone. Helping someone didn't mean you had to sacrifice your own emotional well-being. The difficulty in this case was that he was uncertain of Connie's mental state. She might throw a temper tantrum, she might succumb to a complete mental and emotional breakdown, or she might come out fighting, determined to prove she could manage on her own. You just never knew. 'Right.'

'Is there something else?'

What the hell? Doddsy was his friend and if you couldn't be honest with your friends, who could you be honest with? 'I don't want people seeing me with Connie and thinking there's something between us. You know my heart's elsewhere and I'm pretty certain she does, too, but she still sees a vacancy.' Connie didn't want love. She wanted company.

'Is there something happening between you and Becca, then?' asked Doddsy, with interest.

'No, and I don't think there will be, but right now I'm getting on fine with her and as long as there's a chance — even the tiniest chance — she'll change her mind, I don't want to close that door.' Adam was already in Becca's ear about Connie, though the fact that she'd called him to tell him about that particular conversation implied she wasn't taken in by it, but he'd detected a hint of resentment in her voice and although he'd hastened to reassure her, he wasn't sure she was convinced. Now he remembered seeing Adam loitering in the street the day that Connie had come home and Jude had walked her back to her hotel.

You could care too much for people. To reinforce that he looked across to where Ashleigh was looking down at her phone and he knew from the focused look on her face that she'd be messaging Scott. 'You know the problem, Doddsy? I care a lot about a lot of people, and after a while it becomes…almost competitive.' You could care for people who had competing interests. He cared for Mikey and he cared for his father, but the two of them never spoke and both were notoriously touchy every time he mentioned the other one. 'You do something for one and the other perceives it as a slight. I ought to be able to do a good turn for Connie without anyone misinterpreting it, but it seems I can't.' And he ought not to care, but it seemed he couldn't do that either.

Doddsy followed his gaze. He was a charitable man but he was no way as much emotionally invested with Ashleigh as Jude was. Detachment, in this case, lent him wisdom. 'I don't expect you need to hear this, but maybe it'll help to hear someone say it. You have to let other people make their own mistakes.'

Mikey, his father, Ashleigh, Connie, even Becca.

Doddsy was right. You couldn't take control of people's lives. All you could do was be there to pick up the pieces for the people who mattered to you if they ever needed you to. 'You're a wise old bird, Doddsy.'

'So I've been told.'

'I'll speak to Connie about it when I get the chance.' And he would definitely give a pass to Ashleigh's drinks do.

EIGHTEEN

'That's a good job,' said Connie, standing back admiringly to look at the empty bookcase that now stood in the corner of her tiny living room. 'Thank you. I don't know what I'd have done if you hadn't been here.'

'I'm sure you'd have managed.' Jude stood back, too, but he was careful to keep a distance between them. Taking Doddsy's advice and applying it with care, he had fulfilled his promise to help Connie with her move but had been as perfunctory as possible. He had rescheduled it to a narrow time slot on Saturday evening, between returning from the football and to an unspecified unavoidable engagement (definitely not Ashleigh's Christmas drinks, to which he had no intention of going). While there, he had been careful not to laugh or indulge in anything she might interpret as flirtation, and he had looked as his watch on numerous occasions to reinforce the point. He did so again, obviously, but if Connie noticed she chose to ignore it.

'There's just one more thing. The Christmas tree.' It

had been standing in the corner, an artificial one, still in its box. As she spoke she reached for it and began to unpack it.

'I should head off, now. I've something I said I would do.'

'Surely it's nothing that can't wait a few moments? I need you to tell me if the tree's straight, and to get the lights on. And to get the star on top.'

The tree was a big one, a six-footer, far too big for the living room in this shabby rented flat, where it would take up half of the available space. Not that Connie had much else to fill it, beyond the new bookcase and a few odds and ends. If he'd been a bit braver he'd have arranged to meet Becca on some slender pretext, but his courage had failed him. The problem was that Connie would have no hesitation about interrogating him on what his plans were and he was reluctant to tell her anything too personal. He sighed. 'Okay.'

'It won't take long, and it would be nice if you could help me decorate it. I hate decorating a tree on my own. It should always be a social thing.'

A social thing, yes, but also a family thing. He was wary of it. Back in the day the Satterthwaites' Christmas tree decorating had been a complicated ritual which, because Mikey was so much younger, had endured long after Jude might otherwise have got bored with it. Every year meant picking over hand-made decorations, souvenirs, gifts. It meant unpacking feelings and memories, some of them still raw. These days he made only the barest effort in his own house and his mother, he thought, only bothered so that the house wouldn't look cold and unwelcoming for festive visitors. 'Do you think so?'

'I had boxes of decorations,' she said, 'all the old ones from when I was a kid and the ones I'd made for Mum and

Dad. We always did the tree together, and Dad made a point of keeping that tradition going after she'd gone. I went back and asked the people who moved into the house if by any chance they'd kept them, but they hadn't, so I went down to Sainsbury's and picked up a job lot. Next year maybe I'll have some more memories to decorate it with. Because I'll just pick myself up and start all over again, like I always do.'

It was almost impossible not to feel sorry for her. When he thought back, Jude realised that this resilience was one of the reasons he'd first been attracted to her. To Connie, everything ought to be simple. She wore her heart on her sleeve, and saw love and life — and fairness and unfairness — as no more and no less than what was in front of her at any given time. When he was younger that had seemed honest and authentic, even courageous, but now he saw that it did nothing but obscure the more complicated undertones. Life wasn't simple. People loved and weren't loved in return, cared and weren't cared for, misunderstood and were misunderstood in turn. Too many times, he'd seen just how this harmless misunderstanding could turn to violence and end in death.

There was no help for it. 'Connie, can we talk?'

'I'm dreading Christmas,' she said, ignoring or not hearing him, 'and not just because I won't have the boys, though I'm sure when Christmas Day comes it'll near break me. But it'll be the first Christmas without Dad and I've barely started grieving for him.'

'I expect that'll be tough,' he said, cursing because this turn in the conversation made it more difficult to be brutally honest with her.

'It really will.' She set the tree in its stand and began to fold down its branches, one by one. 'Tell me if these look balanced, okay?'

He went and stood on the opposite side of the room and watched, making approving noises while she tweaked the tree, watching as it expanded, plastic branch by plastic branch, a lurid green behemoth dominating the room.

'Now the lights,' she said, opening another box. 'Here's the end. Can you start at the top and wind them round? I got a long string, so you've plenty to work with. I feel this flat needs a hell of a lot of cheering up, and so do I.'

He did as he was told, and this time it was Connie who stood back and gave him advice. 'It's a bit sparse on your right,' she said, reviewing it, critically, 'but pretty good otherwise. You have an eye for this.'

'It's not exactly hard.'

'Dear Lord, can't you at least take a compliment?' she said. 'We can do the decorations later. Why don't we have a drink? There's a bottle open, and surely you can walk to wherever you're going.'

'I'd love to but I can't. I have to go down to Wasby. Mum's cooking supper.' Now he'd made himself into a liar. He'd never intended anything more strenuous than a bottle of Loweswater Gold and *Match of the Day*.

'Are you having a big family Christmas?' she asked, wistfully.

'Yes. It's Mum's turn to host the family waifs and strays. There's a three-line whip. Everyone in the family has to attend.' Except his father, obviously. 'Mikey's pouring the wine and I'm carving the turkey.'

'I'm so going to miss the boys. I'm going to get a nice loaf of bread and lots of cheese, and some really decent red wine. Maybe I'll go for a walk somewhere.'

He didn't think it was deliberate, because Connie was guileless, but she was guilt-tripping him. He almost cracked and invited her over to his mother's for Christmas Day, but he could imagine what Linda Satterthwaite would say, and how Mikey would first roll his eyes and then never let him hear the last of it. 'I'm sorry it'll be tough for you.'

'It's not like I didn't know that when I decided to come back. It's just that, like I said before, I thought I'd be in my own house and able to see Dad and here I am in this crappy little flat, and not likely to see a soul until people start waking up from their food comas.' She sighed. 'I know you've got a lot on, but maybe we could meet up? I could cook you supper on Christmas Eve.'

Becca was having a drinks party on Christmas Eve, to which the Satterthwaites and all their neighbours were invited. She had made a particular point of checking that he could come and he was looking forward to it. For a split second he found himself wondering if he was any better than Connie, yearning for someone who'd once cared for him but who cared for him no longer. The difference, if there was one, was that he and Becca managed to coexist as friends without any serious complications and that he had enough self-awareness to know when there was hope and, if there was not, that trying to pursue it would only end in alienation.

That was exactly what was happening between him and Connie. He was prepared to offer friendship, she wanted more. The imbalance in their relationship had made it unsustainable. He sighed. 'I'm afraid I'm booked up on Christmas Eve, too.'

'My, you're popular. Are doing anything interesting?'

'Village drinks,' he said, reluctant to mention Becca, for reasons he wasn't entirely sure about. He didn't think Connie was malicious but she could be dangerously tactless and he didn't particularly want her to know how he felt about Becca in case the two should meet. Too many people knew or guessed about that already, and he'd end up making a fool of himself.

'Boxing Day, then,' she said, with a brave smile.

'There's a group of us going to the football.' The Boxing Day fixture, if at home, was the one time his mother went, and Mikey. His father would be there too and Jude, who regularly went with him, would be in a different part of the ground and avoiding him, before quietly detaching himself from the other two and meeting him for a drink. Like Connie, David Satterthwaite would be spending Christmas alone, but he didn't mind. He had plenty of friends elsewhere.

'There's bound to be somewhere in town where people —' he went on, but Connie's expression told him exactly what she thought of that idea, even before she held her hand up to stop him in his tracks.

'Please. I'm not a charity case. Christmas is for family and if you don't have family you have friends, right? And I thought you were my friend.'

They were both staring forty in the face and here they were, involved in an emotional standoff like a pair of sparring teenagers. Everything had to be a drama. 'Of course I am. But that's all it is, Connie.'

'Spending some time together doesn't signify anything,' she said, but she was pouting in disappointment. Yes, just like she had done when she was sixteen. In this sense, at least, she hadn't matured. He could understand how two marriages had gone so badly wrong, how she found herself in public fights with other women, even how she hadn't been able to maintain a relationship with the father she loved.

'It doesn't.' Others might think it did. 'But I've got other people in my life, and I have my job.' One of the bones of contention Becca had had with him was the amount of his free time that got taken up with work and he was keen not to let her see him making too much of an effort to spend the time with someone else. She might misinterpret it.

'And I don't. I don't have a job, or any friends.'

'There's Adam.'

'I suppose so, but he has his family, too, and I don't think they ever liked me. And I enjoy your company.'

'I enjoy yours, too, but as I say, my time is limited.'

'I didn't think you were that selfish,' said Connie, and looked hurt.

She sounded like Mikey, as a teenager, whenever he hadn't got his own way. *Mum, you're so selfish.* He almost smiled. 'It's not about selfishness. We both have our own lives.'

'I did think…' she began, and tailed off. 'Okay. I don't suppose you can help how you feel.'

'I'll always be very fond of you, and I like to think we'll aways be friends. I'm obviously always here to help you if you need me.' That was a concession he hadn't intended to make. 'But that's all. I'm not looking for anything more.'

She turned her back and started fishing about in the box of decorations. 'I'd better do this by myself, then. Could you get me a chair so I can put this on?' She produced a silver, sparkly star from the box and flourished it at him. Her expression was wounded.

'I can do that bit at least,' he said, taking it and reaching up to fit it onto the scratchy top branch of the tree. She had, he noticed, brought a bunch of mistletoe tied up with a scarlet ribbon. At least he'd said his piece before she had the chance to wave that at him. 'How about that?'

'Thank you,' she said, in a subdued voice.

He picked up his coat from the sofa where he'd deposited it, put it on and headed for the door. 'Let me know if you need any help with anything else.'

'I doubt if I will. I'm very self-sufficient. And you'll be busy.'

'I'll see you.'

'Have a wonderful Christmas. I don't expect we'll speak before then.'

'Have a great Christmas, Connie.'

He let himself out and headed out of the flat. After a few steps he paused to look back. Connie's window was uncurtained and the lights of the undecorated tree shone brightly out into the street. She wasn't decorating it. She was sitting in an armchair with her head in her hands.

For a moment he fought his better nature, but it was Doddsy's advice that tipped the balance. Resisting the temptation to go back, he turned towards home.

NINETEEN

To Connie's great astonishment, Vivien had agreed to meet. The text message had come through after Jude had left on the Saturday night which, on balance, was a good thing because she was sure he'd advise her against it, and with some to-ing and fro-ing they had fixed a time of four o'clock on the following day.

I don't know why I put myself through this, Connie said to herself for the umpteenth time, setting two glasses and the remains of the bottle of red wine (opened at lunchtime to calm her nerves) on the stained worktop in the cramped kitchen, and she wasn't just thinking of her half sister. Jude's rejection of the previous day, while not entirely surprising, had been painful. She'd hoped for something positive. He was exactly what she needed, for the moment, at least, but she should have known he wasn't a man to buy into something so obviously temporary. Not everyone saw being single as a problem, and she knew she shouldn't see it that way either, but by God, it was lonely. And now she had arranged to see the woman who had walked in her skin for years without her knowledge, and she was shaking at the very thought.

I really shouldn't have done it. She'd briefly wondered about asking Jude if, despite his inevitable disapproval, he'd come along to support her and if necessary keep the peace. His common sense alone would help her keep control and manage whatever came her way from that entirely unknown entity that was her half sister, but she'd lost her nerve. Even now she thought that if she did call he'd come along, but that would be because his curiosity was driving him, not because he particularly wanted to spend time in her company. Knowing that, she wasn't going to give him the satisfaction, wasn't going to take something without giving back. She might have lost everything else, but she still had her pride.

But it would have been good to have someone there. She already loathed Vivien and wasn't sure she was capable of keeping her feelings under control. Every time she thought of the woman her soul boiled upon into an insane fury. It wasn't about the money, which was unarguably hers; the fraud had been discovered and it was only a matter of proving it and getting it back. The inconvenience of it had been brutal, and that was marked in bold in the minus column of Connie's mental balance sheet. She was jealous, not of stout, grey, ageing Vivien herself, a woman too dull even to squander her ill-gotten gains, but of the time she'd spent with their father.

It was my time, said Connie to herself, shaking a little in her fury. *He was my dad.*

Several times that morning she'd sat down at the tiny kitchen table with pad and pen and tried to map out how she'd deal with this. She liked a list to work from, even though she inevitably abandoned it early. A list of bullet points gave a framework of things she shouldn't say, accusations she had better not make, but the one thing she hadn't actually considered was why, in the name of all that was holy, she was even thinking about this meeting when she had no idea what she wanted from it. Now it was too late. Vivien would arrive any minute and there wasn't even enough time to sink another glass of wine and top up her Dutch courage.

Leaving the pad accusingly blank she returned to the living room and stood by the window, watching as the afternoon hastened towards darkness. Her flat was in the town centre and she had a clear line of sight down Great Dockray, where the pre-Christmas excitement was in full swing despite a thin grey drizzle that made the streets shine. The few shops that were still open were preparing to close but the pubs were doing a roaring trade. A car drove past, a white Citroën like the one that had attracted Jude's attention at the cemetery. There were two people in it. So Vivien had thought it prudent to bring someone with her, as if Connie were a threat,

How insulting. She had no ill intention towards her sister. Her hatred didn't translate into violence, only festered so that, as always, the only person who would get hurt was Connie herself. Her life would be so much easier if she was capable of turning her anger and self-loathing outwards, hurting someone else.

The car drew up on a single yellow line on the other side of the road. Vivien, clutching a bottle, got out of the passenger side and a thin grey man who must be her husband got out of the driver's side. They kissed one another on the cheek and then separated.

At least, thought Connie as Stephen Warrington hurried away in the direction of Costa and Vivien hesitated for a moment before walking past the window with her eyes deliberately averted, they weren't coming in together. Stephen would no doubt be keeping a watching brief, waiting for a call for help if his wife's nerves got the better of her, and then he would come charging in like the white knight Connie so desperately needed and had begun to think she'd found. She shook her head, but there was no time to think about Jude right now. Her enemy (as she had now begun to think of her sister) was at the door.

After the merry chime of the doorbell she took a moment to straighten her cuffs (she had dressed smartly for the occasion, in her best black jeans, white shirt and a Christmas jumper she'd picked up for a song in Arnison's) before she answered it.

'Here goes.' she said aloud, and headed for the door. 'Vivien.' A bright smile she didn't mean. She was good at those. 'Do come in.'

Vivien stepped in and leaned forward in an awkward embrace, bringing with her a tang of 4711 eau de cologne and a sour smell of damp wool. Even in the short period she'd been out of the car, her hair had acquired a sheen of drizzle.

'How nice to meet you,' she said, and held out a bottle. 'I've brought you some gin. Do you drink gin?'

'Yes,' said Connie, accepting the gift graciously, 'though I have wine if you'd rather.'

'I'm afraid I don't drink wine these days. It stops me sleeping.'

Connie took her coat and hung it on the back of the door, waved her through to the living room, put the wine bottle and glasses back in the cupboard and opened the gin. It looked decent and she could finish the wine later. She had plenty of ice and tonic, and she had a small plate of German ginger biscuits from a local deli. They, too, had been on offer. When you had no job and you'd been robbed of your inheritance, you had to watch every penny.

She carried the tray with drinks and nibbles to the living room and, manoeuvring her way around the over-large Christmas tree, set it on a small table between the armchair and the sofa and passed a glass to Vivien.

'How nice to meet you, at last,' said Vivien, very carefully, and smiled politely. She was exactly what Connie had expected — beige trousers with an elasticated waist which couldn't contain a roll of postmenopausal fat across her stomach, a shapeless blue cardigan over a plain shirt. Her hands were speckled with liver spots, her face webbed with wrinkles that came, for sure, from constant disapproval. 'I've been looking forward to it.'

Connie bridled. 'We nearly met at the cemetery, didn't we?'

'Yes. I didn't want to intrude on what must have been your private moment of reflection and grief.' Vivien raised her glass. 'Good health, Connie. To friendship.'

The bloody cheek. Connie drank instead of replying and discovered to her surprise that the gin was more than decent. Trying to frame what she wanted to say, how she could express her fury and her grief and yet contain them, she sipped it slowly.

'And are you settling in?' pursued Vivien, as if she were the president of the local Women's Institute trying to set a new member at her ease.

'Not yet.' Connie sipped again before, inevitably, her woes and her fury got the better of her. 'I wasn't expecting to have to live in a flat. I thought I was going home to live in the family home. My family home. My dad's house.'

That thin, ageing hand stretched out to the plate as Vivien helped herself to a tiny ginger biscuit. '*Our* dad's house,' she corrected, quietly but clearly.

That was unexpected. Connie, who had been bracing

herself for apologies and abasement, was unprepared for a challenge. 'What?'

'Why do you want to see me, Connie?' Vivien asked, with a smile of studied bewilderment. 'I'll be honest. I'm not sure it's a good idea. I don't think we'll have a lot to say to each other. I'll be polite to you, because I try to be polite to everyone, but I'll also be honest.'

'All the better.' Honesty went two ways. She hadn't liked Matt's honest reaction to her decision to leave, or Melanie's to her return. She wouldn't like this, either, but it meant she would be free to reply without restraint.

'Good. You're furious with me because you think I've stolen all your money, and I don't think highly of you because as far as I can see everything you've ever done, or not bothered to do, has been entirely selfish. The way you behaved to Dad was bad enough, but there's your children, too. My nephews. I don't have children but if I did I'd treat them better than you've treated yours.'

What cheek. What absolute cheek. 'They're not your nephews. And how dare you call him Dad!'

'Why not? He is. And they are.'

'Yes, but—' Connie's mind filled with memories. The loss of her mother. Catching her father crying in the armchair late one night and sliding an arm around his shoulders to comfort him. The guilt she'd felt when she was in Australia and hadn't had the time or the money to come back, the time difference that meant she never seemed to find the right moment to call, the phone calls he cut off and the letters he never acknowledged. She'd done a little, but she should have done so much more. 'He was a difficult man. You had to put effort in. I did that.' And got nothing out.

'Really? And yet, for the last two years of his life, somehow I managed to put the effort in.'

Connie crashed her glass down on the table. She'd poured herself a small measure as a precaution, but it had been far too small. 'Why wait until I was safely out of the way?' Fuming, she got up, went to the kitchen and poured herself another, much larger glass.

When she came back Vivien was sitting staring at the tree, cradling her half-empty glass. 'I don't know if he would have welcomed me before,' she said. 'He had a family. He had you. Why would he have wanted me to turn up and change everything? What would your mother have thought?'

'Leave my mum out of this.' Edwin had loved his wife. He couldn't have loved Vivien's mother; she could only have been a passing fancy and Viv herself was nothing more than a by-blow. 'He probably has kids all over the place. He only ever wanted to spend time with one of us. That was me.' She had been his princess.

'Yes.' Vivien's lips set in a thin line, as if this blow had hurt her. 'But he was my father and I had a right to know him.'

To see him, perhaps. 'You had plenty of opportunity.' Connie realised something. 'Wait a moment. How do you know so much about me? I didn't know anything about you. Did you read my letters to him?' In the early days, when he'd been lucid enough to know which of his daughters was which, had Edwin shared reminiscences and memories of Connie herself? Had he spoken fondly of Viv's mother, rather than of his wife? The thought dismayed her.

'Of course. His eyesight was failing. He asked me to read them to him.'

'How dare you judge me!' Connie heard her voice rising to a wail of despair and was powerless to stop it. She shouldn't have had that second gin. She shouldn't have drunk that wine as she'd pored over that empty notepad. She should have had something to eat. It was too late now, and all her mistakes flowed together and locked her into a Gordian knot of recklessness.

'Why not? Don't you think you did things — or rather, failed to do things — you should be judged for? It's time you stopped playing the victim and took responsibility for your part in all this.'

'And what about you? You'll be judged, sure enough.' Connie fought her fury. 'You'll be up in court for pretending to be me. You stole my identity.'

'What nonsense,' said Vivien, crisply. 'Dad always knew who I was.'

'You pretended to be me, to get the money.'

'I didn't pretend to be anyone. My legal name is Constance Sheldon. It's on my birth certificate and Dad is named as my father. I'm his daughter just like you but you had everything from him. You had his love and attention, you had a beautiful house, holidays, everything you wanted. It's my turn, now. I'm entitled to that money.'

For a mad moment, Connie nearly believed her. *All my fault*. But was it? The law was on her side. Yes, her self-esteem was low, and she'd made mistakes, but she didn't need to justify wanting — needing — her own inheritance to this smug, buttoned-up old woman. 'He paid you off.'

'I got nothing. He paid a thousand pounds to buy my mother off.'

'That's all he thought you were worth. Because he didn't want you.'

Viv's lips were narrow and pinched. She, too, must have come to the flat dreading the encounter, but unlike Connie she'd thought it through, had a current piece ready to say. There would have been no blank piece of paper where a plan should be. 'He was young and didn't want commitment. He acknowledged me. If he'd been a different man, a little older or less restless, he would have married my mother and we would have been happy, at least for a while. You would never have been born. I think he knew that. That's why his will was ambiguous. It's why he told me what was in it and didn't change it when he was fully competent to do so. It's why he gave me the key to his house and let me deal with his mail. He trusted me, and I repaid that trust.'

'I don't believe you.' Surely it was untrue? But Edwin was dead and couldn't gainsay it. 'He loved me.'

'When you were younger, perhaps. But let me tell you this, Connie. He talked about you a lot, about how much he used to love you—'

Used to. That hurt. 'Stop it!' She caught her breath. 'Can we play nicely?'

'You started this. You can take the consequences.'

Connie drained her glass, uncomfortably aware of how the alcohol was making her pulse race. A flush of heat rose through her body. Who'd have thought her sister would be such a grade A bitch? It was astonishing how much unpleasantness could be concealed under layers of synthetic beige.

'I don't want to fight,' she said, meaning *I don't want to fight now*. Drunk and taken by surprise, she would lose. 'It's my money. I'm going to get it back. The courts will be on my side. But I'm not so unpleasant as you...as you think. So if you come clean and hold your hands up, spare us both the pain and the expense of taking the will to court, I'll give you—' She wavered. How much should she offer? 'A quarter of it.'

'A quarter?' Vivien laughed. 'Is this really what you wanted to see me about? I didn't think it was because you thought we could be friends, because you aren't like that and I'm careful who I let myself get close to. No, I'm sorry. It's my money. I'll take the rap for the few administrative corrections I had to make on the way, but I'll defend my right to the money. It's the least I deserve. A quarter?' She laughed. 'Unbelievable.'

'Right.' Connie drained her glass. The room began to spin, a result of her fury as much as of drink. 'But you'll lose. Then you won't get a penny.'

'Really? What's a jury going to think when I tell them what he told me? That he said what a disappointment you were to him and that he thought I should have the money? What are a dozen decent, respectable people going to think of your behaviour to your father? And what are they going to think of you, a drunk who runs away at the first sign of trouble and leaves her two children behind?'

'I'm not a drunk!' Connie jumped to her feet and flung her empty glass but her reactions were so slow that her sister moved easily to avoid the missile and in any case her aim was so poor that she missed her intended target by a good six feet. The glass smashed against the adjacent wall in a rain of fake crystal splinters. 'Get out of my house!'

'With pleasure.' Vivien, too, jumped up out of her seat, failing to avoid the tree and setting its lights quivering and its ornaments rocking in a dizzying frenzy. 'My coat?'

'Get it yourself!' cried Connie, and ran from the room and into her tiny bedroom where she collapsed on the bed and gave way to tears.

TWENTY

'God,' said Faye, 'next time you hear me say something's straightforward, stop me, will you?' She had erupted into the office Jude shared with Doddsy without so much as a knock and she was plainly furious. 'I've never seen so clear a case of fraud, I swear it. We even have the bloody woman admitting what she's done. This is news I definitely didn't need on a Monday morning.'

The door banged behind her, rattled on its old hinges, and settled. Jude had been on a call but the minute he saw her he'd terminated it, laid his phone down and turned to her. 'There's a problem?'

'You're master of understatement.' She was furious. 'Yes, there's a problem. At least, I think there is. Our friends in the CPS don't seem to agree with me, or rather they don't think there's quite the same problem.'

He took a moment to consider the worst-case scenario. 'Don't tell me they don't think this is fraud?' He could imagine how Connie would respond to that. Foolishly (he'd been in the job long enough to know better) he'd assured her that charges would be forthcoming, as if it was in his power to do so.

Faye pulled up a chair and sat down. 'Maybe it isn't quite as bad as all that. But I've just spoken to an awfully nice CPS solicitor.' Her tone was devastatingly sarcastic. 'And do you know, Jude, this is *actually quite difficult.*' In air quotes, accompanied by a scowl. 'Because, you see, our woman Vivien *is actually called* Connie Sheldon. And she *did actually spend an awful lot of time looking after her father* and because the documents from Eden's End have gone missing — so unfortunate, by the way, and *can we try a little harder to find them—*'

Jude laughed, bitterly.

'Exactly. And the staff at the home seem to think that he was very fond of her—'

'Even though the ones we've contacted who were there at the time hardly ever spoke to her and never really saw the two together?'

'Yes, but he definitely introduced her as his daughter Connie, and he was totally mentally competent—'

'When he first arrived. We don't know when that changed or why. You'd have thought care home staff would have been trained to spot coercion.'

'You'd have thought so. But our friendly CPS solicitor actually seemed to think it might be easier if we let the two of them fight over the will in court and spend our time elsewhere. Can you believe it?'

He was as astonished and as angry, though not so visibly, as Faye. To him, as to her, the fact of wrongdoing was clear and there was evidence to be collected. 'There's definitely fraud.'

'In my view there is. But unfortunately we're going to have to provide a lot of evidence we don't currently have if we want the CPS to get off their backsides and move this matter forward.'

They were busy, that was the problem, like everyone else. So was the CPS, which might have something to do with the reluctance to run with the case as it stood. 'Okay. Did you explain to them that it's not just financial fraud?'

'Do you think I'm a child? I've pointed out that what Vivien Warrington did was wrong at every level, that she's caused immense distress to Connie Armstrong and that she's admitted to identity theft.' She drummed her fingers on the table. 'But actually I hate to say they might have a point and it makes sense to set the bar for prosecution rather higher than they otherwise might. Nobody knows for sure what Edwin Sheldon intended and there's actually a possibility he may have had a hand in deceiving Connie himself. Which would be extremely unpleasant but not, you will agree, illegal.'

He digested this unwelcome news. 'There must be some point in the process where Vivien broke the law.'

'There must be, but it may turn out to be a very small infraction. She says he gave her the keys to the house and we can't prove that he didn't. She says he gave her permission to use it, permission to have her mail redirected there. The same applies.'

'She never gave a reason for that.'

'She'll just say it's convenience, or some other excuse. If we can't prove she didn't have the right to do it, I don't know what else we can do.'

He sat back and put his hands behind his head, thinking furiously. Like Faye, he detested it when someone got the better of him. He had misjudged Vivien Warrington badly; he'd thought she was an amateur who'd make mistakes and in doing so he had overlooked the one trump card — her real identity.

'Any ideas?' Faye asked. Her fury had ebbed until it was a concentrated irritation, a determination to move on. 'I don't want to give up on this.'

'One or two. There are weak points in her story. Eden's End, for example. They didn't question Connie's identity and they should certainly have done that. It's pretty basic record keeping. There might be something there.'

'Yes, but the woman responsible for that was chaotic, destroyed the documentation and is now dead. Which is a shame because she would almost certainly have had a lot of interesting things to say.'

Jude thought back to his dealings with the maneger, Karen Grant. She had been under investigation for a murder within the home and the strain had been too great for her. Karen had been dead for three years, and was beyond their questions. Or was she? 'Only up to a point.'

'Really?'

Faye hadn't been in Cumbria at the time. What she knew of Karen would be a footnote on an old murder case and if she'd looked back over the notes on this unconnected death she would have paid her little attention. Karen's vulnerabilities had been complex. She had been a depressive, a compulsive eater, a compulsive spender. She had lost money in bad investments she'd hoped would make her rich enough to buy her way out of her unhappiness. 'I think so. Karen Grant was an embezzler.'

'Was she ever charged?'

'No, but if she hadn't died when she did she'd have gone to jail.' When Karen died she was lost to the investigation. The details of what she'd taken and from whom had never been fully investigated and probably still languished on someone's to do list, slipping ever downwards from the moment that Eden's End's owners had taken the decision to write off the loss. There was no prospect of a conviction, so why waste time on it?

'And?' Faye leaned forward.

'We started off following the money.'

'We did, and while Vivien Warrington's account of events leaves a lot to be desired I think I'm right in saying we know where every penny of Edwin's estate currently is.'

'She's given us a full account but it'll be the new year before we can get that followed up.' That Vivien had not provided any obstacles was an indication of how sure she was of keeping the money. 'I've been thinking about her motivation. She claims her main reason for pursuing the matter was that she wanted her father's love and approval, and that the inheritance was something she came to believe she deserved and, when Connie wasn't around, it almost became hers by default. But that doesn't add up for me.'

'No. You can get love and approval without paperwork. All she had to do was be kind to him, and his acceptance of her and rejection of Connie would be her reward.'

'Yes and as far as I know she got both of those things.'

'Which isn't a crime,' pointed out Faye, though her expression suggested she'd like it to be.

'No. The staff had accepted who she was. Once he died, everything she did increased the risk of her being caught. It makes sense that she would have taken control of the funeral, and the sensible option would be to disappear. Connie would have come back at some point and found him dead, assuming the solicitor hadn't got to her with the information once it came to settling probate, but either way it would have been Connie who inherited. But Vivien didn't do that. She stayed and took risks for the inheritance. That makes me think the money was a very powerful motive for her.'

'She benefited from the chaos at Eden's End,' said Faye, 'for sure. But there was no way she could guarantee it.'

'I'm not so sure. Every time she went in she'd have seen what was going on and perhaps she spotted an opportunity. Karen Grant needed money. I wonder if Vivien bribed her to 'lose' all the documentation relating to Edwin Sheldon.'

'You say she was an embezzler?'

'Yes. It would be much easier for her to remove Edwin's file — contract agreement, Power of Attorney document, Connie's contact details, the lot — and take money for it than to keep on cooking the books.'

'I want to say that would be highly irregular,' observed Faye, 'but so is embezzling from your employer and she did that. Are you really telling me no-one investigated her finances?' She looked sceptical.

He shrugged. 'It would have been a matter for the parent company and they saw no point in pursuing it. I expect it's still a live investigation somewhere. If not, then I imagine it could be reopened. It couldn't hurt to have a look at her bank accounts for that period, could it?'

'No,' she said, thoughtfully. 'And there's another thing I'd like to consider. Did Edwin's medical notes get destroyed?'

'No. We have copies and everything seems legit.'

'That's a relief, because I did find myself wondering whether Mrs Warrington's determination to get her hands on the money might have been so great she might have felt the need to hurry her father along to his grave,' said Faye. 'Don't look at me like that. I know it's a bit off-the-wall but it's our job to think about things like that. You've just told me Vivien was motivated by money as well as jealousy. If you're correct and she was prepared to bribe for it, she might also have been prepared to kill for it. And now I'm looking at that drug mix-up with new eyes, as they say.'

He, too, had wondered. 'We asked her about that. She was abroad when her father died and claims she didn't know about his allergy to penicillin, and there's no real reason why she should.'

'Unless someone told her.'

'Or she saw his medical records. But she wasn't there. It looks like a horrible, probably criminally negligent, mistake, and as the next of kin she wasn't keen to pursue it, but that will be because it suited her and she didn't want to draw attention to herself.'

'I'd like you to have a look. Look at everything. At some point in this process that woman committed a crime and we're going to find it.' She stood up, and the scowl was back. 'I hate it when someone gets the better of us.'

'She hasn't,' he said, thinking of Vivien skulking at the bottom of the hill at the cemetery, watching Connie at their father's grave and not approaching. Why not? Fear?

'Yet.' Faye replaced the chair where she'd got it from and left the room as abruptly as she'd entered it, leaving the door to bang and rattle once more in the draught from the corridor.

Jude sat for a moment, tapping his fingers on the desk and staring out of the window towards the River Eden, a silver snake in the middle distance. If you followed its route for a few miles as it coiled through the fertile green fields of the broad valley, you would come to Eden's End. Care homes were tied so tightly in safeguarding red tape it ought to be impossible to abuse or mistreat residents, let alone kill them, but a dozen incidents in his recent caseload demonstrated that wasn't the case. If only a slight lapse in monitoring, record-keeping or DBS checking left elderly patients vulnerable, how much higher was the risk in Eden's End at a time when the management was under the control of a woman with a damaging set of vulnerabilities?

It had occurred to him that Edwin Sheldon might not have died naturally, but it was hard to see how his death could be laid at Vivien's door. He'd been there for two years with Vivien visiting him faithfully and regularly. Eventually he would have died anyway. Why would she have had the need to hasten him on?

Unless, of course, she had reason to suppose that Connie might come back.

TWENTY-ONE

Are you in? Can I pop round? I know what you said yesterday but I really need to see you.

Jude picked up his phone and sighed. Connie. He'd been in the kitchen and the phone had been charging in the hall so he'd initially missed the notification. It was now five minutes old and Connie's flat was barely a fifteen-minute walk away. She'd be at his door before he could come up with an excuse and once she arrived it would be too awkward to turn her away from his doorstep. He'd have to find an alternative, and one was immediately obvious. He picked up his phone and called Ashleigh.

'Sorry to bother you.' He listened for background noise to see if she was alone, but all he heard was canned laughter from a TV sitcom. 'If you've got an hour to spare I'd appreciate your help.'

'Is this about Connie?' she asked. 'I've been thinking about it.'

'Yes, but it's not work. She messaged to say she's on her way to see me about something. She didn't say what. But yesterday I told her, pretty clearly, that I'm only interested in friendship and no more and I'm afraid she didn't get the message.' That irritated him. He was a private person and was careful about sharing details of his personal life. The extent of both his previous relationship with Connie and his current one, such as it was, wasn't something he'd ever intended to discuss widely and now he felt he'd been pressured into sharing it with Ashleigh. She'd be discreet, and he reckoned she would have guessed most of it already, but that wasn't the point. Connie had forced his hand and, as a result, a portion of his sympathy for her evaporated.

'Oh dear. And where do I come in?'

'I was hoping that if you aren't too busy you might think of something very urgent that needs my attention and come running down here, preferably looking flustered and important.'

She chuckled. 'You want me to be your beard, eh? Isn't that what they call it? Or do you want me as your bodyguard?'

He laughed. He didn't think Connie was remotely dangerous, but he couldn't spare the emotional effort her visit would require. 'She can talk and I don't have the time or the energy.'

'That's fine. I can easily do flustered, though I'm not sure about the looking important bit. Drop me a quick text when she arrives and I'll head straight out. That'll give her a few minutes to unburden herself before I interrupt.'

He lifted his head. There was a noise on the doorstep. 'That's her now, I think.' He was right; the doorbell rang, not in an apologetic way but in a long howl, as if Connie was resting her hand on it.

'Okay. I'll see you as soon as.'

He shook his head as he went to the door. Connie's case was complicated enough without the suggestion that Edwin had been helped out of the door of his life before his time. If nothing else it would be another trial for Connie to bear. He wrenched the door open.

'Hi, Connie. I just got your message. Sorry, I didn't get the chance to reply or I'd have asked if it could wait. Ashleigh's on her way down here right now. Apparently there's something she needs to talk to me about.'

A shadow of disappointment crossed her face, like a fleeting passage of cloud over a stormy Lakeland sky. 'It won't take five minutes.'

Jude looked beyond her. On the other side of the road, as he'd expected, Adam was watching them. He had positioned his chair in front of the window and kept the curtains open, even on a winter night when a chill draught must be creeping in to his living room, but it seemed to be a price he was prepared to pay for minding Jude's business. It could hardly be worthwhile, but Adam's self-martyrdom wasn't his problem.

He stood aside and allowed Connie over the threshold. 'Come on in. No point standing on the doorstep on a night like this.'

'Everybody seems to be out every night at this time of year,' she said, unwinding her scarf and taking off her coat without being invited. 'I'm surprised you aren't.'

'It feels like I have been. That's one of the reasons I have so much to catch up on.'

'I really appreciate everything you've been doing to help me. Not just you on a personal level, but all of the police. I hope it'll be sorted soon.'

Faye's tirade of the morning niggled at him. 'The bad news is that it could take quite a long time before the matter is resolved.'

'Oh,' she said, and he sensed her spirits dip. 'I'd hoped…'

'Fraud always takes a long time. It's not just about

knowing who did it and why. We have to understand how they did it, and we have to be able to track the money. That can take a long time, even though Vivien Warrington was reasonably forthcoming.'

'Then I'd have thought it would be pretty straightforward.' She followed him into the living room and sat down. 'We know where the money went.'

'We do, but one procedural error and the case collapses.' He sat, too, without offering her a drink, though knowing Connie it was unlikely that she'd pick up on the hint and if she did she'd probably ignore it. 'How can I help you?'

'Do you know,' she said pensively, picking up the tarot deck which he hadn't got round to putting away after her first visit and shuffling it without any great focus, 'I have so many regrets about what I've done with my life.'

'Doesn't everybody?'

She picked up a card, held it up, shuffled it back in the pack, took another one. 'I don't think there's a card here that's the right fit for me. I haven't behaved very well. I've been thinking about it and I need to tell someone about it.'

'Okay,' he said, as neutrally as he could. It was always a mistake to get trapped in an emotional quicksand with Connie. 'Go ahead.'

'It's bloody Viv. My so-called sister. And yes, I believe she is my sister. You can see it when you look at her. She's so like Dad, especially the nasty side of him.' She held up her hand to stop an intervention he had no intention of making. 'She has exactly the same twist to her mouth when she's angry but not saying anything, like she's saving it up for later. I mean, I loved him, of course, but he wasn't perfect. None of us are. And as far as I can see she has all his faults, like his stubbornness and his lack of forgiveness, and none of the things that made me love him despite them.'

'Wait,' he said, when she'd ground to a halt, 'you mean you've seen her?'

'Yes. I invited her round for a drink.' She put the cards down. 'Why shouldn't I?'

'That's not altogether wise since you're a witness in a fraud investigation—'

'Can we get this right? I'm the victim. Not a witness.'

'Yes, okay.' His patience, already thin, strained further at this unwelcome news. 'You're the victim in a fraud investigation and she's the suspect.'

'She isn't the suspect, Jude. She did it and she's admitted it. She's the criminal.'

He sighed. There was no point in trying to explain the nuances of legal language to Connie. 'These things take a long time and anything that compromises them is best avoided. Meeting her is one of those things. You shouldn't have done it.'

'It's such a bore,' she said, fretfully. 'It's bad enough having to keep away from Melanie. I don't want to have to run down dark alleys to avoid Viv, too.'

'No-one expects you to do that, but you don't need to go out of your way to meet up with her, either.'

'Point taken. Anyway, I won't do it again. It didn't go well. I invited her round because...' She hesitated.

'Why?' Jude prompted.

'I don't know. I suppose I wanted to see what she was like. It's a weird feeling, knowing there's someone out there who's pretending to be you and it gets even worse when it turns out she almost is you. Same name, same father, ugh. Horrible. But you know me, I can't leave anything alone. So yes, of course I invited her round.'

'What happened?' He was prepared for anything. You never knew with Connie. You just never knew.

'I behaved really badly. I deliberately provoked her. I'd had a couple of drinks before she got here, just to give me a bit of Dutch courage, and she brought me a rather nice bottle of gin so we had some of that. But when I saw her, it upset me so much. It really did.' There was a tear in her eye. 'I could see him, there in her face.'

'What did she say to you?' he asked. He could read Connie like a book but Vivien was a stranger to him. He had no idea of her thinking, her reactions, why she might have agreed to go along with Connie's suggestion, what she thought she could possibly gain. All he knew was that she was clever, thought possibly not as clever as she thought she was, and stubborn.

'I offered to give her some of the money if she just owned up to everything.'

This was too much. 'What the hell were you thinking?'

'There's no need to get so wound up.' She looked at him, in wide-eyed innocence. 'I wasn't thinking anything.'

'You should have been.' The suggestion, when it had come from the CPS, had been ironic. From Connie, it potentially placed the chances of a conviction in jeopardy. 'You say she's committed a crime—'

'She has!'

'And now you're trying to buy her off? That's against the law.' He'd have to disclose this, too, to Faye and she would be as angry about it as he was, almost inevitably framing it as somehow his fault.

'How was I supposed to know that?' said Connie, injured. 'It seems the obvious way to put an end to this nightmare. I'm falling to pieces and no-one is helping me. Maybe deep down I thought she might help me, since she's my flesh and blood, but of course she wasn't having any of that. She said she thinks she's entitled to it, she wants it all and says I don't deserve it.'

You just made it more difficult. He didn't say it. 'I told you. You need to trust the process.'

'But I don't, and I don't trust her. She's a first-grade bitch and I hate her. Some of the things she said will never leave me. About me. About Dad. There are things she says he said about me and they were awful, but I didn't believe her. He'd never say anything like that about me. But even the thought that he might have done is so painful!'

'I wish you hadn't done it, for your own good.' He was mightily put out, but had he really expected anything else from her? He'd warned her and she, inevitably, had ignored him.

'It won't seriously compromise the case in any way, will it?' she asked, anxiously. 'I really need that money.'

'It won't do it any good, that's for sure,' he said, drily.

'Oh dear. And actually, do you know the worst thing? I was so angry I threw a glass at her and stormed out and passed out in my bedroom. And when I woke up, do you know what?'

'What?'

'She'd cleared up the broken glass and tided everything away before she left and left me a little note telling me that was what she'd done. I never heard her go. I never even realised she hadn't already left when I went to my room. And I thought, that's exactly the kind of passive-aggressive thing that Dad would have done, and it upset me even more. Because if she's so like him in all these other ways maybe he did decide—'

'Sorry.' The doorbell, which Jude had been listening for, finally rang, in time to stop Connie from further compromising her own case. 'That'll be Ashleigh.'

'Oh God. I suppose I'd better get going then,' said Connie, but she made no move.

He went to the door and opened it, rolling his eyes at Ashleigh to let her know she should play the part they'd talked about, and she replied with a conspiratorial smile.

'Sorry I'm late, Jude,' she said, raising her voice just enough to make sure she could be heard in the living room. 'I got held up. Can we get on? I don't want to rush, but you know how it is.'

'Hello again,' said Connie, now looking rather woebegone. She'd picked up the cards again and was still showing no sign of leaving. 'Are the two of you going to discuss solving all my problems? I'm not saying the answers are here.' She tapped the deck. 'It's all nonsense, after all. But if I'd known what the future had in store…' She checked herself. 'No that's a stupid thing to say. I mean, if I'd listened to the warnings in my own head. Then things might have been different.'

'In what way?' asked Ashleigh, curious.

'It wasn't long before he died. I almost came home. Do you believe in Fate? I used to, but if this is it, it's cruel. I was lonely and I was homesick, and I missed him. It was about this time of year, which always makes it worse. Australia is lovely but I missed the cosiness of winter here, and the Christmas lights and the snow. I think that was when I really started to hate being there. And there was a point where I thought I should come home, but I never said anything because I thought if I did it would be such a surprise for Dad, and he would love it. But I didn't, and a month after that, he was dead.' She reached in her pocket for a tissue. 'I'd better go. You two have things to discuss.'

'Work never stops,' said Ashleigh, with a straight face.

'Even at Christmas? Still, it's nice to know the public guardians are onto it. Whatever *it* is.'

She got up, and looked inquiringly at the hallway and Jude, preceding her, produced her coat. 'They say a lot of police meet their partners working together, don't they?' she said. 'I mean, working nights and stuff, long lonely shifts. Is that how you two met?' Without waiting for an answer, she shrugged her shoulders into her coat, wound her scarf round her neck and headed for the door. 'Bye Jude. Maybe I'll see you soon.' A perfunctory air kiss that just missed his cheek, a brisk wave to Ashleigh, and she was gone, disappearing into the pool of streetlights that danced their way down Wordsworth Street.

'My word!' said Ashleigh. 'Does she have any filters?'

'She never did.' He laughed. 'Now you're here, come in and sit down. How about a drink?'

'I'll take a small one, if you're offering.' She went into the living room and sat down. 'So now you've got Connie reading the cards, have you?'

She was teasing and he knew it, but he resisted it anyway. Connie's visit had unsettled him and now Ashleigh's was doing the same, but for different reasons — two women he cared about, both, he was sure, in the process of making disastrous life choices which he, as a concerned onlooker, could only stand by and watch unfold.

'No,' he said, picking up one and looking at it. The Fool. That included just about everybody, at some level, with the possible exception of what he now saw was the very hard-headed Vivien Warrington. The card, however, still made him smile. When Ashleigh had bought him the deck it had been because each card contained the addition of a tiny, smoke-grey cat engaged in extravagant gestures that mimicked its theme. It had reminded her, and reminded him, of Holmes. Sometimes, when he was feeling unusually sentimental, he would get them out and look at them and the thought of Holmes, who in this card had eyes crossed and tongue out like a bored child, would segue to thoughts of Becca. Tonight, like the night when Connie had first erupted onto his doorstep out of the winter darkness, had been one of those nights.

'She doesn't strike me as the type, in fairness.' Ashleigh picked one out as well, looked at it and put it back in the deck with a sigh.

'I haven't heard you talk about the cards for a while,' he said, for something to say while he went to the kitchen and poured them both a miserly glass of red wine from the bottle left over from the weekend.

'I don't, these days. I used to have a very good relationship with them, but then I tore one of mine up and that made the whole pack worthless. I don't think they've forgiven me.'

He knew the story. The card she had torn up was the one she associated with her marriage and it was ominous that she now seemed to regret it. 'Didn't Raven leave you hers?' he asked, thinking of a mutual friend who had died too young.

'She did, but I was fond of the old ones. They belonged to my grandmother and of course I projected onto them what I thought she'd say to me. Now I wonder if her advice might not have been right for me.'

He handed her a glass and sat down. 'Maybe you're asking the wrong questions,' he said, poking fun at her gently in return.

'It's not unlike life, is it? You have to know what questions to ask to get the answers you need, and you have to listen to the answers, and even anything that doesn't seem like an answer, to get to where you want to go.'

Jude sipped his wine. Connie's presence had him on edge but with Ashleigh he could relax. For a start, she could take a joke. 'The more I hear you talk like that the more I think you only ever saw the cards as just a concentration aid.'

'I don't think I've ever said anything else. I've never thought they have the answers, not really. They just help you to settle your thoughts so you can find them for yourself.'

There was a short silence, in which Jude would normally have made a joke and she would have snapped one back at him until they were both laughing, but tonight it appeared that neither of them had anything of value to say.

'I don't suppose there's going to be much movement on Connie's case until after Christmas,' she said, after a while.

'If then.' He filled her in on what Faye had said.

'Oh dear. So it's back to dealing with the drunken assaults and the petty thefts until the New Year, then.' She sneaked a look at her phone.

'There's no shortage of other things to do, that's for sure.'

They talked for a few moments about mundane things, about Christmas and what they were doing and how much time they were taking off. Neither of them was on call over Christmas, for once, and even a year ago it might have been a chance to spend some time together, but things had changed since then.

'I really ought to go,' she said, snatching another look at her phone. 'I'm supposed to meeting someone for a quick drink. You know how it is at Christmas. Everyone wants a piece of you.'

'Is it Scott?' he asked, taking a not-too-wild guess, and was rewarded, if that was the word, by seeing her turn slightly pink.

'It is, yes. He's thinking of going back to Manchester over Christmas and so we thought we'd catch up. He was at my drinks do on Saturday. But of course, you never turned up.'

There was a difficult silence. Jude disapproved of Scott Kirby, Ashleigh's ex-husband, and Ashleigh knew it, though he never said. She knew because she disapproved of him herself, her life littered with the last chances she kept offering and which he repeatedly squandered. Every reconciliation was temporary and each one ended with her tears. This would be the same. Jude often thought it ironic that she, the most intuitive judge of human beings he had ever met, constantly failed to make an accurate assessment of the man she loved.

'You know how it is,' he said, when it became clear that she was expecting an answer. 'I had something else on.'

'It's a shame, because I'd really like it if you and Scott got along. You're both my friends.'

'When are you meeting him?' he asked.

'In half an hour. But actually,' Ashleigh said after a moment, 'to hang with it. It won't do him any harm to wait five minutes. I'll have another glass of that red if there's one going.'

'Are you back together then?' he asked, reaching for the second bottle from inside the kitchen and twisting the metal cap.

'No. Yes. Sort of.' She raised her glass in salute. 'I don't know. But I'm a few years older now, and so is he, and people learn their lessons, don't they?'

'Some of them,' he said, and thought of himself and of Becca and wondered whether life was a lesson he would ever learn.

TWENTY-TWO

It had been a long, lonely fortnight, made worse by the false promises of December. Connie had thought she was getting it together. She had the flat, and the previous day she'd had the offer of a job — not exactly what she wanted, but a secretarial post in a large agricultural unit out on the industrial estate, starting in the New Year, one she could walk to and which would keep her mind off things she couldn't control — so she was all set for yet another new start.

Or she should have been. Somehow it never turned out like that. The previous evening she'd Facetimed Australia, and the boys had been both delighted to see her and crestfallen to learn she wouldn't be back for Christmas. Then Matthew had had a go at her about that and just about everything else, it seemed, even down to her small triumphs (*Secretary, Connie? Is that what you went to university for? Weren't you going to be a high achiever?*) in that whiny tone of his that irritated her more every time they spoke.

She went to stand by the window. It was the Wednesday before Christmas. The schools had broken up and there were kids skipping through the street beside their parents, teenagers hanging out by the cafes, workers heading for the pub. She always drank too much over Christmas, but didn't everybody? Even Jude, who had a puritan streak to him that she had always found bizarrely appealing and which she occasionally tried to prod towards outrage, had complained about how many nights he spent socialising and how hard it was to avoid drinking, yet still drank. But he would confine himself to one or two whereas Connie, like most of the rest of the population, or so it seemed, found it easier to fall for the illusion, join in the fun and worry about detoxing when she came face to face with January, a month even more austere than her ex had become and entirely joyless with it.

She delayed getting herself a drink while she thought of Jude. When they'd dated at school she'd never thought it would be permanent. They'd both been far too young and it was inevitable that life would come between them. When she returned to Penrith he'd naturally been the one she turned to and he had proved good company. Because he was single, and because in Connie's experience of men very few of them actually enjoyed the single state even if they were understandably reluctant to commit, she'd thought they might have had a second chance, but it seemed he wasn't having it.

She shouldn't have said anything, but loneliness was a desperate place. When she thought about it, there was only one thing worse and that was rejection, something which had come to her in spades. It wasn't only Jude (in the end, she didn't really care that much because there were other fish in the sea) but there was her father. That hurt, more than she could imagine. Had he really told her usurping half-sister how much he hated her, how selfish she was? There was Matthew, refusing to budge from his life plan, prioritising his desire to live on the other side of the world over hers to return home, and playing hardball over the boys. She might try for custody but if they wanted to stay in the country where they'd been born, she had little chance of victory.

But it was her father who hurt most. 'Dad,' she said, out loud, 'you didn't really say that to her, did you?'

She'd got into the habit of chatting to him, not just because there was no-one else for her to talk to but because there was so much she'd meant to say to him that he would never now hear. Sometimes it felt as though the words were trapped inside her like bubbles in a bottle of champagne, pressure building until eventually it burst and they all came tumbling out, an unholy mess for her to clear up.

'I got it wrong,' she said, looking at the clock on the wall and seeing that it had had finally nudged towards six. It was too early for her evening meal — she ate late — but not for a pre-dinner drink. She went into the kitchen and poured herself a large slug of the gin that Vivien had brought her. 'I shouldn't have left you like that. I should never have agreed when Matt wanted to go to Australia. I should have stayed here and made sure you were all right. We should have been there for each other.'

She took the gin through to the living room, ice clinking in the glass, and sipped it. 'I don't make friends in this place. Is it me? Am I just unlucky? Am I too needy? Is that it?' The problem was that she'd chosen to cut herself off from so many of her friends. Jude was too busy to see her, or didn't want to. Adam had made it clear that he had other things to do and other friends, and that she wouldn't fit in with them. The only other person she had kept in touch with was Mel, and she'd hardly call that being in touch. It was more that Mel had leeched on to her, with the occasional caustic comment on a Facebook post, or pointed posts of her own about friendship and fidelity. It was no surprise that that relationship had turned toxic.

She should have blocked her at the start, but she'd wanted to let her see how happy she and Matthew were in Australia, determined to show the woman that her former husband had no regrets. Karma, then, that the dream had gone sour and she was back in a place where her predecessor seemed to have little better to do with her own life than stumble across her path and spit abuse at her. There had been a message to her via social media that morning, wishing her a lonely Christmas, and she'd replied to it, with a sarcastic message telling Mel to pop round for a drink so they could be miserable together. Yes, Mel was a bitch and a grade-A one at that, just as Vivien was, but she couldn't argue that she didn't deserve it.

Halfway down the first glass was always the moment where she was most honest, and therefore harshest, with herself. There was only one way out of it and that was to drink through it.

'Do you know what, Dad?' she said, drowning the rest of it and heading back to the kitchen to pour herself another, 'I'm so looking forward to dry January. Everything will be bloody good next year.' She just had to get there.

She paused, head cocked on one side as if to listen to him, as if he could possibly reply from the heaven or hell to which he had gone without even saying goodbye. 'I want to show you,' she said to him, 'and Matthew, and the boys, that I'm worth something.' Because just then she didn't feel worth anything. She felt as if she'd failed at everything she'd turned her hand to and she wasn't yet forty, which meant there was plenty more failure still to come.

The doorbell rang. For a moment she indulged in the most impossible fantasies of who it might be. Jude, or even Adam, knowing she was lonely and come to visit. Matthew, having somehow faked the video call from Australia, announcing that he'd brought the twins to spend Christmas with her. A huge flower arrangement from an unknown admirer. Anything would do. She was expecting nothing. She opened the door.

'You invited me round for a drink, didn't you?' said Mel Trotter, grinning. 'Don't tell me you didn't mean it. *Welcome any time*, you said. And so here I am, Connie, because you and I need to have a little talk where there's no-one to hear.'

Connie still had the glass in her hand. For a moment she thought of dashing the gin into Mel's face as she'd tried to do with Vivien, but that would be a gift and Mel would delight in calling the police. 'It was a joke, and anyway I'm busy.'

'I've come all the way in from Carleton,' said Mel. She was a skinny blonde and was clad in a sporty fleece and leggings which suggested that in fact she was only passing on her way back from the gym.

'I don't care. I've got nothing to say to you.'

'We have so much in common, Connie. We can call ourselves the Matt's Ex-Wives Club and bitch about whichever woman he's shacked up with now. I've been through all your pain. I'd love to hear you talking about it.'

'I'm busy.'

'A little bird tells me you've got a job. I don't think you were listening to what I said before. You aren't welcome here. Go somewhere else. Anywhere else. I work up at the industrial estate, too, you know. It'll hurt my feelings if I see you up there, which I will.'

How did she know about the job? The only person Connie had told was Matt. Her heart sank. That meant they were still friends. 'Mind your own business, eh, Mel?'

'I don't imagine you'll last long up there. Every time I

see you, you have a drink in your hand. You can't have people like you working on sites where there's heavy machinery, can we? It's dangerous. You wouldn't want your new boss to know you're a drinker.'

I drink because I'm unhappy, Connie wanted to say to her, but that would have been conceding defeat. 'It's Christmas, Mel.' *I can stop any time I want to. I just don't want to stop now.*

In time to avoid a worse confrontation but too late for her own well-being, she did what she should have done as soon as she realised who her visitor was and slammed the door. Mel didn't go away at once, but stood there for a moment, ringing the bell and shouting through the letterbox. Walking into the living room, Connie slashed the curtains shut before her predecessor could appear there, pressing her pretty face up against the window. She felt ill. She slumped down on the sofa and the tears began to fall. How had she ended up like this? She wasn't a bad person but somehow the last twenty years had left her feeling corrupt and rotten, so helpless.

'Cooee! Connie! You invited me, remember!'

She struggled to her feet and turned on the radio. Cheesy Christmas tunes filled the air. Her father had loved classical music and always had the radio on. Had anyone at Eden's End thought to find out what he liked, and make sure there was something tuneful to break the silence of his old age and direct him towards memories that were pleasant rather than painful? Had there been music playing at the very end, and if so what had been the last sound he heard on this earth? Brahms, Britten, Beethoven? She hoped he hadn't met his end listening, as she now found herself doing, to Slade.

Her nausea heightened, until it became a sharp pain in her gut. She should tell someone about the meeting. She should tell someone she felt ill. It must be stress, maybe a stomach ulcer. She needed help, but who was there? Adam wouldn't come because (she now understood) he wasn't a man to put in any effort for someone else unless it afforded him some amusement, and helping a sick woman definitely wouldn't qualify as entertaining. Jude would want to know about Mel's visit for sure, but she hadn't missed the way he'd managed to carefully deflect her when Ashleigh O'Halloran had arrived; his priorities, too, were elsewhere. But Ashleigh O'Halloran, the detective sergeant, had struck her as both sympathetic and outgoing. She would want to know about Mel, too, and she would know what to do. She might even come and help.

Her phone was on the table and when she got up to fetch it she was overwhelmed by dizziness. Her legs gave way under her and she tumbled to the floor. She felt sick, faint, her heart beating, her hands suddenly cold. But she reached the phone in time and, with her hands sticky with sweat and slithering across the screen, she managed to dial the sergeant's number.

TWENTY-THREE

'You should read those bloody tarot cards of yours,' said Scott Kirby, draping an affectionate arm around Ashleigh's shoulders as they sat side by side on the sofa just as they used to do, 'and see what kind of future it has for us.'

'Us, eh?' said Ashleigh, amused. She was constantly amused by Scott. Even when their marriage had been at its lowest ebb, just before she'd taken the decision to end it, there had always been some tiny thing to make her smile. It was often intangible. It might be the slightest inflection in his tone that hinted his words, though cruel, came from love or could equally be turned back on himself, or it was the tiny gesture that said *I know, I know*, when he was being too obviously unreasonable. It could be the raised eyebrow that always asked a question about how she felt about him, knowing the answer she'd rather not own up to, or it could be this, the affectionate mockery with which he regarded so many things about her.

It was why it had taken her so long to leave him and why it was so tempting to return.

'Yes, us. Like it or not, Ash, the best days of my life were when we were together. Weren't they for you?'

The problem with *us*, for Ashleigh at least, was that she and Scott were the classic couple who could live neither together nor apart. This had never troubled him. He had always confronted her objections to his infidelity with wide-eyed innocence, though that had never stopped his behaviour crossing the line from assertive to coercive and controlling. She told herself that even as she enjoyed the touch of his arm against her shoulders and the closeness of him. She'd missed that. They'd been childhood sweethearts and your first love was always special. 'I suppose they were. Yes. Such a pity it all went wrong.'

'I know. Do you think we married too soon? Before we'd finished growing up, I mean? Before we learned about relationships?'

'Some people never learn,' she said, thinking about Connie Sheldon.

'That's the cynical detective in you coming out,' he teased her. 'I've learned. Look, I'm a proper grown up now. Do I have to abase myself? I know now I was a bad husband. I know I didn't behave well. I know I didn't give you enough space and I know I didn't let you live your life the way you wanted to.'

That was the textbook definition of controlling behaviour. Ashleigh could imagine Jude's reaction if he could hear it. His lips would have twisted into a wry smile and he would have shaken his head in a way that showed his disbelief. Once, she might have listened to him, but he wasn't always such a good judge of relationships himself, and it was natural for two men she'd dated to be suspicious of one another. She couldn't trust his judgement on this. 'That's right. You didn't.'

'And now I'm heading for my forties and looking back

on the younger me with horror. God, I was a piece of work. And I look at you and you haven't changed. You're all I ever wanted.'

'Apart from all the other women.' Before he had a chance to answer that well-justified accusation, Ashleigh shrugged off his arm and got up. 'That was a good idea of yours. I'll get the cards.'

Leaving him sitting on the sofa sipping at a glass of wine, she got up and ran upstairs to her room to fetch the pack of tarot cards bequeathed to her by Raven, the New Age woman who had died, quietly and at peace with the world, earlier that year. Jude had put them into her mind earlier that week and now Scott was doing the same. If she was honest she wasn't in the mood for them, but they were a distraction from Scott and his flattery and would give her control of the conversation. She stood for a moment with the silk-wrapped packet in her hand, weighing up whether it was really wise to get into this kind of game with her ex, but it was the briefest hesitation before she ran back down again. 'I haven't read these for a while.'

'I'm flattered you're prepared to do it for me.' He pulled up a small table in front of him. 'Here, sit next to me again. I liked that.'

She did so, unable to suppress a shiver of delight. When she'd been with Jude their strong physical attraction had overlain a rock-solid friendship but that elusive thing that was love had been absent. At the time she'd thought it was good thing because love, which too often began pure but became corrupted by jealousy and possessiveness and fundamental inequality when one partner was unable to give as much as the other needed, appeared too often on her desk as a damaging, toxic emotion, a motive in a violent crime.

But in her job she only ever saw it when it went wrong.

When love worked, it did so quietly and unobtrusively, without any need to trouble the police.

'What now?' he asked as she shuffled the deck. 'Do you deal them out? Do I pick one?'

'Hush,' she said, and touched his hand, very briefly, before dealing the cards out in a horseshoe. It was difficult. She was distracted. 'I don't know if this is a good idea.'

'Oh?'

'I need to concentrate. And I'm not used to these cards.' Out of the corner of her eye she watched for a sneer. Jude never hid his cynicism and she was always concerned that it undermined her credibility in his eyes but Scott remained untroubled, his clear expression gazing at the cards, then at her.

'That's a shame. I did want to know what they say about us. Not because I need to know, but because you do. Don't you? Because you don't trust yourself. But actually, I think you know what you think and you know what you want, and you have an idea of the way things should be between us and you know that's right. But you're afraid of it and you need something to tell you.'

'Nonsense.' Abandoning any pretence at the reading, Ashleigh picked up one of the cards at random. It was the *Three of Swords*. In the past its negative connotations had always reminded her of Scott but now she found herself wondering if that had been projection, if her feelings had influenced her interpretation. She replaced the card, face down, before he could see it and ask questions.

'Is it my turn now?' he asked, light-heartedly picking up a card and putting it back. 'No, I don't like that one. There's too much blood. Let's have a look and see what else there is.'

'Idiot,' she said, laughing as he picked up the pack and

began to rifle through it. 'You know that's not how it works.'

'Isn't it?'

'I know exactly which card you're going to pick out of that.' It would be The Lovers. Scott had many qualities to balance out his faults, but subtlety wasn't one of them.

'No. I'll be totally random.' He picked out a card and held it out.

'That's the *Six of Wands*.' She smiled at its message; it meant she was in control of her own destiny. It could mean other things, of course; everything was double-edged. It could be a warning against an unwise choice, but today she preferred not to dwell on that.

'I picked a good 'un, I see.' He looked at her meaningfully. 'I always do. What about this?'

'Go on with you. That's the *Queen of Cups* and she means happy and healthy relationships.' But when he'd drawn it from the pack it had been reversed, and so meant the opposite — a manipulative relationship with no recognition of boundaries.

'You see? The cards are speaking to us, Ash, and for once I'm all ears.' And now the final card and yes, it confirmed how predictable he was. 'Oh, look. Even I know this one. It's *The Lovers*. And I know what that means. Do you?'

'Yes. It means you shouldn't make relationship choices lightly.'

'And I'm not. I'm not listening to the cards. I'm listening to my heart.'

She was trying not to listen to hers, but it was impossible; it was hammering away so loudly he must have been able to hear it.

'See?' he said, and took her hand and placed it against his chest.

She left it there. It had been a long time, but she still remembered when they had first touched like that. She'd thought then that there could never be a moment like it with anyone but him, and she'd been right. There never had been.

Her phone buzzed on the table beside her and she turned to it, briefly. 'I expect that's Jude.'

He put his head to one side and gave her a quizzical look. 'And?'

'And nothing.' She wouldn't answer it. It would be about some triviality, because they had fallen into the habit of calling each other about nothing as friends did and, as friends should, they wouldn't let an unanswered call cause discord between them. 'He can wait.'

'Are you sure you don't want to answer it?' he said, watching her closely as if to see a moment of weakness, a flash that indicated she might care more for someone else than for him.

'I think there are more important things for me to do right now,' she said, as the ringing stopped.

'Correct answer. So shall we do them?' he asked, and she'd barely breathed her assent before he kissed her, and she kissed him back, and her hand pressed against his chest moved on to his pressed against hers and it was like being in love again.

'It's just as well Lisa's not here,' she said, because her housemate, who detested Scott and could have been relied upon to make his visit highly uncomfortable, had gone for a week's skiing before the season got busy.

'Yes, but even if she was, you know what? We'd have found one another.'

'Do you think so?' she whispered, her forehead against the warmth of his cheek.

'Yes. because your cards are a meditational aid, but that's all they are.'

'It's all I ever said they are.'

'Yes. And the brutal reality of it is that we're in charge of our own destiny and we have the power to make ourselves happy or make ourselves miserable.'

'We've tried that both ways,' she said, as their hold grew even tighter.

'And I know which one I liked more. I still love you. I know you probably don't like it but I can't help it.'

'Who said I don't like it? I'm just more practical about it than you are.'

They kissed again, more slowly this time, with intent. It wasn't an end in itself, but a beginning, an unstoppable force that would end only one way, for better or for worse.

'Do you want to be unhappy for ever, Ash?' he asked, as his hand slid down her back. 'Do you want me to be unhappy? Surely we've done that already? Where do we go from here, darling? Where can we possibly go now?'

Another kiss, deeper than ever, a kiss that reached down to her soul and set her body aflame and left only one, obvious answer. 'Upstairs,' she said, and finally surrendered her head to her heart.

TWENTY-FOUR

'I only just picked up the message,' Ashleigh said, sounding panicked in a way Jude was quite unused to. 'I have a friend round and we were chatting. I missed the call. Connie left me a message saying she feels really ill and some woman had turned up her door and harassed her, and she sounded awful, Jude, really awful. I called 999 and they're sending an ambulance but I can't get down there right now, I've had a drink.'

'I'll go down,' he said, already reaching for his shoes, which he'd slipped off to warm his stockinged feet in front of the fire. 'Did they say how long they'd be?'

'No, only that they'd get there as soon as they can.'

'When did she call you?'

'It was over an hour ago. She sounded incoherent.'

'Connie drinks too much,' he said, feeling disloyal as he said it but knowing it was the brutal truth. 'Did it sound like that it was that?' She was too quick to drown her many sorrows, and he'd seem too many people drink themselves to death.

'No, it didn't. She was struggling for breath and

sounded as if she was in pain. I called her straight back but she isn't picking up.'

'Leave it with me.' He ended the call, finished tying his laces, fetched his coat and jumped into the car, pushing through the evening traffic as fast as he could. Connie's flat was on the ground floor and the curtains, wrenched shut, still showed a chink of light. Leaving space for the ambulance he pulled up to a sharp stop on a double yellow line, slammed his hazard lights out, got out and ran to the flat. There was no answer when he rang the bell and no movement behind the lighted, opaque glass panes of the door; he barely waited long enough to be sure of that before moving swiftly to the window to investigate the crack between the curtains.

He swore, under his breath. He couldn't quite see what was going on in there because circumstances were conspiring against him — condensation blurring the not-very-clean window, the narrowness of the gap, the arrangement of the furniture — but he could see enough to know that someone, surely Connie, was slumped on the floor in front of the sofa. He rapped hard on the window, not expecting an answer. His options narrowed; he went back to the door and rattled it, experimentally, to test how robust it was, and found it firm.

The glass it was, then. This kind of job had once been routine, breaking into properties to investigate elderly or sick folk whose concerned relatives or neighbours hadn't seen or heard of them for days. He already had his gloves on, and for good measure he wrenched off his scarf and wound it round his wrist. After that, he punched the glass pane out of the door and slid an arm through.

The key was still in the door. The last thing he needed was to dislodge it and have it spin away out of reach, so he unwound the scarf from his left hand and removed the glove, sliding his fingers through the gaping space in the glass and nicking the back of his hand for his pains, but he soon had the key firmly between finger and thumb. It was stiff in the lock and he struggled to free it, but it took a moment before he got it safely to the outside of the door, set it in the keyhole and turned it.

She'd put the chain on. Damn. 'Connie!' he called though the gap into the void, and got no answer, only his voice echoing back at him from the sparsely-decorated hallway above the sound of Christmas music from the lounge. He pulled the door to, slid his hand back through to release the chain and opened the door.

It had barely taken him a minute. Another second and three steps across the splattered glass in the hallway took him into the living room. 'Connie!'

She was slumped on the floor, curled up in the foetal position, and a miasma of alcohol fumes hung over her. He dropped to his knees beside her. 'Connie, it's Jude. Are you all right?'

No pulse. He tried again, unsure. Was that a flutter of life? 'Connie, can you hear me? There's an ambulance on its way. The paramedics will look after you. They'll get you up to the hospital, and you'll be back on your feet before you know it.' If she survived there would be no-one to look after her, and he'd find himself embroiled in a commitment, but that was better than the alternative, which was that she was dead. He feared that, feared it very much, but he was almost certain it was already too late.

If she'd gone, her last breath had barely left her body. She was still warm, tears glistening on her waxen face, lips slightly parted. He moved her into the recovery position and went through to the hall, where he guessed her bedroom would be, and fetched the duvet to cover her. Then he went back and sat beside her.

'The ambulance isn't far away, now.' That was all the comfort he could offer her. He couldn't even promise her that her family would visit. In this half of the world she had no-one but those distant cousins and the half-sister who'd wronged her. 'Let's get you back on your feet and we can work everything out for you.'

The Christmas music switched from pop hits to *Away in a Manger*, a bizarre and unconnected jump. Still sitting beside her, he looked around the room. He was dripping blood on the carpet, so he got out his handkerchief and wound it round the back of his hand to staunch the flow. What would happen if Connie was dead? Would the CPS give up on the prosecution and leave Vivien triumphant? A sour feeling, defeat, crept into his mind at the thought.

'Not if I can help it,' he said aloud. 'I've got your back on this one.'

He scanned the room, trying to work out what had happened. It was no surprise to see an empty glass on the table, and the phone on the floor told a tale of a fall that had sent it spinning away from her. In his mind, the sequence of events formed. Connie, feeling ill, overcome by alcohol or sickness, calling Ashleigh, who hadn't been available. Why hadn't she called him? He frowned. He would have come straight away, no matter what. She must surely have known that. No matter; she must have dropped the phone, tried to reach it, fallen and lain there for the hour or more it had taken for someone to notice.

Outside, flashing blue lights announced the arrival of the ambulance. Thank God.

'Okay,' he said to Connie's still form. 'Here we go. We'll get you sorted.'

'Okay?' said the first paramedic at the door. 'What's the story? Drink? Choked?'

There had been no sign of vomit. 'No,' said Jude

pointing them through to the living room. 'I don't think so. There's drink involved, for sure, but I don't think that's the whole story. But I think we're too late.'

He left them to it, not wanting to watch the indignity that would ensue as they tried to revive her, and went into the kitchen. Poor Connie, dying (he was sure of it now) alone and in pain, afflicted by some strange sickness or allergy.

The gin bottle was on the table, almost empty. On impulse, he put on his gloves again and picked it up. Connie had been alone. No-one could have harmed her, but somehow he didn't like the look of whatever had happened to her, and it would do no harm, when whichever uniformed officer was on duty arrived to fill in the requisite forms, to hand the bottle over to them and make sure that someone had a good look at it.

He took a moment to call Ashleigh. 'It's not good news, I'm afraid. Nothing official, yet, and I'm not a medical professional. But I don't think it's looking great.'

'Oh God. I'm so sorry! If I'd only picked up—'

'You weren't on call,' he said, though what she said was undeniable. 'Look, that's the uniforms now. I'd better go and talk to them, see what's what. We can speak tomorrow.'

When he glanced into the living room he could see the paramedics had all but given up, and were manoeuvring Connie's body onto a stretcher. He stood back, respectfully, to let them pass. The flat had been locked and it was entirely typical of Connie to drink to excess, alone, but there was something about this whole thing that bothered him, and it wasn't just the tragedy of her untimely end, or the grief about to be visited on two small boys half a world away.

TWENTY-FIVE

'What the hell,' said Faye when Jude brought the bad news to her office first thing the next morning, and this time it wasn't the fury that had accompanied the revelation of the CPS preparing to wash their hands of the case, but a controlled, white hot irritation that bordered on anger, 'what the actual hell do you mean?'

'Exactly what I say. Connie Sheldon was taken to hospital last night with suspected alcohol poisoning. She didn't make it.' He rubbed his temple. His head ached. Somehow he felt as if he'd failed her, and now there was nothing he could do except carry on the fight.

'She did have a self-destruct button,' said Faye calming down, 'from what I understand, and a drink problem too, by the sound of it, although God knows with what she'd been through I can hardly blame her for taking to the bottle. I'd be tempted to do the same myself. I was worried you were going to tell me there's foul play, but at least it sounds straightforward.'

'Yes.' Nothing with Connie had ever been straightforward. 'It looks like it.'

She pounced. 'You have doubts?'

Did he, or was he just letting his own feelings obscure his judgement? 'I'm sorry. I think I do.'

There was a silence, in which Faye stared at him with narrowed eyes and he watched her, imagining her brain ticking over behind them. It wouldn't just be concern that there might be something suspicious about this death. Like him she would be joining the dots and connecting it to the live investigation, noting that if Connie had survived and the justice system got itself in gear, she would have come into a lot of money at her sister's expense. 'Who found her?'

'I did.'

'Okay. Were you just there on spec, or did she call you?'

'She called Ashleigh, but she didn't pick up the call until about an hour later. Ashleigh called an ambulance, then me, and I went straight down to see what was going on.'

'Right.' Faye got out her phone and flicked off a quick message. He couldn't see it but he could imagine the content, and the tone. Faye's rages were fortunately short-lived but they were never pretty. 'Then we'd better get her up here and find out exactly what happened, hadn't we?'

There was another silence while Jude prepared himself for the scene he knew would follow and struggled to suppress his own concerns about it, and Faye tapped her fingers on her desk. The open plan office where Ashleigh was based was at the other end of the corridor, but it took longer than normal for her to appear, tapping on the door and coming in looking pale and anxious. 'Sorry. I was on the phone.'

'No problem,' said Faye, indicating a chair. 'For a moment I was worried that you hadn't picked up my message.'

'No, I was just...' Ashleigh stumbled to a stop. Too often, Faye put her on edge and Jude wasn't remotely surprised to see it happening again. He risked a warning glance at Faye, who ignored him. 'I came as soon as I could get away.'

'Good. So Jude tells me that Connie Sheldon called you last night but apparently you were too busy to answer.'

'I—'

'I should have mentioned that Ashleigh wasn't on call.' Jude nodded, to let her know he had her back.

'So who was?' Thankfully Faye was too busy glaring at Ashleigh to scowl at him. 'Perhaps we should be speaking to them, too.'

'Chris Marshall, but Connie didn't call 999. She called Ashleigh directly.'

'Why would she do that?'

'I don't know,' Ashleigh said. 'I've been wondering that all night.'

So had Jude. If Connie had called 999 they might have got to her in time. 'I don't know, but perhaps she was in such a state that she forgot. Got out her phone and rang the first name in her contacts, or the first name she thought might help. A,' he pointed out, in case Faye had forgotten her alphabet, 'being at the top of the list.'

'Hmm.' She didn't sound convinced by that, but not everyone was as relentlessly organised and logical as Faye. Sometimes she failed to understand that there was no reason for an individual to undertake a particular action, and that sometimes people just did things, and wondered about their own reasons afterwards. Inevitably, she turned to Ashleigh. 'And what exactly were you doing that was so important you couldn't answer your work phone?'

'I was on a date,' said Ashleigh, shuffling her feet like a naughty schoolgirl.

'A date?' said Faye, with ice in her tone.

As if it was any of her business. Jude moved it on. 'Can we hear the message?'

'I doubt if it'll enlighten us much,' said Faye, still put out, 'but you never know.'

'It's not easy to listen to.' Ashleigh gave Jude an apologetic look.

'Of course. You and she were close, weren't you?' Faye asked him, showing the first sign of sympathy.

'Once,' Jude said, but he didn't think the message could trouble him too much now that he'd seen Connie's body slumped on her living room floor. 'Come on, Ash. Let's get it over with.'

She placed her phone in the middle of the desk. A notification popped up and she swiped it away, but not before Jude saw who it was from. He could guess, now, what had kept her so preoccupied, and who the date was with. Arms folded, he sat back and listened while Connie's voice, cracked and faltering, filled the room. *Sergeant O'Halloran? It's Connie Sheldon. I need your help, I don't know what to do. I've just had a horrible experience...Mel...my husband's...oh god. I feel so ill. I don't know what to do. Please help me.* And then the tone as the message ended.

Faye looked at Ashleigh. Ashleigh looked down at the desk. Feeling the outsider, Jude watched them both.

'So,' said Faye after a moment, 'that doesn't sound to me as though she was calling because she was ill, does it? And it doesn't sound to me as if she felt immediately threatened.'

If she had done, Connie would have called someone better able to respond with blue lights and sirens. But because the threat wasn't obvious didn't mean it didn't exist, and because Connie didn't think it was immediate didn't meant it wasn't urgent. 'This reinforces my concerns,' he said.

'About what?' she said. 'An officer not answering her phone to a call for help after which a woman was found dead?'

This was too much. Faye was his boss but that was out of order. 'Could you and I have a word in private?' he said to her. 'Ashleigh, maybe you could step outside for a second.'

'By all means. You can go.' She nodded curtly to Ashleigh. 'I think I've heard all I need to from you right now and I'm sure you have other things to be getting on with.' When Ashleigh had backed out of the room in even more of a fluster than when she'd come in, Faye turned back to him. 'Well?'

She knew. He took a second to think how to approach her. 'I mentioned to you that Ashleigh wasn't on call.'

'Nevertheless, if she'd answered her phone this might have been avoided and we wouldn't be having this conversation now.'

'We're all entitled to a private life.'

'That's a very wholesome theory and while I'd very much like to concur, I'm afraid I can't. This message will be played at the inquest and everyone will hold us responsible for what happened.'

Personally he thought most of the general public were a little more forgiving than that, but Faye had a terror of the press that sat ill with her responsibilities. It was one of the subjects on which they most often disagreed. 'Ashleigh puts in way more time than she gets paid for. As her line manager I—'

'And as your line manager I should remind you to keep a civil tongue in your head,' she said, crisply. 'The message will be played in public, and questions will be asked. What a gift that'll be to the people who like to tell us they pay our wages. But I take your point. Is there anything else you have to say on this matter?'

'Yes. I took a bottle of gin from the kitchen,' he said, 'as evidence.'

'Evidence?'

'Yes. I don't think it was drink that killed her.'

'That's all I need. First you present me with a Christie-esque mystery with an inheritance at its heart, and now here's a gift-wrapped locked-door murder. Are we suddenly back in the Golden Age of detective fiction? Because that's what it feels like.'

'I don't think I said it was murder,' said Jude, carefully.

'Do you think it is?' Faye, now that the storm of her irritation had passed, was more receptive. 'That message tells us Connie had had an unfortunate experience with her husband's first wife. Is that relevant?'

'It might be. I saw the same woman approach her in town a week or so ago and speak to her very aggressively. So while I wouldn't want to stick my neck out, I think it's worth looking at very closely. I'll be very interested in the outcome of the post mortem—'

'Let's hope she didn't die of fright, because that would add Sherlock Holmes to the mix,' said Faye, sourly.

'I don't know what she died of. I only know she'd been drinking gin and that there's a good chance it was the gin that her half-sister brought her.' It had been a good quality bottle, from a local craft distillery, and he knew that as a matter of course Connie would drink wine when offered a choice. But she might have run out of wine, or simply preferred a change. 'If the gin's clear and Connie died of alcohol poisoning, then fine. It was a tragic accident. But I want to see both of those things established before I get too complacent about what happened.'

TWENTY-SIX

It had been a long day. Faye's unjustified aggression had only amplified Ashleigh's guilt at not having answered her phone, but she'd had no time to dwell on it. She'd spent much of the day with Jude, chewing over this and that, picking over Connie's movements and connections, and all the while worrying away at the process of achieving justice for Connie, briefing the police in Australia to break the news to her husband and family, making arrangements for them to fly over and spend the most miserable of Christmases. At no point in the day had she had the chance to have a word with him alone, and it wasn't until she saw him putting on his coat and scarf and heading towards the exit that the opportunity arose.

'Going down to the car park?' she asked, a false and obvious conversation starter.

'Well done, Sherlock.' He smiled, but it was a thin smile. He looked exhausted.

'I've been looking for a chance to talk to you.'

He could have said *I don't think that's a good idea* or, worse, *I don't know that we've anything to talk about*, but he said neither and they walked out of the building in a sober silence. A few years earlier, on a dark night not unlike this when the lights had pooled silver on the tarmac of the car park, Scott had accosted her in this very place. She'd only recently transferred to the Cumbria force and the ink had not yet dried on her application for divorce. That night he'd been at his worst, drunk and possessive, furious at her move to break away from him, and Jude had rescued her by offering him a lift to the hotel where he was staying. She'd never found out what passed between them that night but it was a reasonable bet that it formed the basis for their mutual dislike. Of the two of them, she understood Jude's attitude the more clearly. Scott was Marmite, loved or hated in equal measure, and she now understood that she did, after all, love him.

She had been working on a case at Eden's End then, too. It was no wonder the more excitable locals talked in hushed voices about the place being cursed and the more practical ones realised that its problems stemmed from chronically poor management and were reluctant to take the risk of consigning their loved ones to it. What went round came around — Scott and herself, unexplained deaths at Eden's End — and yet some things had changed. She had realised the impossibility of being happy without him and he'd realised he could no longer behave as he had done before. In a better world she would have been truly happy, but she had Faye's fury and the fatal delay in getting help to Connie weighing on her conscience.

They reached Jude's car first. He must have been in early; it was parked close to the entrance.

'That was a hell of a day,' he said, opening the boot and placing his laptop bag inside it with care.

'Yes,' she said, pausing beside him, 'terrible.'

'Faye was out of order,' he said abruptly. 'I spoke to her about it.' In the lamplight, his shrug was telling.

'What did she say?' asked Ashleigh, apprehensively. Her relationship with Faye went back a long way and had always been fraught. An excellent detective and equally effective administrator, Faye was less good as a manager, a woman who forgave and forgot nothing.

'I think she understands she shouldn't have spoken to you like that.'

It was, she noted, a very carefully framed explanation. Everyone knew what Faye was like. She encouraged informality within the ranks but only to a certain point, beyond which no-one was allowed to step without the risk of insubordination. It took newcomers a while to learn where it was. Jude's challenge to her, though entirely reasonable, had been high-risk and Ashleigh recognised it was as close as she would get to an acknowledgement that Faye was in the wrong.

'I know,' she said, 'but actually I wonder if she has a—'

'There's no *actually* about it and you need to stop wondering. She doesn't have a point. I don't have to tell you we're all entitled to our free time and we're under no obligation to do any work while we're off duty. The only mistake you made was telling her you were on a date.' He was shaking her head at her. 'What possessed you?'

'It slipped out.' That was another thing she had to blame Scott for, more damage he'd caused without ever understanding what he'd done. Way back in the darkness, when Ashleigh had been in another force and Scott had been flirting with every blonde who crossed his path, she had had a rebound relationship with Faye Scanlon. At the time she hadn't understood why she'd done it but now she saw, with startling clarity, that it was because Faye was as unlike charming, feckless Scott as it was possible to be.

Jude knew it. 'It's none of my business, but was your date with Scott?'

'It isn't any of your business, no, but because we're friends, I'll tell you. Yes. It was.'

'I just wondered, because, as you say, we're friends, and because if you're going to be seeing him again I'm bound to bump into him and if I know then I'm more likely to make the effort to be polite.'

If she hadn't been feeling so guilty about Connie she might have laughed. That was so typical of him. She almost thought he was teasing her. Jude was fair, that was the thing. He cared for her and he knew how much Scott had hurt her. If only they could have fallen in love. 'He's very different now.'

'Of course he is,' he said, deadpan. 'Thank you for letting me know. I'll behave myself, now.' He opened the car door.

Ashleigh lingered. 'I know I didn't do anything wrong, but I do feel so bad about Connie.' She could still remember the buzz of the phone, the instinctive move to answer it, the way that Scott had so gently turned her away from it. Then they'd gone upstairs and left the phone behind and for the next hour, while Connie had been on her way to heaven or hell, Ashleigh had been in a heaven of her own. 'If I'd answered it—'

'*If ifs and ands were pots and pans*, as my mother used to say...' He trailed off. 'Don't feel bad. It happened. If it's any consolation I feel bad about it too.'

'Why? You almost saved her.'

'Because I don't understand why she didn't call me.'

She knew him well. When a relationship ended it would be much easier if you could lose the accumulated knowledge of years of close interaction, shared jokes, thoughts, ambitions and aspirations. It could be uncomfortable finding yourself privy to someone's feelings when your star was no longer yoked to theirs. It had been like that with Scott and now it was the same with Jude.

'Perhaps because you told her you weren't interested?' she suggested.

'I don't like to think it was that, but yes. She had her pride.'

'You can't reproach yourself for that,' she said, with spirit. 'It was obvious she was very keen on you and obvious she didn't want to take no for an answer, but I don't see what else you could have done, or you'd never have got rid of her.'

'She might still be alive.'

She might, and there were consequences that might have come from it, particularly in terms of Connie making Jude's life difficult, but obviously that was unsayable. Instead, she turned her mind to sharing the blame. 'She might still be alive if I'd answered the phone, too.'

'Why didn't you?' he asked. 'Not that you should have done. Don't get me wrong. But you usually do.'

She was glad that in the patchy light of the car park it was easy for her to take a half step backwards and draw a cloak of darkness across her face. Normally she couldn't resist the tantalising ring of her work phone, the jeopardy of an unwelcome call or a breakthrough piece of information. 'I thought it might be you.'

'Right,' he said, sounding unsure, and then he laughed, but the laugh was a bitter one. 'That's two women not wanting to speak to me in the space of a few minutes, then. I hadn't realised I'd become that...' He searched for a word. 'Antisocial.'

'Don't be ridiculous,' she said, crisply. 'You know it isn't that.'

'Then what is it?'

'I could hardly take a call from you when I was on a date with Scott, could I?'

'Most people wouldn't have an issue with that.'

She accepted the challenge in his voice. Scott was a jealous man. It was in his nature. If she'd answered a call from Jude, no matter how mundane the subject, it would have put his back up and the evening would have been ruined. His charm would have descended into injured feelings and spite, as if he was punishing her for having other friends. 'I think Scott feels threatened by you.'

This time the laugh was a more straightforward one. 'I don't see I'm a threat to anyone. Those days are gone.'

They were, though they'd been good while they lasted and the relationship had been emotionally uncomplicated, which was something she would miss. Scott required so much effort. 'I know what you're going to say.'

'I'm not going to say anything about how you live your life. My only advice is not to tell Faye about it.'

He, too, had shuffled back out of the light and it made him curiously easier to talk to. 'It's so difficult, Jude. I do know what you think and I know you're right to think it.' And she knew, too, why he couldn't say it. 'You know what he used to be like. But we were together very young and maybe we married too soon, and maybe neither of us knew how to manage a relationship.'

'From what you've said,' he remarked, managing to sound more detached than she thought he probably felt, 'and from my own observation of him, he has a lot of bad relationship habits to unlearn.'

For sure. 'He knows that.'

'And do you think he really will change?'

Who knew? He'd promised before. 'It's like this. We care for each other. And if we don't try again then perhaps we'll never actually be able to make it all worthwhile.' All the rows, his womanising, his jealousy. She had wasted so much emotional energy on him when she was younger that she didn't dare try and work out how much. She had left him, gone back to him, finally left him again, and now, after he'd followed her up to Cumbria and kept his distance for a couple of years, they had become friends again. In the oxygen of that friendship, it had been inevitable that the embers of their romance would flare up anew. 'I think he's changed.'

'Time will tell.'

'If I'm wrong, you're at liberty to say *I told you so.*'

'I'd never do that.' He said it with certainty. 'But you can promise me one thing.'

'Of course.' Unlike Scott, Jude could be relied on never to ask her for something unreasonable.

'If you ever need my help, don't be like Connie. Don't be too proud to ask.'

'I can safely promise you that,' she said, as he got into the car. 'One more thing.'

'What's that?'

'Is Scott the reason you didn't come to my drinks?'

'Not exactly. But no-one wants an ex hanging around, do they?'

'Didn't you say to me that Becca was having a drinks party? Are you going to that?'

'That's different.'

But it wasn't. 'Me being with Scott doesn't change anything between us.' Or it wouldn't if he allowed that. 'Can I be honest with you?'

'By all means,' he said, rather dryly, she thought, but there was a hint of a wry smile on his face.

'I'm going to make it work with Scott this time. I won't take any of his crap, but I have to do that. So if I were you I'd make Becca fully aware of that and then maybe you can try and make it work with her. Because that's what you want.' It was why they managed to be so civil with each other, maintain their friendship once the physical side of their relationship had died. They understood one another.

'It doesn't matter what I want. It has to be what she wants, too.'

'Have you asked her recently?'

'Not recently, but that ship sailed a long time ago.' He shook his head and laid his hand on the inner handle of the open door, keen for the conversation to end. 'Good luck with Scott, though. I really hope he makes you happy. But remember what I said. I'm always here if you need me.'

'I'll remember,' she said, and read his relief as he closed the car door, started the engine and drove away.

TWENTY-SEVEN

'What have we got?' said Jude as he, Chris Marshall and Ashleigh gathered at the table in the incident room. It was a matter of days until Christmas and already the place was thin on personnel. Doddsy, who he would normally have wanted to have on his team as the voice of calm and reason, was already off on annual leave and Faye, thank God, had something else to do. The forensic labs, too, were starting to slow down as the holidays took hold, and though Faye had leaned on everyone she knew to try and hurry the post mortem reports through, there was as yet no sign of them. To a degree their hands were tied until those results came through and there was no realistic evidence that Connie's death had been anything but misadventure, but Jude was no less sure of it for than that. 'I want to know everything we can find out about Connie's last few days.' Then, if the lab results showed something criminal, they would be ready to act.

'I've already been looking at that.' Chris Marshall, one of the detective sergeants in the team, looked pleased with himself. He hadn't known Connie and so this investigation was less of a burden for him, nothing more onerous than another series of routine checks in an unfortunate accident.

How refreshing that must be. There was an ugly taint when it came to investigating the death of someone you knew well. 'Have you come up with anything?'

'These Ring doorbell things. What an invention!' said Chris, merry as Father Christmas. Like Doddsy he had managed to get in early with his request for Christmas leave and his enthusiasm for it was showing through. 'They've made my life a lot easier. Fortunately Connie's flat had one fitted. We know how many visitors she had and, apart from the post, there were just the three. There was your good self.' At this point he nodded familiarly towards Jude. 'Then there was Vivien Warrington.'

'We knew she'd visited,' said Jude, 'because Connie said so. It was at her invitation.' He bit back his criticism of Connie's motivations. It was irrelevant now, and the fight to inherit Edwin's wealth was one for her husband to take up on behalf of her sons.

'Right. Mrs Warrington appeared, alone, on the Sunday afternoon at just after four o'clock, carrying what looks like a bottle.'

'It was a very decent gin,' said Jude, 'and it's at the lab right now.'

Chris gave a low whistle. 'Okay. That's what we're looking at, is it?'

'Yes,' said Ashleigh with a gusty sigh. 'I don't know about you, but I'm very much inclined towards poisoned gin.'

That had been Jude's initial thought, but you couldn't jump to conclusions. Faye had tried to lean on the lab to get the bottle of gin tested, too. The results would be illuminating.

'Mrs Warrington stayed about twenty minutes and then appeared to leave in a hurry. There are CCTV cameras that confirm she was dropped off, and picked up, by her husband.'

So far, nothing new. Jude had no reason to doubt Connie's version of events and this confirmed it. 'Who was the third one?'

'Wednesday evening, at 6.04 pm. Female, fortyish maybe, wearing gym clothes. Someone who identified herself as Mel.' He extracted a printed image from a folder and laid it on the table. 'Does that mean anything to you?'

'Yes,' said Jude, because the image was blurred and distorted but nevertheless immediately identifiable. 'That's Melanie Trotter, formerly married to Connie's husband.'

'The plot thickens.'

Oh, it did. 'In her message to Ashleigh,' Jude said, deliberately avoiding her eye in case she should see some kind of criticism in it, 'Connie mentioned that Melanie had been giving her a hard time. I can vouch for that, because I saw her approach Connie one day in a pub and tear a strip off her, for no obvious reason.'

'Drink talking, you reckon?'

'I think so. But I never heard anything I would interpret as threats of physical harm.'

'There's a transcript of the conversation, if you can call it that.' Chris distributed that, too. 'Again, not what you'd call threats of violence, more along the lines of you'll-never-work-in-this-town-again. But there's clearly no love lost between them, and eventually Connie shut the door on her.'

'Did Melanie go in?' asked Jude, intrigued.

'No, and she didn't appear to bring anything with her

either. But she's clearly someone who had an issue with Connie and for all I know she's dreaming of dancing on her grave.'

Wishing someone dead didn't mean you killed them, but it was interesting nevertheless. 'She cared enough about Connie to turn up on her doorstep and harangue her. I think we need to talk to her, sooner rather than later. I know from other sources that she and Connie interacted on Facebook, and possibly also on other social media, and not always positively, so that might be worth an hour or so of your time.'

'I'll do it as soon as we're done here,' said Chris, obligingly. 'I'll run a quick search for you and I can always drill down a bit later on. What am I looking for? Any interactions with Melanie Trotter, obviously, but is there anything else?'

'I'm still thinking of the gin,' said Ashleigh. 'I can't get away from that.'

'Melanie didn't give her the gin,' said Jude, thoughtfully, 'and I'll be astonished if Vivien interacted with Connie on Facebook under her own name.' But she might easily have been there under another name, or have searched Connie's very public profile just as Jude himself had done. 'If the gin turns out to be poisoned and if it came from Vivien, I doubt we'll find the reason on Facebook.'

He looked at the two of them. Chris was already making extensive notes on his tablet and Ashleigh had that slight frown on her face that he recognised as concealing the germ of an idea. 'What are you thinking, Ash?'

'I'm still thinking about the gin and there's something I'm just not getting. Something about Vivien. It's a gamble that Connie would drink it, if it was poisoned. But we know Vivien is a gambler. She gambled that Connie wouldn't come home, for example, which could have happened at any point without warning, and then the cat would have been among the pigeons. So I'm absolutely convinced that she'd gamble with poison, wherever she got it from.'

'The nursing home's the obvious place, isn't it?' said Chris.

But that had been three years before. It was easy to see how Vivien might have obtained drugs that could kill from Eden's End around the time of Edwin's death, but to acquire them and keep them for years, on the off-chance of murder? Jude cast his mind back to Faye. *I did find myself wondering whether Mrs Warrington's determination to get her hands on the money might have been so great she might have felt the need to hurry her father along to his grave.* And there had been Ellie Jack. *Chaos in the drugs record with stuff unaccounted for. It would never have happened on my watch.* But when Edwin had died, Vivien had been well out of the way.

'Something occurs to me.' He read out the date of Edwin's death. 'I want to know if Connie says anything in the preceding few weeks — say, a month — about coming home?'

'I can do that now. You carry on and I'll do it while I'm listening.'

'Have you got time to have a chat with Melanie this afternoon?' Jude asked Ashleigh.

'Yes. I'll look forward to that.' He thought she said it with a trace of relish, as if Melanie's antics at Connie's doorbell had annoyed her on the dead woman's behalf. 'Even if she didn't actually kill her she certainly played a part in making her life a misery. And let's face it, we can't rule out that Connie took her own life, in which case if I was Melanie Trotter I wouldn't want to look at myself too long in the mirror.'

'We can't rule it out. No.' But Jude thought not. Whatever Connie went through (sometimes he thought it was things she put herself through, avoidably, as a form of self-harm) she somehow always came out of it upbeat and moved on to something else. Her resilience had been extraordinary, her life punctuated with the optimism of fresh start after fresh start. 'Let's see what we get from the toxicology report and the gin bottle.' But even then the poison could have been self-administered.

'Okay,' said Chris, turning his iPad towards them. 'I've done a very brief sweep of Connie's socials and it's worth a closer look. There's a post here, a couple of weeks before the date of Edwin's death. She says she's tired of Australia. She complains about the heat and the flies and the wildfires. Dear me, she doesn't sound very happy, does she?'

She hadn't been. Jude knew that, but he was nevertheless surprised how soon the gilt had come off the Australian gingerbread. 'Does she say anything specifically about coming back?'

'Let's see. Yes, she does. She says *I can't stand this place any longer. We're going to have to have a big discussion about how long we can stay here. I never thought I'd say I miss cold and wet old Cumbria but I need to get back and soon.* Though, as I flick through, it appears she didn't come back and if they did have that big discussion she hasn't posted about it.'

'Good work. Can I ask you to keep on looking?' Because Melanie Trotter would have known about Connie's return, too. 'And Ash, I think it would be opportune if we can find out where Melanie is this afternoon and you pay her a visit and see what she has to say for herself.

TWENTY-EIGHT

'I hated the bitch,' said Melanie Trotter. 'Someone else will tell you if I don't, so I might as well be honest about it.' She sat back and gave Ashleigh the long and resentful stare of someone who'd been well and truly ambushed.

'I see,' said Ashleigh, severely. She wasn't surprised by Melanie's attitude; after all, the woman had come back from lunch not expecting to find a police officer in reception. Some people might have retreated behind a defensive silence but it was entirely in line with what Ashleigh knew of her character that Melanie would come out fighting.

'But I didn't kill her. Don't go thinking that.'

'No-one's suggesting it.'

'It's why you're here, isn't it?' She brushed aside Ashleigh's much-practiced speech about *routine*. 'I'm not saying I wouldn't have liked to, and I'm not saying I wouldn't have taken a swing at her if I'd a few drinks too many and the red mist came down, and I'm not saying I wouldn't have enjoyed it, because I would. But it didn't happen.'

'You went to her flat on Wednesday evening. Why was that?'

'I never meant to.' Melanie was starting to look anxious, as if she'd reviewed her position and realised it might be serious. 'I was passing. I'd been to the gym and I'd come the back way home because there was traffic on the roundabout, and it took me past her flat. Matt — that's my ex — had told me where she was living. I think he thought I might pop in and be nice to her.' She snorted. 'Not a chance. I didn't mean to go anywhere near her. But as I say, I was passing, and a bit mad that he thought I'd do that, to be honest, so I just stopped the car and rang the bell. Shouted at her a bit and went away.' By now she had the grace to look ashamed.

'Did you go in?'

'No,' said Melanie. They were sitting in the cramped office on the industrial estate where she worked as office manager for an agricultural supply firm. The room was draped in gold tinsel but the banner wishing customers and staff a merry Christmas sagged and some of the fairy lights that adorned Mel's desk had gone out.

'Why not?'

'She wouldn't let me.' Melanie shrugged. 'Look, I know what I just said but I'm sorry she's dead, because you always are when it's someone that dies young. It makes you think. And that's a hell of way to go, all on your own, like they say she did. But at the same time I wonder if I really am sorry. Because Connie was the most selfish woman I ever met. She trampled over everyone on her way through life, she didn't care about anyone else. It was me-me-me with her, all the time.'

'Did you know her well?' asked Ashleigh, torn between a deep dislike of this woman's attitude and admiration at her honesty.

'For a bit, aye.' Melanie looked down at her hands, as if to avoid Ashleigh's gaze. 'It was what made it worse. We lived in the same street growing up. I quite liked her, once. She could be funny and she could be kind.'

'You just said she was the most selfish person you ever met,' Ashleigh reminded her.

'Yes.' Still Melanie stared at her hands, her nails polished scarlet with stars set into them, manicured for a Christmas do. 'But at the time I fell for it. She was a leech, you know the sort. If you showed her the slightest bit of kindness she'd be back for more, and more. I invited her to meet my friends, because I felt sorry for her. She came round to the house. I went to hers, too, met her dad there once. He was a miserable old sod.'

'When did Connie's relationship with your husband start?'

'I don't know.' Melanie allowed herself a wry smile. 'I suppose I took my eye off the ball. She's not the femme fatale type, though I suppose she's pretty enough. There's a vulnerability about her, though, and I think that appeals to a certain type of man. It certainly did to Matthew. He always saw himself as a bit of a he-man, you know? He's big on protecting women, providing for them. It didn't occur to me that Connie would strike that note in him. I'm a bit tougher. I can look out for myself and I've never been the kind of woman who simpers over a man the way she does. So when he told me he was leaving me…well. I was broken.'

Ashleigh let the silence endure while Melanie dwelt on her grievances. It didn't matter what the rights and wrongs of the matter were, only how Melanie understood them. It might be that Connie and Matthew Armstrong had been perfect for each other; it might be that Matthew was the one to blame; it might be that Melanie was impossible to live with. None of that mattered. The only thing that was important in the context of this conversation was what Melanie thought, and how she might have reacted.

'What was your response?' she asked, as the silence became heavy and she'd spotted Melanie looking at what looked suspiciously like an engagement ring, now worn on her right hand.

'I had a right go at Matthew,' she said, slowly, 'because he was nearer, you know? And I probably had a few words with Connie, too, though my mam probably wouldn't approve of some of the things I called her.' She gave a sheepish grin. 'Or maybe she would. Whatever. She deserved what I said. I can be quite fierce.'

'Did you think you had a chance of getting your husband back? That he'd become tired of Connie, perhaps, and she of him?' asked Ashleigh.

'I don't know. Maybe I did. I don't remember. Maybe. But then the pair of them took off to Australia, and she got pregnant. Me and Matt had talked about kids but I didn't think the time was right. And then that protector instinct kicked in. He'd never abandon his kids. He'd probably think twice about abandoning his wife if he thought it meant he wouldn't get to see them. But that cow didn't even stay to look after them.'

'When you knew that Connie was back, how did you react?'

Melanie thought about that for a while. 'I laughed, I think. I heard the story, how she'd come back to sponge off her old man when the marriage broke down, and he was dead and someone else had done the kind of thing to her that she did to other people. Funny, because I used to go and visit my nan in Eden's End and saw Edwin's name on the door, and I used to think about her leaving him there on his own and how I'd never do that. Yeah, I thought it was karma and if anyone deserved karma it was Connie Sheldon.'

'I believe you had at least two encounters with her before that last one. Did you just see her about? Or did you make an effort to try and find her?'

'A bit of both, I think.' Melanie rubbed at the fingernail of her right index finger, as if to buff it to an impossibly high shine. 'I think she was staying in the middle of town somewhere. I was in town quite a lot, on my way to and from the gym, drinks with friends, Christmas shopping and so on. She was always somewhere, in a bar or in a cafe or a restaurant, and it was always obvious. If I'd done what she did I wouldn't be putting myself in the shop window. I'd be hiding away out of shame. But Connie was a nosy cow and she liked to see what was going in. So yes, I kind of felt she was putting herself in the way of trouble.'

'You approached her and warned her to get out of town, I believe.' Ashleigh recalled Jude's description of the interaction he'd overheard.

Melanie's eyebrows lifted in surprise. 'How do you know that?'

'Someone saw you.'

'God, you guys have eyes everywhere, don't you?' Melanie's glance was almost admiring. 'Yes. I'd had a drink and there she was, kind of asking for it. So I did tell her, exactly what I thought.'

'Would you say you were threatening?'

'I didn't think so. Not that I wanted to make her welcome. I wanted her to know exactly what everyone she used to know thinks of her. Because they all do. All of them.'

'Okay. Do you remember what you said?'

'No,' said Melanie, and her lips narrowed. 'Does it matter? I didn't do anything to her.'

'We're examining the circumstances of Ms Sheldon's death as I explained to you.'

'Are you trying to say I drove her to suicide? Is that it?' Suddenly Melanie was wary. 'I didn't do that. I didn't make her drink. She was a sad woman at the end, for sure, but I don't think I've got enough power over her for that.'

'And yet,' Ashleigh reminded her, 'when she'd moved into her flat you made a point of going there and harassing her.'

'She made me so angry, you know? Swanning round. And then when I'd seen her she had another bloke with her, and I thought to myself, that's her sinking her claws into some other poor innocent soul, probably married to someone else because most people that age are, and she hadn't wasted any time over it.'

She must be talking about Jude. Ashleigh suppressed her smile at the description of him; he was possibly the most knowing and cynical person she knew, and she knew a lot. 'That was an old friend of hers.'

'Right. That won't mean Connie didn't have designs on him.'

'But it made you angry enough to go out of your way to see her.'

Melanie shifted in her seat. Her phone rang and she looked at it hungrily, as if it might prove a distraction, then looked away. 'I know I ought to have been able to let it go, but I couldn't. Funny. I thought I'd got it out of my system after I called to see her. She'd got the message, and she wouldn't let me in anyway. She was already drinking by then and she looked pretty rough. I didn't need to punish her any more. There was no way Matthew was going to take her back, so after that, I didn't care about her any more.'

'Do you still love your ex-husband, Ms Armstrong?'

asked Ashleigh, interested. The clues were there. The engagement ring. The fact that Melanie still sometimes used her married name. That several years had passed and she hadn't moved on, when the objects of her love and her hatred were on the other side of the world.

There was pause while Melanie thought about it. 'I don't know. If you'd asked me I'd have said I hated the bastard and never wanted to see him again, but then it was her that came back and I think I knew. I thought they might come back here when her dad was in the home but no. I wanted Matthew to come back, not her. So yes. He didn't deserve it, but I suppose I do. Maybe I always did.' She reached into her pocket for a tissue. 'Anyway, I've got a horse now, instead. They're a whole lot nicer than people, and a whole lot more useful, too.' She blew her nose. 'Is there anything more you need to ask? Because I've got a meeting in ten minutes, and stuff to do before I get there.'

'No, that's fine.' Ashleigh had heard enough.

Melanie picked at the tissue. 'Do you think I did...kind of make her do it?'

'At the moment we don't know what happened.'

'Right.' Melanie got up and moved towards the door. 'Look, if it was me...I never meant it.'

'I understand.' Ashleigh followed her, intrigued. There was time, perhaps, to slip in one last question. 'Do you think your husband will come back to you?'

'No. He won't want to live here again,' said Melanie, wistfully, but her face gave away how much she cared for him. 'And yeah, do you know what? If he did, I think I'd forgive him anything.'

TWENTY-NINE

Just as Vivien closed down the call the hum of Stephen's work van throbbed on the driveway outside. She laid her phone on the side table and made the most of the few moments' peace before he clattered his way in through the front door, unaware how everything had changed on the instant, reflecting on the sheer isolation of her position.

The clock ticked. The noise of the van shut down. This was him off for Christmas, now.

Christmas. For families. Now he was all the family she had left, and who knew how that would turn out?

He didn't come in immediately. She could hear him faffing about, the door of the van opening, a pause before it closing again, the bleep of the alarm three seconds after and then, ten seconds after that, the sound of his key in the front door.

Home for Christmas.

'Don't look!' he called, jovially, and rustled about through the kitchen and up the stairs. She went through to meet him as he came back down again, still in overalls, still in his boots. 'Bottle of wine tonight, Viv. And look, I've got chocolates. From Janice.'

She supposed Janice had to make a show of giving all her employees chocolates. 'Very nice,' she said, taking a step towards the kitchen unit where he'd placed the box of white chocolate truffles — her least favourite, sickly and expensive. He must have told her. *Viv doesn't like those.* Like a coded message that excluded her from her own Christmas, in her own home. For a moment she imagined Stephen and Janice sharing the truffles (his favourites, of course) and laughing at her.

'You all right?' he said, realising. 'Has something happened? You're white as a sheet.'

For a second she stared back at his anxious face. 'Yes. Something has.'

'What is it? What's gone wrong?'

'It was the police. They just called.'

'Again?' She detected a rise in his mood, as if this was good news. Maybe he thought it was. He might have been expecting she'd found out about him and Janice and would be pausing for a frozen second to decide what he should do, to choose between defiance, denial and silence. The police wouldn't concern themselves with that. In fact, under the circumstances, the best news for Stephen might be her arrest and imprisonment.

He must take her for an idiot. She had known about Janice for years.

'It's Connie. My sister.' She looked at the chocolates. She would open them that evening, to make a point. She would say: *my goodness, you know I'm not a fan of white chocolate but these are gorgeous*, just to spite them both. 'She's dead.' Poor Connie. Well, after a fashion.

He came up to her and hugged her, so good at pretending, at being solicitous. 'What happened? No wonder you look so shaken.'

She leaned into his familiar shape. If it hadn't been for Janice she would still have loved him instead of holding him in a silent sneering contempt he'd never imagine she could feel. If it wasn't for Janice she would have told him the whole story long before, asked for his help in hiding the money, or secreting at least some of it away in case the courts decided against her. But Janice existed and had been having an affair with her husband for years, and Vivien knew it and never forgot.

How like her father she was. She could hold a grudge for decades, its anger and its violence compounding with every turn of the earth.

'It was just the shock,' she said, releasing herself from his grasp. 'Go and get out of those overalls, love. Why don't we order a takeaway, to mark the start of the holidays, and then we can open those chocolates afterwards?'

'That would be nice,' he said, still watching her. 'So what happened to Connie?'

'Oh, sorry. Yes. They don't know, the police said. They had a call yesterday. She'd phoned someone saying she was in distress.' The police sergeant, Ashleigh O'Halloran, had seemed more shaken by Connie's death than you'd expect from someone who must have delivered that kind of message so many times before. Drink or drugs, accident or illness. People died suddenly all the time. 'By the time they got to her it was too late.'

'But they didn't say what caused it?'

'They said all the usual things. Routine, still investigating, waiting for test results. I imagine she drank herself to death.'

He had soft brown eyes, like a cow's she used to think,

and she was watching him now exactly like a cow that was trying to make up its mind about the intentions of someone crossing its field. He suspected her. Fair enough. She had a lot of reasons to want Connie dead. 'When did it happen?'

'Yesterday evening. Just think. The two of us sitting down for dinner and she…' It would be prudent, even with Stephen, to pretend she felt more sympathy for Connie that she did. 'The poor girl. I wish we could have been friends. And to think we were sitting having that lovely meal and she was—' She dabbed at her dry eye and turned away so he wouldn't see just how fake she was. 'She was my last living relative,' she said, quietly, 'and now I don't have anyone.'

'You have me,' he said, and began to unfasten his overalls. 'You'll always have me.'

She waited until he had removed them, to reveal an incongruous Christmas jumper and a pair of un-plumber-like red corduroy trousers he brought out every year in a show of festive jollity, held out her hand for them, and thrust them in the washing machine.

You'll always have me. Surely he said that to Janice, too, in those cosy hours when he was *working late on a job that overran*, or *had to go to the estate out at Penrith, drains needed rodding.*

Rodding Janice's drains, she thought, coarsely, and smiled at how shocked he'd be if she said it out loud. 'Thank you.'

'I thought something terrible had happened when I came in,' he said, 'and I suppose it has. But in another way it's not terrible at all, is it? Be honest. She was a nasty piece of work and you'll be glad to see the back of her.'

You must tell me when the funeral is, she'd said to the sergeant, *so I can send flowers. Of course I can't possibly attend. It would look bad, embarrass her poor husband and those little children.*

And besides, who knew what would happen between now and Connie's funeral? Nevertheless, as long as Connie was above ground and not laid in the same lair as their father, the two of them fighting like rats in a sack in the hereafter, she wouldn't be completely at peace.

'Viv? You seem so distant. Are you sure you're all right?'

'It's just the shock.' She rallied. 'Sorry.'

'I'll get you a drink, eh? Since it's nearly Christmas and I'm not on call tonight.'

He was on call over Christmas, of course. Viv smiled sweetly, sure there would be at least one callout that wasn't for real, probably on Boxing Day when Janice would be on her own. 'You're right. It's not all bad. I mean, she can't argue about the money, now. It's mine.'

He got a beer from the fridge for himself and fixed her a gin and tonic. 'Let's drink to the future, eh?'

'You should give up work,' she said, watching as the gin gurgled into the glass and thinking of Connie, downing drink after drink without thought. 'We could go and live by the sea, in Cornwall, maybe. You know I've always wanted to. Somewhere abroad, even.'

It was unfortunate that he had his back turned to her. The expression on his face would have been priceless. 'Oh, I don't know, love,' he said, after a telling second's hesitation. 'I know we've talked about retiring. But I love my job.'

'You never used to.'

'No, but I need something to keep me busy.'

'Now she's dead we have enough money.'

'Aye, but we'll still have that. I could go part time, maybe. But I think I'd like to keep my hand in. Work and play, like.'

'Have your cake and eat it, you mean,' she said,

keeping a straight face as she always did and he, as he always did, missed the hidden meaning.

'If you put it like that,' he said and handed her the glass. 'Cheers, Viv. Here's to a new start.'

'A new start,' she echoed, and smiled.

THIRTY

'Do you two have five minutes?' Jude had shouldered his way into the incident room. It was nearly time to shut up shop and go home, and everyone who didn't have something they couldn't put off had already started packing up but, as he'd expected, Ashleigh and Chris were both still there. The two of them were working side by side, and he pulled up a chair between them, iPad in hand. 'I'd like a quick catch up before you go off home for your Friday night pints or mince pies or whatever. It shouldn't take long. We had a good catch up this morning, but since then I've had the results of the toxicology tests and they're giving me a lot to think about.'

'That doesn't sound great.' Chris stopped what he'd been doing and swung his chair round to face him.

'It's not. The tests show excessive levels of a drug called Immobilon.'

'What's that?'

'It's a horse tranquilliser.' said Jude. 'An opioid. Usually injected, and there are no signs of any puncture wounds so it's unlikely Connie would have administered it herself.'

'A horse tranquilliser?' said Chris, perking up. 'Am I right in thinking Vivien Warrington used to work for a vet?'

'Yes. I'd be treating this as homicide anyway,' he said, because if there was any doubt that was what they were all trained to do, 'but I might as well come straight out with it. It's possible Connie could have obtained it herself, but I don't think so, partly because it's not widely used any more and I'm not aware she had any contacts with the kind of large animal practice where you might still find it. But it wasn't the way Connie was wired. She never, ever gave up. I thought there was something fishy about it on the night she died.' That was why he'd taken the gin bottle, an action he now thought was prescient. 'We've searched the flat and there's no sign of any drugs, or needles, or any empty blister packets, or anything else in the house.' It hadn't taken long. Connie hadn't had much.

'I agree,' said Ashleigh, looking thoughtful. 'Unless Connie decided to kill herself and then neatly removed all evidence, then someone else introduced the drug into her system in some way and the obvious way is through the gin bottle.'

'Precisely. That's why I'm so keen to get the analysis of that gin back from the lab.'

Chris looked at his watch, as if that would hurry things on. 'Vivien does seem the obvious one, doesn't she?'

'Given that her father died as a result of medical negligence while she was conveniently out of the country and her sister as a result of poisoning while she was also conveniently elsewhere?' said Jude, drily. 'Yes, I'd say she is.'

'Has anyone spoken to her about it?' asked Chris.

'Not yet.' Ashleigh sat back and sighed. 'At least, not

since we told her about Connie's death, and I have to say she seemed rather more upset by that than I'd expected, though maybe she's a better actress than I gave her credit for. I can make the transcript of that chat available later, but the summary will have to do just now. Vivien's assumption was, or she pretended it was, that Connie had either taken her own life or drunk herself to death. She said she'd visited at Connie's request and Connie had offered to split the money with her, but she'd refused.'

'She's still insisting it's rightfully hers, then?' said Chris, with a whistle that was almost of admiration. 'That's what I call brass neck.'

'I know. She wouldn't give an inch on that. She managed to imply that Connie was unhinged and said her husband had warned her about going along and had insisted upon going with her, but had waited outside. She had taken a bottle of gin, one they'd been given as a gift—'

'Unopened?' asked Chris, alert.

'She claims it was sealed but we can't prove that one way or the other. She went in and she and Connie each drank a gin and tonic. She didn't see Connie making them, but she assumed they came from the bottle she brought. She says the visit was short and difficult. Connie became aggressive and threatening, Vivien refused to give an inch because, as she says, it was a matter of principle.'

'She doesn't like Connie, does she?' asked Jude, interested. It had struck him, as he mulled over the case, that Connie had had an extraordinary capacity to inspire dislike, even hatred, without ever having been someone who hated in return. He'd always found her appealing and attractive, but perhaps, as Mel had remarked to Ashleigh, it was because he spotted her vulnerability and was moved by it.

'I would say she definitely doesn't. I didn't get the

impression she hated her in the way Melanie said she herself did, but this was a phone call rather than a direct interview so it's harder to tell. I certainly think Vivien's smart enough to know she's in enough trouble already and that venting about someone whose death is being investigated isn't that smart.'

Interestingly, Jude noted, that hadn't stopped Melanie from holding forth. 'No, it definitely isn't.'

'She said the gin had been her husband's suggestion, by the way, to keep Connie sweet, as she put it. We only have her word for the fact that she drank it, of course. Eventually Connie threw a glass at her and flounced out to her bedroom. Vivien waited for a while to see what would happen next and when there was no sound she peered in and found Connie sobbing incoherently on the bed. She cleared up the broken glass and left.'

'What a bizarre thing to do,' said Chris, wrinkling his face in puzzlement.

'Connie thought that was passive-aggressive,' said Jude, 'and I can see that. It would mean that when she got up and went to clear up there would be a subliminal message left for her, the same message that Vivien had tried to send whenever she talked about how much she loved her father. It basically tells Connie: *I'm better than you. A better person, a better daughter.* Better all round, in fact. That would be a blow to Connie, but not enough to make her kill herself, in my opinion.'

'That's pretty much psychopathic behaviour, don't you think?' asked Ashleigh. 'She wanted me to think she felt sorry for her. But, as I say, I might have felt differently if I'd seen her face to face.'

'I'm leaning towards Vivien, for sure,' said Jude, 'but let's have a think about the alternative, too. That's Melanie. We know her behaviour towards Connie was aggressive, and we know she's threatened her at least twice, once when she called and once in the pub when I saw what happened. There may have been other occasions.' He looked at Chris Marshall. 'I know you were following up on this. Any joy?'

'Plenty,' said Chris, promptly. 'To the extent that I'm pretty clear in my head that she was proactively ill-wishing Connie very publicly, so who knows what she might have done to take that a step further?'

'What about her socials?'

'Melanie followed Connie on every platform she was on. There's nothing I'd call incriminating and nothing illegal. It's more a constant stream of abuse. Every time Connie posted, Mel was in there with a negative comment. She tagged her in sarcastic posts and reposts — a meme about women letting other women down, for example. I'm astonished that Connie didn't block her.'

'Maybe she didn't care.' But when he thought about it, it was more likely that Connie had thought she deserved this kind of abuse and accepted it as a punishment, as her due. 'Can you pin it down to anything particular? Any threats?'

'I don't think so. If nothing else, if Melanie had been too explicit the post would have been removed or she would have had her account suspended. You can only go so far before someone reports you.'

'So, an undercurrent of abuse, but nothing particular?'

'The nastiest was where she announced she was leaving and coming back and Mel made some comment about it.'

Jude nodded. He remembered that one from when he'd been sitting on Becca's sofa peering into the mirror of Connie's life that she had chosen to present to the world. 'But that was ages ago. And pretty mild.'

'Yes, three years back. Not that long before her father died, but we know she didn't come back.'

He swiped his iPad and opened it up. The swift summary Ashleigh had sent of her interview with Melanie had drawn his attention and he scanned it for the relevant comment. 'Here. Melanie was visiting her grandmother in Eden's End while Edwin was there. She took positive pleasure in the thought of him being alone. She would have known Connie had talked about coming back and she would have had the same opportunity to acquire drugs that Vivien had, or anyone else in the place. And she's still visiting. Her grandmother is still in the home.'

'She works at an agricultural supplier, doesn't she? I wonder if she has any contacts with vets?'

'I don't know about that,' said Ashleigh, suddenly alert, 'but she does have a horse.'

Lots of people locally did. They lived in a rural area. Jude's train of thought was broken by Faye's appearance, erupting through the door to the incident room opening and scanning the room before her eyes rested on them. As she crossed the room towards them, Jude struggled to read her expression, and failed. 'Is there any update?' he asked.

Chris jumped up and pulled up a chair for her. She eyed it as if she didn't intend to stay, then changed her mind and sat.

'I take it you've been discussing Connie Sheldon?' she said. Her tone was clipped.

'Yes. Obviously we don't know for certain what happened, other than that she overdosed on a horse tranquilliser.'

'Then you're obviously considering suicide.'

It would make their lives a whole lot easier if Connie had finally broken. 'I don't believe she took her own life, or that it was an accident. We know she antagonised people.

She had very public fallouts with Melanie Trotter in the days leading up to her death, and she was also aggressive to Vivien Warrington, who has an unhealthy dislike. Vivien used to work for a vet and Melanie has a horse.'

'And Vivien Warrington has the money and thinks she can keep it,' said Faye, with distaste.

'I don't know what Vivien thinks. She may have considered the prospect of losing the money and thought that Connie's death would put an end to it, but it won't. She'll still have to prove it's hers.' Connie's claim would have been inherited by her children and there was every possibility that her husband would take up the fight on their behalf.

'Ah,' said Faye. 'So you're telling me you think it's Vivien Warrington. The Vivien Warrington who stole Connie's inheritance and took a bottle of gin to her. The bottle of gin you very thoughtfully collected and sent off to the lab. Well, I have news for you about that bottle of gin, and I don't think you're going to like it.'

'You've got the results back from the lab?' he said.

'I have. They came through about five minutes ago so I thought I'd come down and tell you straight away. There's nothing at all wrong with that gin. If you want to prove that someone murdered Connie Sheldon, you're going to have to find another way for them to do it.'

THIRTY-ONE

'See you Monday,' said Chris, as Jude popped his head around the door of the incident room to let them know he was on the way home.

'Yes. We'll talk again then. I'm damned if I'm letting this one get brushed under the carpet.'

'Tough one, aye,' said Chris cheerfully. Jude didn't answer, though Ashleigh, who was putting on her coat in the corner of the room, gave him a sympathetic look. Another time they'd have gone for a drink, discussed the case, but everything was different now She'd no doubt be off to meet Scott and fan that rekindled flame, and he would sit at home and fume about how no-one seemed to see the Connie he'd known and, for a brief teenage moment, thought he'd loved.

He headed out of the building in an uncharacteristically bad mood, leaving doors to bang behind him as he went. People showed different sides of themselves to different people, but it bothered him how everyone seemed to have misunderstood Connie while she was alive and continued to do so after her death. She'd had a good heart and honest intentions and her behaviour towards those close to her, while it could not be condoned, could be ascribed to the circumstances in which she found herself.

He frowned as he got in the car. Faye, who remained committed to throwing the book at Vivien Warrington for the fraud she had perpetrated, was somehow less adamant that Connie's death was murder. To Jude, there was an obvious logic that the one should follow on the other. The law didn't allow for an individual to profit from the proceeds of a crime. If Vivien didn't realise this, she might think that her chances of inheriting the entirety of Edwin's estate would be hugely improved should Connie meet an untimely end. Melanie Trotter, who had hated Connie as much as Vivien had done but for different reasons, might have had access to the drugs on which Connie had overdosed, but he couldn't see how she'd administered them and in any case his gut instinct was that the woman was more talk than action. That left Vivien, who had turned up to visit Connie with nothing to gain from it and possibly a lot to lose if her half-sister had become violent towards her, but she claimed that they had shared the gin.

And the gin had not been poisoned.

It was Vivien who fascinated him more as he reviewed the crime they knew she had committed. Her honesty, which (he thought) she'd hoped would convince them that her actions were justified, had related only to areas in which it was inevitable she would eventually be caught. She'd played a long game and had failed only because she hadn't realised the inevitability of her discovery. Her father's death had been fortuitous in its timing, perhaps, but the planning around the fraud had been impeccable and she must have assumed that once she had the money she couldn't be forced to give it back. She'd certainly made a brave show of insisting on her right to it.

So, she was a planner and she was driven but when it came to motivation his impression of the Warringtons, with their pleasant house in an upmarket suburb of Carlisle, was that they didn't need the money. Four hundred thousand pounds, the value of Edwin's estate, would be a handy sum of money, but they would have been well enough off without it.

Wills caused many crimes. Different people had different ideas of their entitlements, as to whether they inherited as a right or a privilege. Connie, who would have benefited from the money, had seen it as secondary to the time she might have spent with her father had she known of his condition, and Vivien had claimed the care she had given him, and the circumstances of his death, as her own virtue.

He couldn't see past Vivien. That was the trouble. It was the planning. It was the fact she'd changed her name and yet made sure she was still Connie Sheldon when it suited her. She had, he was sure, either bribed or coerced Karen Grant to lose the relevant paperwork or overlook its inconsistencies, but Edwin Sheldon could have lived another dozen years. Connie would have come back and proved her identity beyond doubt. She would have produced witnesses to say who she was, Jude himself among them, and Vivien, for all her plotting and planning would have achieved nothing. If Connie had returned when she'd first intimated on that Facebook post that Chris had uncovered and read out, Vivien would have been found out. Edwin had died just weeks later, in the nick of time.

In the nick of time. He'd been waiting in the queue of traffic in the lights at the Kemplay roundabout, ready to turn off through the town towards home, but this thought galvanised him. On a sudden impulse, he flashed his indicator to change lanes to the great irritation of several drivers around him, and turned off down the A686 towards Eden's End.

The nursing home was in semi-darkness, heavy curtains drawn in all its rooms and the only light coming from the fanlight above the front door. The car park was busy, because this was the time when a shift change brought the night carers. He reckoned they would overlap for about fifteen minutes at most, and he was lucky. He had hit exactly that spot. He pulled up in a narrow space at the end of the car park and squeezed his way out between the car and the thick hedge that marked the boundary. Ahead of him, an incoming carer swiped her key fob across the door and, seeing him beside her, stood to let him in.

'Are you visiting a resident?' she asked him. 'We allow visitors any time, but right now we're starting to think about getting our residents to bed.'

'Not visiting.' Stepping inside, Jude saw exactly what he was hoping for — Ellie Jack, with her coat on, heading purposefully towards the door. 'It's Ellie I was after.'

Ellie Jack stopped when she saw him. 'If it isn't Santa Claus himself, with that merry smile.' She grinned at him. 'What is it now? We must just about be running out of people for you to arrest. It had better not be me. There'd be no-one to do the drugs round tomorrow.'

'I'm not arresting anyone,' he said, as the woman who'd let him in hurried off down the corridor. 'Not today, anyway. I was on my way home and I thought of something you might be able to help me with.'

'About old Edwin and his warring daughters? I do find myself thinking about that. It's all a bit King Lear isn't it? A proper tragedy.'

'It is a bit. And yes, it is that. I'll try not to keep you too long because I know you'll be busy, but I'd like to pick your brains. How good's your memory?'

'It depends. If I do the same thing over and over again I can't tell one occasion from another, but I like to think if there's something unusual it might stand out.' She regarded him with interest.

'What do you remember about Edwin Sheldon's death? I know you weren't there when it happened, but you must have heard the chat.'

She stopped to consider, getting her gloves out of her pocket and slapping them on the palm of her hands as she frowned. 'The main thing was that his daughter — the first one, not the one in Australia — couldn't have been nicer about it. She'd always been an absolute sweetie with him, and she was a nice woman in general. She brought him his favourite chocolates, looked after him, that sort of thing.'

'Gave him his drugs?'

'Not that. But she made life a bit easier for all of us. Especially after the...' She paused to pick the right word. 'The confusion over the drugs. Edwin was prone to wandering about. I can see how it happened, but there's no question there was a failing of care and no question that some folk would have kicked up a fuss about it. She wasn't like that. She said perhaps it was for the best, and that she hated watching him dying.'

'Was he dying?'

'We all are,' said Ellie, sombrely. 'Some just cling on, you know, and fade away so they're almost like tiny ghosts watching you as they go past and some of them get to the point where they've had enough and they just let go of life. I always thought Edwin would be one of the first type. He wasn't a man to let go.'

Edwin's death, irregular though it had been, was a closed matter, but Jude still had questions. 'I don't want you to be insulted by my next question, Mrs Jack, but is there any way the drugs dispensed in the home, specifically penicillin, could have been…acquired by an outsider?'

Her eyes widened. 'You know they could, though not without breaking every rule in the book. But if you're suggesting it was me, it wasn't. I know I did that sort of thing once, but it was only once, and I was a hell of a lot younger then. I swear there's no-one more conscientious than me.'

'But you weren't the only person with access to the drugs trolley. There was Karen Grant, perhaps?'

'Well, no. Karen would have had no need to.'

'But she had all the keys?'

'Yes,' said Ellie, thoughtfully. 'She did.'

'Isn't that bad practice?'

'Yes, but by that point Karen was doing anything to make her life easy.'

There was a pile of suggestion slips on a small table next to the visitors' book on whose open page he noticed Melanie Trotter's name. He helped himself to a slip and noted what Ellie had told him, and put the piece of paper in his pocket.

Ellie watched him carefully. 'Am I allowed to ask where this line of questioning is going?'

'You can ask,' said Jude dryly, 'but I won't give you an answer, because I don't know myself. And if you don't mind, I'd rather you didn't mention this conversation to anyone else.'

'You know me. Quiet as the grave when I have to be, and sometimes this place feels a bit like the grave. But if there's anything else I can help you with, let me know.'

'One more thing. Do you know Melanie Trotter?'

'Maggie Graham's granddaughter? Yes. She's been coming here every week for years, and I expect she'll be doing it for years more. Maggie's one of the ones who'll cling on.'

She swiped the key fob to let them out and he followed her into the car park, which was rapidly emptying as the shift finished and the majority of the staff headed home, squeezed back into the front seat of the Mercedes and sat there for a moment, frowning. He could make a case for Vivien hurrying her father into his grave so she could pre-empt the risk of Connie returning and discovering her pain to inherit, and he thought there were plenty of people who might consider that either a pragmatic or even a merciful move, certainly not something that should be treated as criminal. But it was criminal, if Edwin didn't want to die. He could see how Vivien might have leaned on the unfortunate Karen Grant, how she might have added interference with the drugs trolley to the request to lose all the relevant paperwork. He could see that her fury at Connie might have been so overwhelming that the only punishment was that she should follow Edwin to the grave at her sister's hands.

There was the penicillin. That might have come from the confusion within the home, or it might have been brought in by someone who knew of Edwin's allergy. Aside from Connie, who had been on the other side of the world, that knowledge would be limited to someone with access to his medical records.

But Vivien hadn't been there, just as she hadn't been there when Connie had somehow been murdered behind her locked front door.

He sighed. It was cold, and crystals of ice were beginning to form across the windscreen. He turned the heating up and sat there watching as it melted and his vision cleared.

Ice. He slapped his forehead. Of course! And immediately he got out his phone and called Faye.

'I don't think I was wrong about the gin and tonic,' he said to her, when she answered.

'Really? You're calling me on a Friday evening to tell me you think the highly-trained professionals at the lab have missed something? I'll get on to them first thing in the morning and let them know your thoughts. Though they won't get my message until Monday, and probably not until after Christmas.'

'They didn't miss anything,' he said. 'We did. When we searched Connie's flat.'

'The tonic was in cans. It can't have been that.'

'No. What else goes into a G&T? Ice.' Ice, that would keep until Connie made herself a drink. Ice, which when Vivien had so carefully tidied up after Connie's meltdown could have been easily replenished in the freezer and left for another day. By then Vivien would be a long way away — just as she had been when Edwin died. 'I want to go back and search that flat again, and this time, I know exactly what I'm looking for.'

THIRTY-TWO

She'd only gone and left him.

Dear Stephen. We've been together a long time, I know, but anniversaries stopped mattering when I found out about your mistress. I've known about her for seven years, I counted those, and I bet it's been going on for longer than that. Are you the reason her husband left her?

Bloody hell. He swallowed. How had she known all that time and not said anything? She just kept smiling and cooking his supper and agreeing to everything he suggested, accepting his excuses for emergency callouts and jobs overrunning. He read on.

I've taken everything I want from the house and I'm moving abroad. There's much more money in Dad's estate than I told you about, so I'll be able to live very comfortably on it, and on my own savings. I didn't tell you I started saving money as soon as I found out about the affair. I've transferred most of it abroad. Feel free to tell the police this. They won't find it. Oh, and I've cleared out our joint savings, but don't worry. I'm leaving you the house.

And the mortgage. Cow. She had money he didn't know about, as well as the money he did? And a lot of it?

If he'd known that, he might have been tempted to stay with her.

You won't hear from me again. I've changed my phone number and by the time you read this I'll be out of the country and on my way to a new life. Good luck with Janice.

I'll never forgive you.

Vivien.

THIRTY-THREE

In the morning Ashleigh, who was the unlucky one on call over the weekend, went down to Connie's flat armed with a warrant no-one was alive to ask for and accompanied by two uniformed officers, and returned with a tray of ice cubes from the freezer compartment of the tiny fridge. Once these were dispatched to the lab she returned to the incident room, where she wasn't surprised to find Jude waiting for her. Faye's presence was both less expected, and less welcome, and was a mark of how seriously she was taking matters.

The two of them had been locked in what looked like deep but fruitless discussion when Ashleigh arrived, and neither stopped frowning when they saw her. Jude at least sat back and waved her to a seat but Faye ignored her.

'I should have guessed this would happen,' she said, finally noting Ashleigh's presence and nodding as her junior officer sat down. 'We should never have let the Warrington woman go. It's the quiet and unassuming ones that are the worst. Always. I don't know why we didn't throw the book at her earlier.'

'We could hardly lock the woman up on the basis of what we knew at the time.' Jude nodded to Ashleigh. 'Mission accomplished?'

She nodded. 'Has something happened?'

'Only that Vivien Warrington's done a runner,' said Faye, and her scowl deepened. She would see this as a failing and, as someone who was reluctant to accept that some things were unavoidable, would be looking for someone to blame.

'Just herself?' she asked. 'Or both of them.'

'Just her,' said Jude. 'Her husband called us just now. She left a note saying she's left him and gone abroad.'

'It would have been helpful if he'd done that when he found it,' said Faye, rather scornfully, 'but it seems he has a mistress, his wife knew about, and he wanted to discuss the matter with her first, no doubt to make the two of them look as innocent as they can.'

'I think they probably are innocent,' said Jude, 'under the circumstances. If she'd left and there hadn't been a long-term affair I might have been a bit more sceptical and thought it was just a set up, so that she could disappear and he could join her as soon as the coast was clear. But it seems he's more than happy to move in with the other woman, or have the other woman move in with him, and a part of me wonders if it therefore suits him to have her make a clean getaway.'

'How long has she been gone?'

'He found the note yesterday. He'd been out all day, at his allotment in the morning and then at the pub with friends. When he came back he found a note saying she'd gone and wasn't coming back, that the money's stashed abroad, that she knows about the mistress and she's off to live the rest of her life on her ill-gotten gains.'

'I expect she'll have left the country by now. Whether it

was planned the whole time or whether she got cold feet and panicked, who knows? But that was entirely avoidable.' Faye scowled.

Jude's expression, inevitably, was more forgiving. 'I think it's probably a collective failing, Faye, and it would have been disproportionate in terms of use of resources to keep tabs on her when she hadn't even been charged. As we didn't know what we know now, I don't think any of us can be held individually responsible, and if any one of us was to be, it ought to be myself as the investigating officer.'

'I'm not pointing the finger,' said Faye, as though she wished she could, 'though I daresay someone will be if we don't catch her. My worry is that she's going to try and do the same thing again.'

'But why would she? She's already got the money,' said Ashleigh, thinking of Vivien Warrington. 'I don't think she's a serial offender.'

'No?' asked Faye, sceptically.

'No, but it seems she may have been planning this for a very long time. The fraud, for certain, and the ultimate escape. And if she was planning it for that long she would have had plenty of time to cover her tracks.'

After all, it was no surprise that Vivien had been so accommodating about providing them with details of what she'd done with the money. She must have known it would take a long time, weeks perhaps, to verify. Once that was done the clock had begun ticking and she would have had to make her move. 'We're looking for her, of course?'

'An all-ports alert,' said Jude 'and all the rest of it. But if she's that smart she'll be long gone. If she left as soon as he went out yesterday morning she could have been on a flight out of the country before he was home, and I wouldn't be remotely surprised to find she's got another alias as well.' He looked glum.

Ashleigh considered. 'Maybe. But something tells me she hasn't gone far.'

'Let's hear your thinking,' said Jude, encouragingly, his smile balancing out Faye's frown.

'Despite how it might look, I don't think Vivien did it for the money, at least, not entirely. By which I mean, if it hadn't been for the inheritance I think she would have done what she did anyway.'

'Right?' said Jude interested. 'I'm fascinated to hear that, because yesterday I called in on Eden's End and spoke to Ellie Jack, and she had quite a lot to say for herself. She told me how wonderful Vivien was with her father and how she always brought him his favourite chocolates. And now I'm sitting making a connection between putting poison in ice cubes and putting penicillin in chocolates. And that makes me think that she hurried her father off the face of the earth when she thought Connie was coming back and that's precisely because she couldn't risk losing the money.'

'Before you came in,' said Faye, by way of explanation, 'we were discussing whether or not we have enough evidence to revisit the investigation into Edwin's death, but I'm afraid I think that with the amount of time that's passed it'll be very difficult to establish anything.'

People forgot. Edwin had been gone for years and noone would have thought to look in a box of chocolates, left like a ticking time bomb for him to consume while Vivien was away. It would be a neat and elegant solution to the problem of an old man, stubbornly in the way of an inheritance.

'He was the big obstacle,' agreed Ashleigh. 'Of course. He was old and he may have been persuaded that Vivien was Connie, but perhaps he'd reached a point where she couldn't be sure he wouldn't give her away.'

'You can be old and confused,' said Faye with an unwarranted degree of bitterness, 'and not recognise people who love you, even your close friends and relatives, but every now and then old people do have flashes of clarity. I wonder if Vivien had seen signs of that and had thought the risk was too great.'

'I'll be interested in your thoughts,' said Jude, who always made a particular effort to be encouraging when Faye was in a bad mood, 'about what Vivien's motivation might have been if you think it wasn't just the money. It's obviously to her material benefit to have both her father and her half-sister out of the way.'

'But the Warringtons don't actually need the money. They were reasonably comfortably off. She could just have left her husband and got half of everything, moved away if she wanted to. She had a decent pension. I agree you have to have a motivation for two murders and I agree that the money makes it easier to get away with it.'

'Vivien definitely wanted the money,' Faye reminded her. 'Connie offered to split it with her and she refused outright.'

'Yes.' Ashleigh visualised Vivien, the intensity of her gaze, the set of her shoulders. There had been a coldness about her which she'd failed to hide. 'It was important because of what it represents. I don't know how confused Edwin Sheldon was. I don't know whether he really did understand she was the daughter he hadn't seen for a while. It's possible he did, and believed he was leaving the money to Vivien.'

'I'm not sure his intentions carry a lot of weight here,' said Faye with a sigh, 'given the man is well beyond our reach.'

'No. But it's what mattered to Vivien. This whole thing was about establishing herself with her father. I don't know whether you can say she really loved him. He was absent, through his own choice, for the first fifty-odd years of her life and she must have resented that.' There had been no softness in her tone when she'd spoken about him, only a proprietorial pride. 'I think his love became her obsession and her resentment became a weapon to use against him.'

'That sounds like a trailer for a particularly corny movie,' said Faye, but her interest was caught. 'Go on.'

'I think she was obsessed with Connie. When her mother finally told her who her father was, she planned to make contact. She told us that. Then she discovered that Edwin had another daughter, a baby girl he doted on. Vivien was so upset by that that she went to the lengths of changing her name. I thought it was odd. It's completely out of proportion.'

'It sounds to me she was rejecting her father the way he'd rejected her,' said Faye, 'not being desperate to connect with him.'

'That may be what happened at the time. It may be what she thought she was doing. But she said something in that first interview I had with her. She said she'd watched Connie growing up, and if, as she claims, she was never in touch with her father she must have done it surreptitiously.'

'It would be easily done,' said Jude, thoughtfully, 'given that Edwin didn't know who she was and wouldn't recognise her if he saw her.'

'Yes. You can see how it might work. Someone who knew their movements, who could pretend to be a local who might be coming along the street at the same time as Connie's mother was collecting her from school, or who would regularly be seen in the neighbourhood. Perhaps they were even on speaking terms.'

She saw Jude's expression sharpen. 'Connie had a

phobia when she was smaller. She used to joke about it when we were younger, all a bit dark but her sense of humour was like that. She was always afraid that someone was following her. She had dreams about waking up and finding a strange woman bending over her, and her mother always said it must be something that had happened when she was a child. Some neighbour who'd scared her, perhaps. Maybe it was Vivien.'

'Such a shame you didn't remember that before,' said Faye, with a gusty sigh.

'I wish I had. I doubt we'll be able to prove anything unless Vivien was so obsessed she kept a record, but I do wonder if she was a much greater presence in Connie's life than Connie ever realised.'

Ashleigh could imagine her, the missing child, always on the outside looking in at the adored princess. For a moment she had some sympathy, but then she remembered Connie's anguished message. 'She certainly seems to have be fully aware of what Connie was up to, throughout her life.'

She saw Jude's expression change to one that was somewhere between enlightenment and amusement. He understood. Perhaps he found it funny that Vivien might have watched him and Connie as they blundered through their adolescent romance. 'Connie was never shy about posting her life on social media, that's for sure.'

'No. She left everything public, too. I have a little bet with myself that Vivien will have been lurking there, saying nothing, seeing everything. It will have been more salt into the wound. This child, who could do no wrong, making a series of increasingly disastrous life choices and then, as Vivien would see it, dumping her father in a care home and running away to the other side of the world.'

Faye tapped a restless finger on the desk. It was an indication that she was listening. 'But the money?'

'The money represented how much he cared for her. It's how some people express value.' How the world expressed it, in too many cases. Your value was what you got paid. 'That's why she wanted everything, but there was much more to it than that. What she stole from Connie was the last years of her father's life. She stole her identity. She walked in her skin. She persuaded a confused old man that she was his daughter and that he loved her.' Maybe he hadn't. Maybe he'd yearned for Connie but seen instead someone he didn't recognise. And, at the end of it, when she'd won his love and his trust she had concluded her vendetta and paid him back for those years of neglect by killing him.

'I'm not a psychologist,' said Faye, thoughtfully, 'but I think a psychological assessment of Vivien Warrington would be very interesting indeed. I do wonder if you might be right.'

Ashleigh looked at Jude, who was nodding. She could tell that, now she'd drawn his attention to it, it all made sense.

'That's why she was at the cemetery when Connie and I went up there, I expect. With hindsight I'd say that was an entirely deliberate move.'

'Are you suggesting she knew Connie would be going up there?' asked Faye, incredulous.

'No, but it would be a reasonable guess. Connie had just discovered her father was dead and had been buried without her knowledge. It was a safe bet she'd go within a few days of coming back and an even safer one that she'd go on his birthday. I expect Vivien had been loitering near there keeping an eye out ever since Connie came back.

That was what struck me as odd at the time. She wanted to be seen.'

'Yes. If all she wanted was the money she'd have kept well away, not taken the risk.'

'Exactly. But she obviously couldn't keep away, even when she saw Connie wasn't on her own. That's why I noticed her. She came right up behind us, well within sight, and then left her wreath, clearly labelled who it was for and who it was from, on a random grave where there had to be a chance that Connie would see it.'

'With you watching?' asked Faye. 'Really?'

'She obviously didn't know who Connie was with,' said Ashleigh, trying not to smile at Jude's slightly smug expression, the chance of having been in the right place at the right time. 'If she had, maybe she'd have cut her losses, but I think not. If I had to put money on it I'd say that, no matter how risky it was, she just had to see Connie suffer.'

'Lovely,' said Faye, after a moment's pause. 'I confess, I shouldn't be surprised that ordinary people have extraordinary obsessions, but somehow I always am. Most of them don't have the courage or the strength to pursue it, though.'

That was what was different with Vivien. 'It was worth it for her. She won.'

Faye's expression twisted once more into a scowl. 'Indeed. And unless we find her she'll keep on winning.'

'Is she done with Connie, I wonder?' asked Jude, thinking aloud.

'I would imagine so, if she killed her. What more is there for her to gain?' asked Faye, rhetorically.

'Not much, perhaps,' said Jude and turned to Ashleigh, 'but I think there might be one thing.'

'Closure,' she supplied, immediately.

'Yes. She needs an end to the adventure. Maybe

Connie's death is enough, but given the risks she took to watch her half-sister grieve I think there's every chance she'd take the risk again.'

'I don't follow,' said Faye.

'Okay. Let's assume Ashleigh's correct about how she feels. In that case, if I were Vivien, my triumph would only be complete when I saw my enemy buried in a ceremony with no mourners, all alone.'

'Except that won't happen because Connie has a husband, two sons and presumably one or two friends beside yourself.'

'Yes. Connie's burial is a matter for her family. But I don't think Vivien needs to know that. Do you?'

There was a short silence. 'What are you suggesting?'

'I think Vivien will be desperate to turn up at Connie's funeral.'

'She'd be mad to do so. If she hasn't left the country already she will have done by the time the funeral comes around. It'll be weeks, what with the festive period, and her husband having to arrange things from Australia and then plan to come over.'

'I was thinking,' said Jude, 'that with her husband's agreement, perhaps we could sort something out. Sooner, rather than later. Something to tempt Vivien out in the open.'

They looked at each other, and then Faye slapped her hand on the desk. 'What do you mean? A sting? Fake funeral? Empty coffin? Police officers as pall bearers? Notice in the local paper saying *private funeral, no mourners*?'

'Exactly that.'

'My God,' said Faye, and her eyes lit up. 'I like it. I like it very much. Just leave it to me…'

THIRTY-FOUR

Hi everyone, Matt here. Thanks for all the condolences on Connie's death. After a lot of thought I decided not to disrupt the boys at Christmas and bring them back for the funeral. It'll be a private event in Penrith on Christmas Eve morning, no fuss, no flowers. There will be a memorial service some time in the new year and you'll all be welcome at that.

I'll be deleting Connie's FB after the funeral. Further details on my page. Follow me if you don't already.

Matt xx

'Here you go, love.' The taxi pulled up at the entrance to the cemetery while Vivien was checking that final post on Connie's Facebook feed for the umpteenth time.

'Thank you. Could you wait? I might be half an hour, but maybe not that long, and I have a train to catch.'

He gave her the thumbs up, and well he might. He'd keep the meter running and it would be money for old rope for him, well worth it for the clean getaway for her.

She'd see her sister buried with no-one to mourn her, no-one to see it but the funeral directors, and then she'd head off to the cruise she'd booked, jump ship on the continent and no-one would be any the wiser.

She got out of the taxi. There was a weak, low sun as she made her way along the short stretch of pavement on Beacon Edge outside the cemetery. Her nerves were taut. It wasn't just this, the funeral, the final send-off. It was everything else she was leaving behind. But she'd had no alternative, other than to live the rest of her life quietly seething while Stephen continued to see Janice in secret, unable to challenge him because if she did he might leave.

She'd had enough rejection. She wouldn't risk any more.

How had he taken the news of her departure? Perhaps it was as well she didn't know. Meekly, probably, because he was a man for the quiet life, or with a degree of glee because now he could play away as much as he wanted. The police would give him grief because they wouldn't believe she was capable of doing all this alone, and with luck they might even charge him. After a while they would have more important things to do than worry about her. She imagined Stephen and his mistress, a few weeks down the line, sitting in the living room and eating the last of the Christmas chocolates, raising their glasses and toasting a life together.

She struggled for breath a little as she approached the cemetery gates, stopping to glance at her watch. Ten to twelve. The police must have concluded that Connie had died by accident or the funeral surely wouldn't be being held so soon, but she was still too smart to draw attention to herself — no treacherous rainbow hat this time. She'd watch from a distance and see her half-sister lowered into the grave and then, when she was sure she had gone, she would leave and sink into obscurity. She had no idea what she would do with all the time she would have, when she was no longer obsessed with her sister and her globe-trotting life.

She got out her new phone and checked again, hoping she wasn't too late. Turning up her collar and pulling down her hat, she turned into the cemetery. There was a cortege leaving, an empty hearse and three funeral cars, but she didn't recognise any of the mourners and in any case there were far too many of them for the funeral to be Connie's. She had no-one left to cry for her but those two boys. Even her husband, it seemed, didn't deem her worth the effort of seeing her off personally.

When the funeral party had cleared the gates she headed towards the chapel, past a bank of floral tributes in red and white and yellow, an arrangement that must have cost hundreds that said MUMMY in bronze-coloured chrysanthemums. The last of the stragglers, moving away from the freshly filled grave, dabbed at his eyes with a handkerchief and gave her a glazed and incurious look as she passed.

The list of funerals was pinned up on a board in front of the chapel; a second hearse stood outside. The party just leaving must be mourning an Alice Wilkins. At the next service, the notice informed her, they would be burying Constance Armstrong, née Sheldon.

Vivien smiled. 'Hello, my love,' she said, mockingly, to the notice. 'I'm here to see you off, make sure you've gone. Because no-one else wants to, do they?' *See what being Daddy's favourite earned you, little princess. It did you no good at all.*

'Are you bearing up?' said Ashleigh, as she and Jude paused in the foyer of the chapel as the empty coffin was borne to the waiting hearse for its short, final journey across the cemetery.

'I'm glad I'm here to see her off,' he said, lowering his voice in case anyone was within earshot. Behind them, Faye harrumphed in what might have been irritation. He sensed she was shaking her head, but she was as thrilled as he was at the idea of springing a trap. He had no idea what was in Faye's past, or present, that made her so engaged but whatever it was it meant she cared as much as he did.

'Can you see her?' said Faye, under her voice.

'No,' he said, without looking around him too obviously, 'but she'll be here.'

Ashleigh dropped back and Faye moved forward, so the two of them walked side by side, dutifully slowly behind the car. Up on the hill the breeze was keen and the low hum of the motorway traffic drifted across to them.

'Mr Armstrong was a good sport,' said Faye, still under her breath, 'and I do hope his good faith isn't wasted.'

Connie's husband had been suitably grief-stricken, Jude had thought, and had said all the right things, Knowing Connie as he did he thought she'd picked a good man. It was just unfortunate that he'd been married to someone else and when she'd got him she wasn't able to keep him, but this cycle of achievement and self-destruction had been typical of her. He'd attend her official funeral when the time came, but even in this charade of an empty coffin and closed chapel doors he felt her loss keenly, as if a part of his youth and innocence had gone, too. 'He's as keen as we are to see whoever killed her brought to justice.'

'You surely don't have any doubt that it was—'

'None at all.'

'Goodbyeee!'

They both spun round. Melanie Trotter came dashing up the path towards them.

'I almost missed it,' she said, merrily. 'This is Connie's funeral, isn't it? I thought it would be a shame if nobody turned up to make sure she'd gone. I mean, see her off. Who are you? Are you friends of hers? Surely not?'

Faye was staring in complete contempt. Jude stifled a wry smile, both at this and at the turn that Connie's funeral had inevitably taken.

'Yes, I'm a friend of Connie's,' he said, aware that Chris Marshall, playing the part of a pall bearer, was keeping a stern eye on proceedings. He hoped Chris, or one of the others, was also watching out for Vivien, because something told him Melanie was going to want all his attention.

'I didn't think she had any left.' She fell into step beside them. 'We're supposed to talk about people at their funerals, aren't we, say how wonderful they are? That won't take long.' She looked at Faye. 'Who are you? A relative? Or did she steal your husband, too, and you want to wave her off like I do?'

'This is Detective Superintendent Faye Scanlon,' said Jude, torn between dismay at the way matters had gone, because now he had no chance at all of keeping an eye out for Vivien, and an amusement he couldn't help feeling, 'and she and I are here representing the police.'

This, at least gave Melanie some pause for thought. 'Right. Did someone bump her off then?' She smiled.

'There's a live investigation into Ms Sheldon's death, yes,' said Faye, repressively.

'Right,' said Melanie, doubtfully, and seemed to be repressing her feelings.

They had reached the grave. By now Jude had

expected the charade to have played itself out, and for Vivien to have revealed herself, but either she hadn't turned up or she'd seen enough and left. Doubt seized him. He probably shouldn't have come but he thought Vivien would have been expecting him and it would have looked odd if he hadn't been there. He hadn't expected them to have to go through the whole process of the interment.

The minister spoke a few words. The police officers lowered the coffin into the earth. And Melanie Trotter, overcome by her emotions, pushed forward to the edge of the grave.

'Goodbye Connie,' she called at the top of her voice. 'This is how it ends, then, eh? No-one to mourn you but one old friend and a policewoman. Buried on Christmas Eve and not even Matt and your kids here to say goodbye. Well, I'll say goodbye, and good riddance, and when these guys have filled in the grave I'll be the first one to dance on it.'

'This behaviour is entirely inappropriate,' said Faye, furious.

'You don't know what she was like. You really have no idea.'

Jude stepped back, leaving Faye to deal with Connie. He was more concerned that Vivien, who he and Ashleigh had been so sure would turn up, might have slipped the net. He turned and scanned the cemetery while Melanie laughed beside him and Faye fumed, and eventually took her by the arm and guided her away from the graveside.

But there was no sign at all of Vivien Warrington.

It was glorious. It was delicious. It was the perfect send-off for Connie, and the best thing about it was that someone else had taken on the responsibility for it and was distracting that detective (Vivien, sheltering behind a tree with extreme care, had known he'd turn up and so had approached the funeral extremely warily, keeping a much greater distance than she would have liked) which could only be to the good. It was all there, everything she'd wanted. The cortege, the absence of mourners bar the detective who had been so improbably sweet on Connie all those years ago and still seemed even more improbably blind to her many failings. And then Melanie, shouting and laughing and displaying as much glee in Connie's death as Vivien felt, making the scene that Vivien should have made and allowing her a swift getaway.

Because, she knew, the detective might be keeping an eye open for her and she couldn't risk being seen. For once in her life, Vivien allowed discretion to triumph. Perhaps one day, a few years down the line when she was too old to care whether she was caught and when she had little of her life left to live, she could sneak back and leave some flowers and a suitably scathing note on both Connie's grave and her father's. Something like *you deserved each other*.

Melanie was still causing chaos. A severe woman in black, who she didn't recognise was remonstrating with her but she didn't dare wait to see how it played out because Jude Satterthwaite was on the lookout for someone and it could only be her. She'd approached with care, kept a distance, planned an escape. From the protection of one tree to another, round the back of the chapel, making sure she couldn't see the police and that therefore they couldn't see her.

So far so good. Once round the chapel the gateway yawned and there was no-one waiting for her. She'd made it. She ran the last few yards to where the taxi waited and wrenched the door open, flinging herself in. 'The station, please.' If they hadn't seen her they wouldn't look, at least until it was too late and she was safely out of the way.

The taxi didn't start. Puzzled, Vivien glanced out through the window. The taxi driver, grinning, was standing at the side of the road smoking a cigarette.

She tried to open the door but it was locked. Then at last, she turned to challenge whoever was in the driver's seat.

'Good morning, Mrs Warrington,' said Ashleigh O'Halloran with a smile. 'We've been hoping to have a word with you.'

THIRTY-FIVE

'It's a relief,' said Vivien, in a low voice. 'Can I tell you everything? I have to tell someone.'

'I'd be delighted,' said the sergeant, sitting on the other side of the table and watching her with keen blue eyes that reminded Vivien of that cold blue sky above the cemetery on the day she'd watched Connie grieving. That had been her mistake. She hadn't known at the time that the man who was with her was a policeman; she'd recognised him only as Connie's teenage sweetheart and it had never occurred to her that this gangling youth of whom she had been so quietly scornful might have grown up to be a threat.

She'd been disabused of that notion soon enough, but by then it was too late and she was already committed to the path that brought her here, to this bleak interview room on Christmas Eve.

Ashleigh O'Halloran nodded to the duty solicitor, who had already warned Vivien not to say anything and who clearly had no idea of how great a burden a murder could be on a middle-class, middle-aged conscience. 'First of all,

I'm going to explain exactly what I want to talk to you about. I want to ask you some questions about the death of Connie Sheldon, your half-sister, and of your father, Edwin Sheldon.'

They'd found out about her father? After three years? She looked at the sergeant in amazement and thought she saw a glimpse of satisfaction behind the stare, as if the woman had her number. Was that such a bad thing? It had been very lonely, hating the way she had. 'Oh.'

'I'll begin with that, if I may. I'd like you to tell me what happened at Eden's End in the immediate run-up to your father's death.'

Vivien reached into her pocket for a handkerchief. She thought about that often. 'He was dying anyway. He'd given up.'

'Why had he given up, Mrs Warrington?' asked the sergeant, who must surely have some idea.

If she'd had any energy left Vivien would have denied everything. She'd have fought. She'd have clung to the hope of her long retirement with Stephen, living comfortably off the money, and even if they took the money off her she would take comfort from the fact that she'd seen her sister out of the world. But she was tired, and Stephen had someone else. Despite the spirited fight she'd put up in defence of her rights, she had nothing left but the truth, by now so heavy a burden that she had no option but to share it.

'Connie didn't visit,' she said, almost in a whisper.

'Your sister Connie?' said the sergeant for clarity.

She nodded.

'You gave the staff to understand…' said the sergeant, and then corrected herself. 'Your father gave the staff to understand…'

'Yes. Because I told him to.'

The sergeant let the silence drag.

'I told him I wouldn't come again if he didn't. But really, sometimes he thought I was her,' said Vivien, in a rush. 'I kept telling him I was, and he looked at me as if he might believe it.' He'd wanted to believe it. That was what had hurt her the most. He'd wanted her to be Connie. 'But as he got older he stopped pretending. He told the staff he didn't know who I was, but they thought he was just confused.' Edwin had lost his filters. In the end he'd known she wasn't Connie and because of that he had ceased to love her, in as much as he had ever loved her at all. She sniffed.

'Did that upset you?'

'Yes,' confessed Vivien. Regret surged within her. 'I only wanted him to love me. I wanted him to know that I was the one who'd visit him, even though he'd rejected me. I needed him to know he'd been wrong about me.' *I needed to matter to him.* 'It hurt. It really hurt.'

'Did it hurt enough for you to kill him?' asked the sergeant.

The question snaked into her heart like an arrow through a chink in a knight's breastplate. She winced. 'No.'

'Did you kill him?'

'Mrs Warrington,' said the solicitor, suddenly insistent, 'you don't have to answer that question.'

But she did. 'He was old.'

'He was eighty-seven. What did you do?'

'I...I...' She looked up at the woman, felt herself shrinking down in her chair. 'Do I have to tell you?'

'I'll help,' said Ashleigh O'Halloran, briskly. 'You told me in a previous interview that Karen Grant, then the manager at Eden's End,' (she nodded at the recording device, as if she was noting it for someone else to hear) 'had accepted your explanation as to your identity. If we were to look further into her finances and yours, would I find any…unusual…transactions between you?'

Oh God. If she had the courage and the spirit she'd had at the beginning of this adventure, she would at least have made them work for their evidence, but something had changed. Something had broken her defences. 'Yes.'

'What did you give Ms Grant, and what for?'

'Five thousand pounds,' said Vivien, miserably. 'To…to not ask questions. And for…and to get…to get…something from the drugs cupboard.'

'You will be aware, as am I,' said the sergeant, sounding almost stern now, 'that Ms Grant was in an extremely fragile mental state. She was deeply in debt and highly vulnerable. Are you telling me you coerced her into helping you?'

Put like that it sounded brutal. Vivien had never thought of herself as a bully. 'Yes.'

'What did she acquire for you?'

'It was penicillin.' You could get penicillin anywhere, but a prescription would have linked her to it. Karen Grant had been easily pressured, without even asking why and no doubt not realising what the penicillin was for until it was too late.

'And you then gave it to your father?'

'Yes.'

'You knew he was allergic?'

She had found that out by chance. It was so much easier to make it look like someone else's fault than it would have been to use the horse tranquilliser she had obtained for the purpose, but that, of course, had come in useful later. 'He liked chocolates. I bought them for him and the staff gave him one with his cup of tea every morning. I left a box before I went on holiday.'

'And while you were away your father died of anaphylactic shock as a result of taking penicillin which you placed in a box of chocolates in his room.' The sergeant looked at the recording device in the centre of the table. 'I don't want there to be any confusion, Mrs Warrington.'

'That is what happened.'

'Okay. And what, exactly prompted you to take this particular step? You claim to have loved your father. You said you cherished the time you spent with him. Why did you cut short that supposedly precious time?'

Connie. Of course. All of this was because of Connie. 'She said she might be coming back.'

'Who?'

Vivien swallowed. 'My sister, Connie. And if she came back, he...he might have...they would have stopped me seeing him.' Connie would have taken Vivien's place at his bedside, sobbed over him, played the prodigal daughter. She would have won.

'Thank you,' said Ashleigh O'Halloran, in clipped tones that failed to hide her disapproval. 'So, to be clear. When you thought Connie might be coming back and would supplant you in your father's affections, you murdered your father in order to spite your sister, and then you went on to defraud his estate of a large amount of money to which you had no claim. Correct?'

'Yes.' Vivien sniffed again.

Ashleigh O'Halloran got up and fetched a paper cup of water which she placed on the table, then resumed her seat. 'And did you never think,' she asked, now rather more gently, 'about what would happen when Connie came back? Because barring an accident or illness, she was bound to come back.'

Folding her lips into a thin line, Vivien stared back at her. She felt as though all her faults were being laid bare in front of her, as if she needed someone to point them out to her. She didn't. She'd thought of them often since she'd murdered her half-sister. 'Yes.'

'And so, when she did come back…she would have discovered you. That's what happened. How long had you been planning to kill Connie Sheldon?'

Vivien licked dry lips. When had she first realised what the inevitability of Connie's return would mean? There would be uproar, and Connie might become the object of sympathy. She would weep and cry in public and people would pity her. But that hadn't happened. As she always did, Connie had let herself down. 'Since I realised she'd come back.'

'Which was…when?'

'Just after Dad died.' Connie, who was proprietorial, would have hated her calling him that. She rolled it over in her head, enjoying it. *Dad. Dad.* Sometimes when she'd said that and looked confused, saying *you're not Connie*, she'd patted his hand and reassured him. *Yes, Dad, it's me. I'm Connie.*

'Okay. So now can we move on to Connie Sheldon's death?'

The two of them stared at each other, Vivien trying to read the woman's eyes, being met by a blank stare. What did they know?

'We know,' said the woman, as if to prove she was a mindreader, 'that you visited Connie and brought her a bottle of gin. We know that when you left you cleared the kitchen. We know she drank that gin, with tonic, and ice, alone.'

'Yes,' said Vivien, her throat constricted.

'Toxicology results showed Connie died from an excessive dose of Immobilon. Am I correct in thinking that you worked at a vet's practice?'

Am I correct. The woman was mocking her. They knew.

Somehow they knew everything. 'Yes.' Though maybe not quite everything.

'You would have had access to Immobilon, through your job. I notice,' said the woman, who had obviously done her homework, 'that about a month before your father's death there was a break-in at your place of work and drugs were taken. The perpetrators were caught, but I see from the crime reports that you were first on the scene.'

Opportunity had knocked. It often did, if you were brave enough to answer. 'I was the office manager. I opened up the practice. Yes.'

'We have a search team at your house at the moment, Mrs Warrington, and I have been told that a quantity of Immobilon was found there. Did Connie invite you to her flat, or did you invite yourself?'

'She invited me.' If she hadn't, Vivien would have turned up, offering the sealed bottle of gin as a goodwill gesture. Then she would have come back, made a friend of her sister and destroyed her. In the end, Connie's mercurial nature had destroyed herself in a much more satisfying manner. 'I thought I'd cultivate a friendship and there'd be an opportunity…'

'To make her a gin and tonic?'

'Yes. But then I realised it would be difficult not to…to explain myself if I was there and she was sick and I wasn't. I already knew she drank a lot, drank alone, and when she passed out I realised I had the chance to make sure I wasn't there when she died. So I tidied up after me and I filled the ice cube tray and added the Immobilon to it. I knew she'd drink it, later.'

'Did it occur to you that you might have poisoned anyone who came to visit her?' asked the sergeant, severe, now.

'She never had visitors, though. She alienated everyone.' Though when she thought about it, she'd had one visitor, that tall detective who was Ashleigh O'Halloran's boss and who had been the one to read her her rights on the pavement outside the cemetery as his junior officer clasped the handcuffs on her. That would have been awkward, if she'd managed to accidentally poison a senior police officer. But she hadn't. 'She died alone and that was what I wanted.' She smiled. Her father had died thinking he loved her and Connie had died alone and in pain, and so, despite being found out and losing all the money, it had been worth it after all.

'It worked so well,' she said, committed now. 'So well. It was a shame not to do it again.' And again and again. 'Have you ever been rejected, sergeant? Again and again. And again.'

They stared at one another again and this time something flicked into the sergeant's eyes and she jumped to her feet and headed for the door. 'Excuse me a moment.' And was in such a hurry that she was on the phone before she reached the corridor, uncaring of whether she was overheard. 'Jude, this is urgent. We need to get hold of Stephen Warrington. I believe his life may be in danger.'

THIRTY-SIX

Stephen had turned his phone off. There was always someone ringing him, now, workmates or friends, all of them pretending to be solicitous, all of them wanting to know the full story and some of them (those who hadn't liked him and those workmates, in particular, who had been jealous of the perks that came with him sleeping with the boss) taking a gleeful pleasure in his downfall. *I hear the missus has left*, they would say, or *what's this about your Viv?* Some of them, with an eye to the future, perhaps, even pretended. *If there's anything I can do to help, mate, let me know.* And then there were all the people who pretended to be Viv's friends, none of whom had ever bothered with her much beyond what was necessary, phoning to get the gossip.

Yes, a period of peace and quiet was well in order.

He was surprised at how quickly he'd switched from being at ease in his wife's household to slotting so easily into the same role with his mistress. Janice had been delighted. The police had descended on the house he'd shared with Viv (it seemed they thought she'd had something to do with Connie's death, though he couldn't for the life of him think what it might be, Viv being that passive, harmless type) and so it had seemed obvious to follow Janice's suggestion and move in right away while they ripped the fabric of his life and his marriage apart.

It would be a different Christmas, for sure. He and Viv always went out for an Indian on Christmas Eve, a tradition whose origin he could no longer remember but which might have stemmed from an early date, but Janice was cooking, up to her elbows in flour as she made mince pies. The casserole which she'd prepared for the evening was already in the slow cooker, the turkey crown defrosting in the fridge, the veg prepared for the morning. Viv had enjoyed the process of making Christmas dinner and spun it out all through the day whereas Janice was determined that everything would be ready to go and the morning would be relaxing.

He didn't think he'd miss his wife. Sometimes, indeed, he had almost forgotten she was there. She never expressed an opinion, never argued. Now it turned out she'd known about him and Janice all the time and never even had the courage to challenge him on it. It made his life easier now she'd faded out of it. The only difficulty would be if the police ever found her and he had to engage with the process.

'Anything I can do?' he asked Janice.

'It's all under control. Why don't you make us a sandwich for lunch and then we can put the presents under the tree this evening, maybe go down to the pub for a drink later.'

He opened cupboards and drawers, still finding his way around her kitchen as he searched for bread and plates, uncovering things where he didn't expect them, opening a cupboard to find a treasure trove of festive goodies —

crisps, nuts and raisins, sugared almonds, satsumas and the opened box of white chocolate truffles which Janice had given him and which, because they were too good to waste, he had brought with him as a meagre contribution to the feast. He got them out and put them on the counter top, because it was Christmas Eve and he was living a different life, now, one in which he could dip into a box of chocolates any time he wanted without being frowned at. Not that he'd ever paid any attention when Viv frowned, and in fact she probably frowned a lot more than he remembered and he'd never noticed it. All in all, he congratulated himself, the breakdown of his marriage had been entirely without pain.

He glanced out of the kitchen window. The noise of an engine, fast. A police car. A twitching curtain over the way.

'What's going on?' said Janice, seeing it too.

'They must have found Viv,' he said, and headed for the door, opening it to a young policeman, flashing his warrant card. 'Hello.'

'Mr Warrington,' said the young policeman. 'PC Garner. May I come in? I have reason to believe that your wife may have been trying to harm you.'

THIRTY-SEVEN

If Eden's End had been better staffed, it might never have happened. Arriving late at Becca's Christmas Eve drinks after what was at the very least an overstimulating day in the office, Jude paused in the doorway of the small but crowded living room waiting for someone to notice his arrival and found himself thinking too much about Edwin Sheldon and his daughter. If Connie hadn't posted on Facebook, her father would have died naturally and Vivien's deception might never have been discovered. If she'd been in a better mental state and less cantankerous, she might have made a tougher target for her bitter half sister. If Stephen Warrington and his new woman had eaten the chocolates which had so obviously been tampered with (and which, he would bet his house, contained Immobilon)... If he himself had gone round to Connie's one night and taken a glass of Coke with ice in it...

He turned away, abruptly, and found himself face to face with Becca, who was circulating around the room with a large glass jug full of mulled wine. She was dressed in a bright red skirt and a Christmas jumper and wore a twist of golden tinsel in her brown hair.

'You're here,' she said, and leaned in to kiss him on the cheek, putting the contents of the jug at grave risk as she did so. 'I thought you weren't going to make it.'

So, at one point in the afternoon, had he. 'I got delayed.'

'Your mum said. Here,' she said, reaching for a clean glass from a side table and filling it almost to the brim, 'have some mulled wine. It's not as if you're driving, and it is Christmas.'

He accepted it, and drank. 'Thanks. Fair to say I needed that. That was delicious.'

'It's the first time I've made mulled wine, would you believe it? Hopefully I won't end up poisoning anyone,' she said, and then stopped herself half way through laughing. 'Damn. Sorry. I should probably not have got started on this stuff. It's lethal.'

'At your own party, on Christmas Eve?' He contemplated his glass, sticky with a warm, ruby-red, cinnamon-scented concoction. 'Not at all.'

'Are you all right? I don't like to see you standing in the corner all by yourself. And I saw you on Beacon Edge earlier today with Ashleigh and a police car, and you all in your funeral black. So I'm guessing you've had a bad day.'

All in all it could have been a lot worse. They'd apprehended Vivien and got a full confession, and Melanie Trotter had wasted a lot of effort on disrupting a fake funeral and would hopefully have realised how embarrassing her behaviour had been by the time the real thing came around. Probably most importantly (toxicology tests would prove this one way or another) they had almost certainly saved the lives of Stephen Warrington and his mistress, and acquired the piece of evidence that would convict Vivien in so doing. 'It wasn't what it looked like. Ask me another time and I'll explain.' By then he might be able to laugh about it. 'You know I'm not much of a social animal.' He cast a glance around the room. His mother was laughing with the neighbours, one of whom was telling what her hand gestures suggested was a very risqué anecdote. Mikey and his girlfriend, Izzy, were in a complicated clinch under the mistletoe. Adam Fleetwood had not been invited.

'You never change, do you?' She set the jug down on a side table, where it immediately oozed into a sticky red stain. 'Even when it's case closed, perpetrator caught. Which I'm guessing it is.'

'It is, yes.'

'And still people think you ought to be happy but it's much more complicated than that. You have to decompress. It's like when I lose a patient. Even if it's a blessed relief, I can't just walk away.'

'Exactly that.' Except that when Becca lost a patient, as she put it, it was almost always a process that was expected and managed. Vivien's arrest was only another point along a trail of disaster that had cost two lives and ruined others — those of Connie's husband and sons, and of Stephen Warrington who appeared to have been totally unaware of the dark places to which his wife's obsessive love (or was it obsessive hatred?) had taken her.

'And of course. I haven't had the chance to say it to you, because I've been so busy, but I meant to drop you a line to say sorry about Connie. I know you were close.'

He wondered if she'd been jealous. You could never tell with Becca, who had just as many frailties as everyone else but who struggled against them more than anyone he knew, and was hard on herself when she failed. 'A long time ago, yes.'

She reached for the jug and topped up the empty glass she had in her other hand. 'First love?'

'I suppose you'd call it that.'

'You never quite get over that, do you?'

He thought of Connie, flawed, antagonistic and defiant, bereft of her mother at a young age, cursed with a father as stubbornly independent as she was and as resistant to asking for the emotional support which might, in the end, have saved them both. 'I'm not going to lie. That one did hit home.'

'And those poor kids,' said Becca, her Christmas cheeriness softening. 'She lost her mother quite young, didn't she, and now they've lost her. Poor little things.'

'Pretty bad all round,' he agreed, thinking of everyone who had been cursed by Vivien Warrington's targeted fury.

'Come on, Becca,' said Mikey, bouncing across the room. He'd largely extricated himself from Izzy's grip, but the two of them were still holding hands. 'We need more mulled wine.'

'Help yourselves,' she retorted, 'and then take the jug and circulate. Oh, and there are plates of nibbles in the kitchen, so you can do those, too, and earn your drinks. Right now I'm talking to Jude.'

Mikey, who had arrived at the party late and hadn't been about when Jude had arrived home with his bags of gifts for the next couple of days under his mother's roof, took stock. 'Is Ashleigh not here? Shame. She's so easy on the eye.'

'Enough!' said Izzy, rapping him smartly on the head. 'Let's go to the kitchen.'

Amused, he watched them go. 'Young love, eh?'

'I'm sorry Ashleigh couldn't come,' said Becca, also watching them. 'Is she away home for Christmas with her folks?'

'I expect so,' he said, though he thought he knew exactly where she was and who she was with, that though she was on call over Christmas she would have another companion for the quieter moments, that Scott Kirby would have cancelled any other plans and be making the most of his opportunity. 'She wouldn't have come anyway. We aren't together any more.'

'Aren't you? Oh dear. I'm so sorry,' she said, though she knew that the relationship had been fading. 'I mean, it wasn't…well, because of Connie was it?'

He looked for a sign of encouragement, a spark of hope when she heard for certain that he was single again, but all he could see was what looked like genuine concern for him, for Connie, for everyone.

'Time just ran out,' he said, lifting his glass in a salute to God-knew-what and reflecting, as he sipped, on how long-lasting first love could be and how, for better or for worse, it never let you go.

THE END

ACKNOWLEDGMENTS

As always, it is impossible to thank all of the people who have helped me to write this book, largely because so much of it came from people who don't know. They are the people who shared my social media posts, who gave me good reviews, who reached out to tell me they liked my previous books, and even asked for more. Without them, I might well never have written it.

But I did, and in the writing there are those to whom I owe a debt of gratitude. They are, if I may call them that, the usual suspects - Graham Bartlett, who provided invaluable advice on keeping the policing realistic; Keith Sutherland, who is always a willing and eagle-eyed proofreader; the talented Mary Jayne Baker for the cover; and my husband, Alan, for his editorial input. I would like to add a special shoutout to Brian Price, who gave me invaluable advice on the best methods of poisoning someone while well away from the scene of the crime.

Thank you to you all.

ALSO BY JO ALLEN

Death by Dark Waters

DCI Jude Satterthwaite #1

It's high summer, and the Lakes are in the midst of an unrelenting heatwave. Uncontrollable fell fires are breaking out across the moors faster than they can be extinguished. When firefighters uncover the body of a dead child at the heart of the latest blaze, Detective Chief Inspector Jude Satterthwaite's arson investigation turns to one of murder. Jude was born and bred in the Lake District. He knows everyone — and everyone knows him. Except his intriguing new Detective Sergeant, Ashleigh O'Halloran, who is running from a dangerous past and has secrets of her own to hide. Temperatures — and tensions — are increasing, and with the body count rising Jude and his team race against the clock to catch the killer before it's too late...

The first in the gripping, Lake District-set, DCI Jude Satterthwaite series.

Death at Eden's End

DCI Jude Satterthwaite #2

When one-hundred-year-old Violet Ross is found dead at Eden's End, a luxury care home hidden in a secluded nook of Cumbria's Eden Valley, it's not unexpected. Except for the instantly recognisable look in her lifeless eyes — that of pure terror. DCI Jude Satterthwaite heads up the investigation, but as the deaths start to mount up it's clear that he and DS Ashleigh O'Halloran need to uncover a long-buried secret before the killer strikes again...

The second in the unmissable, Lake District-set, DCI Jude Satterthwaite series.

Death on Coffin Lane

DCI Jude Satterthwaite #3

DCI Jude Satterthwaite doesn't get off to a great start with resentful Cody Wilder, who's visiting Grasmere to present her latest research on Wordsworth. With some of the villagers unhappy about her visit, it's up to DCI Satterthwaite to protect her — especially when her assistant is found hanging in the kitchen of their shared cottage.

With a constant flock of tourists and the local hippies welcoming in all who cross their paths, Jude's home in the Lake District isn't short of strangers. But with the ability to make enemies wherever she goes, the violence that follows in Cody's wake leads DCI Satterthwaite's investigation down the hidden paths of those he knows, and those he never knew even existed.

A third mystery for DCI Jude Satterthwaite to solve, in this gripping novel by best-seller Jo Allen.

Death at Rainbow Cottage

DCI Jude Satterthwaite #4

At the end of the rainbow, a man lies dead.

The apparently motiveless murder of a man outside the home of controversial equalities activist Claud Blackwell and his neurotic wife, Natalie, is shocking enough for a peaceful local community. When it's followed by another apparently random killing immediately outside Claud's office, DCI Jude Satterthwaite has his work cut out. Is Claud the killer, or the intended victim?

To add to Jude's problems, the arrival of a hostile new boss causes complications at work, and when a threatening note arrives at the police headquarters, he has real cause to fear for the safety of his friends and colleagues…

A traditional British detective novel set in Cumbria.

Death on the Lake

DCI Jude Satterthwaite #5

Three youngsters, out for a good time. Vodka and the wrong sort of coke. What could possibly go wrong?

When a young woman, Summer Raine, is found drowned, apparently accidentally, after an afternoon spent drinking on a boat on Ullswater, DCI Jude Satterthwaite is deeply concerned — more so when his boss refuses to let him investigate the matter any further to avoid compromising a fraud case.

But a sinister shadow lingers over the dale and one accidental death is followed by another and then by a violent murder. Jude's life is complicated enough but the latest series of murders are personal to him as they involve his former partner, Becca Reid, who has family connections in the area. His determination to uncover the killer brings him into direct conflict with his boss — and ultimately places both him and his colleague and girlfriend, Ashleigh O'Halloran, in danger…

Death in the Woods

DCI Jude Satterthwaite #6

A series of copycat suicides, prompted by a mysterious online blogger, causes DCI Jude Satterthwaite more problems than usual, intensifying his concerns about his troublesome younger brother, Mikey. Along with his partner, Ashleigh O'Halloran, and a local psychiatrist, Vanessa Wood, Jude struggles to find the identity of the malicious troll gaslighting young people to their deaths.

The investigation stirs grievances both old and new. What is the connection with the hippies camped near the Long Meg stone circle? Could these suicides have any connection with a decades-old cold case? And, for Jude, the most crucial question of all: is it personal, and could Mikey be the final target?

Death in the Mist

DCI Jude Satterthwaite #7

A drowned man. A missing teenager. A deadly secret.

When Emmy Leach discovers the body of a drug addict,

wrapped in a tent and submerged in the icy waters of a Cumbrian tarn, she causes more than one problem for investigating officer DCI Jude Satterthwaite. Not only does the discovery revive his first, unsolved, case, but it reveals Emmy's complicated past and opens old wounds on the personal front, regarding Jude's relationship with his colleague and former partner, Ashleigh O'Halloran.

As Jude and his team unpick an old story, it becomes increasingly clear that Emmy is in danger. What secrets are she and her controlling husband hiding, from the police and from each other? What connection does the dead man have with a recently-busted network of drug dealers? And, as the net closes in on the killer, can Jude and Ashleigh solve a murder — and prevent another?

Death on a Monday Night

DCI Jude Satterthwaite #8

An ex-convict. A dead body. A Women's Institute meeting like no other…

It's an unusually challenging meeting at the Wasby Women's Institute, with local resident and former drug-dealer Adam Fleetwood talking about his crimes and subsequent rehabilitation…but events take a gruesome turn when prospective member Grace Thoresby is discovered murdered in the kitchen.

The case is particularly unwelcome for investigating officer DCI Jude Satterthwaite. Adam was once his close friend and now holds a bitter grudge, blaming Jude for landing him in jail in the first place. To complicate things further, the only thing keeping Adam from arrest is the testimony of Jude's former girlfriend, Becca Reid, for whom he still cares deeply.

As Jude and his colleague and current partner, Ashleigh O'Halloran, try to pick apart the complicated tapestry of Grace's life, they uncover a web of fantasy, bitterness and deceit. Adam is deeply implicated, but is he guilty or is someone determined to frame him for Grace's murder? And as they close in on the truth, Jude falls foul of Adam's desire for revenge, with near-fatal consequences…

A traditional detective mystery set in Cumbria.

Death on the Crags

DCI Jude Satterthwaite #9

Everybody loves Thomas Davies. Don't they?

When policeman Thomas falls from a crag on a visit to the Lake District in full view of his partner, Mia, it looks for all the world like a terrible but unfortunate accident — until a second witness comes forward with a different story.

Alerted to the incident, DCI Jude Satterthwaite is inclined to take it seriously — not least because of Mia's reluctance to speak to the police about the incident. As Jude and his colleagues, including his on-off partner DS Ashleigh O'Halloran, tackle the case, they're astonished by how many people seem to have a reason to want all-round good guy Thomas out of the way.

With the arrival of one of Thomas's colleagues to assist the local force, the investigation intensifies. As the team unpick the complicated lives of those who claim to care for Thomas but have good reasons to want him dead, they find themselves digging deeper and deeper into a web of blackmail and cruelty … and investigating a second death.

A traditional British police procedural mystery set in Cumbria.

Death at the Three Sisters

DCI Satterthwaite #10

Three feuding sisters. A faded spa. And a woman, dead in the water…

As they head towards retirement, Suzanne, Hazel and Tessa Walsh are locked in bitter disagreement about the future of the lakeside beauty spa they jointly own. Should they keep The Three Sisters going as their parents wished, or should they sell to a neighbouring hotelier who seems determined to acquire the failing business, even at a preposterously high cost?

When their employee, Sophie Hayes, is found drowned close to the spa one cold January morning it rapidly becomes clear that it's no accident: Sophie has been murdered. But who could possibly want to kill her — or was she mistaken for someone else? As DCI Jude Satterthwaite seeks the answers he and his team dig ever deeper into the complicated and embittered relationships between the sisters and their neighbours.

As the investigation proceeds Jude becomes convinced that Sophie's murder may only be the beginning and it's not long before a shocking and tragic turn of events proves him correct and he and his team find themselves in a race to prevent a further, final tragedy overtaking the Three Sisters. Can he uncover what deadly secrets the sisters are prepared to die — or kill — for, or will he be too late?

Death in Good Time

DCI Satterthwaite #11

A murdered undertaker. A missing clockmaker. A family secret.

In life, eccentric aristocrat Lady Frances Capel was known for her habit of setting challenging puzzles, but the problem she leaves behind after her death looks unsolvable. When the undertaker is found dead at her funeral, DCI Jude Satterthwaite is left with a headache for a whole host of reasons, and a case he'd very much rather not be working on.

Jude's suspicions that the key to the mystery lies in Lady Frances's will and with a decades-old family secret are confirmed when he receives a cryptic message from reclusive local clockmaker Gil Foley, but when he follows up Gil has vanished. Convinced that this has something to do with the undertaker's death, Jude finds the stakes raised sky-high when he realises that his ex-partner, Becca Reid, is involved in Gil's disappearance.

With both Becca and Gil in grave danger, Jude and his colleague DS Ashleigh O'Halloran find themselves in a race against the clock. Can they solve the mystery before time runs out and a second life is lost?

Death on the Small Screen

DCI Satterthwaite #12

In the film world, no-one is what they seem.

When renowned film director Simon Morea's estranged wife Annabel reports him missing, she suspects he's lying low — until wannabe actress Lexie Romachenka stumbles across Morea's body in a lonely spot on the Cumbrian fells. With his death confirmed as murder, the search for a missing person becomes a manhunt.

DCI Jude Satterthwaite has a difficult enough job given that the body has been lying there for days and the trail is cold, but he soon discovers that plenty of people are happy to see the director dead. When the body of the only potential witness turns up, Jude's attention focusses on Morea's complicated love life. Is the killer a jilted lover, a jealous partner, or his vengeful wife?

As suspects emerge and secrets are revealed, Jude and his colleague Ashleigh O'Halloran find themselves in a race against time to save another innocent life…

The Dangerous Friends Series

Blank Space

Dangerous Friends Book 1

He's made a lot of enemies. She has some dangerous friends.

Bronte O'Hara is trying to move on from her ex-boyfriend, Eden Mayhew, but when she finds an injured man in her kitchen in the run-up to an international political summit in Edinburgh, a world she thought she'd left behind catches up with her with a vengeance.

Eden's an anarchist, up to his neck in any trouble around — and he's missing. The police are keen to find him, certain that he'll come back, and that when he does, he'll have Bronte in his sights. What does he want from her — and does she dare trust a handsome stranger with her life?

With danger and romance in equal measure, Blank Space is a contemporary take on the romantic suspense tradition pioneered by Mary Stewart.

After Eden

Dangerous Friends Book 2

In the aftermath of a violent G8 summit when she almost lost her life, Bronte O'Hara finds herself fighting against her feelings for Marcus Fleming, the policeman who saved her. When Marcus is cleared of any wrongdoing over the deaths of three people during the undercover police operation, Bronte isn't the only one who struggles to come to terms with the outcome. The friends and relatives of those who died are determined not to let the matter rest, whatever the cost. Some are looking for closure; some want justice. And someone is determined to use Bronte in a bid to gain revenge…

Storm Child

Dangerous Friends Book 3

Scotland can be a dangerous place.

When their car comes off the road in a blizzard, Bronte O'Hara and her boyfriend, detective Marcus Fleming, stumble across an unconscious teenager in the snow. After he's rescued by two passing strangers, the boy simply disappears, and even Marcus's police colleagues don't believe their story — until the youth's body is found.

It looks like the accidental death of a young criminal, but Bronte and Marcus are convinced that things aren't as straightforward as they seem. Who was he? What was he doing out in the storm? Who else might be in danger?

And who will stop at nothing to make sure that Bronte and Marcus never find out?

Printed in Dunstable, United Kingdom